LOCKED UP LIARS

SAINT VIEW PRISON, #1

ELLE THORPE

WWW.ELLETHORPE.COM

#1

For Jira.

Not only the world's best husband, but as it turns out, a pretty good plotting partner too. Thank you for all your input on this book.

Love you.

Elle x

1

MAE

I would have recognized the tattoo creeping up his neck anywhere.

For years, I'd been slightly obsessed with the way it swirled across his skin and into his hairline. I'd dreamed of tracing my fingertips along the swells and patterns, chasing them beneath his shirt collar, over his shoulders, and finding out how low the intricate design actually went.

I could have asked my sister, of course. She could have told me exactly how far it snaked down the side of his body. But I'd never asked. I couldn't.

Asking my sister about the tats on her boyfriend's skin?

Just no. That would have been awkward.

So I kept my inappropriate curiosity locked away, tucked deep inside, and never voiced it to anyone.

Then they'd broken up.

And I hadn't seen him since.

But one glimpse of that tattoo across a smoky bar was all it took for everything to come roaring back. The curiosity. The desire. The plain stupid, ridiculous fact that the man curled my toes even from this distance.

Inappropriate. Inappropriate. SO inappropriate.

Tori nudged me. "Who are you checking out?"

I jerked and turned to face her. "What? No one. It's nothing."

She gave me the sort of knowing grin only a best friend could. Then she peered through the crowd, past the waiters taking drinks and food to tables, over to the bar where he nursed a short glass full of an amber liquid with ice.

Her eyes widened. "Is that Heath?"

It was my automatic instinct to play dumb. "Heath? As in Jayela's Heath?"

I wasn't fooling anyone. Tori knew it just as well as I did.

Concern puckered her brow. "Please don't tell me you're still harboring that secret crush on him? It's been four years, Mae."

I knew exactly how long it had been. I'd thought I was done with the absurd crush. Who knew it was just simmering away under the surface, ready to explode back in full force at a single sighting? But sitting there, staring at his broad shoulders and the way they tapered down to his narrow waist, it felt like no time had passed at all. All those feelings I'd hidden from him, from my sister, from myself—they all swirled through my system, turning happy cartwheels because we were in his presence once more.

Traitorous frigging feelings. They needed to get their shit under control.

Tori let out a low whistle. "Don't even bother denying it. It's written all over your face."

I didn't want it to be. I tried to school my features into something that didn't look like the heart eye emoji.

Tori's concern morphed into something quizzical. "He's not your sister's man anymore, you know. He hasn't been for a long time. Jaye is over him. She's been over him for years. So, if you wanted to go there..."

A firm grip yanked the chair beside me out from beneath the table, scraping it along the floor. I jerked, the sound shuddering down my spine like nails on a chalkboard.

"Go where?" Jayela sat down heavily on the wooden chair and grinned at me and Tori.

Tori opened her mouth to answer, but I gave a shake of my head, praying she'd remember that I knew all her secrets as well. Even the one about what had happened with Todd Morsely at tenth grade church camp, which I'd never told anyone. So hopefully she'd keep my unhealthy little Heath obsession to herself, too.

She pressed her lips together, the deep crimson of her lipstick flattening into a line.

I breathed a sigh of relief. "Nowhere. It doesn't matter. Where have you been? We were supposed to meet an hour ago. Tori and I are already halfway to tipsy." We'd ordered two rounds of drinks, including some for Jayela, then polished off the lot while we waited for her. The alcohol was already pleasantly warming me from the inside out.

Jaye shrugged out of her leather jacket and draped it over the back of the bar chair. "I know, I know. But things at work went to shit. Boston and I had to debrief with the chief. He's pissed. We let him down."

Tori leaned forward, resting her elbows on the tabletop. "Ooh," she singsonged. She was definitely a little tipsy, too. "What happened? Tell us all the cop drama."

Jaye shrugged. "Same old shit as every other crappy day this month. We had another botched stakeout. And Boston is being a dick about it. He thinks it's a coincidence we've had three with the exact same useless outcomes this month."

Boston had been my sister's partner at work ever since she left the academy. Normally the two of them were peas in a pod. It was extremely unlike them to argue, but this wasn't the first time this month she'd seemed on edge after coming home from a day at work with him.

I made a slightly fuzzy mental note to prod her about it later and tried to keep my gaze from flickering in the direction of the bar. "If it's not a coincidence, then what? What's your theory?"

Jaye raised a hand to signal our waitress over, but the woman was busy. She gave a nod, though, indicating she'd noticed, and Jaye turned her attention back to me. "I think three is too many. Something else is going on. Someone is tipping them off." A muscle ticked at the corner of her eye. "I don't know why Boston can't see it. We kind of got into it tonight in front of the chief."

I bit my lip. Even without her explaining further, I knew that would be eating my sister alive, slowly tearing at her conscience from the inside out. There was nothing more important to my sister than her job. Not socializing. Not men. She hadn't really dated since Heath, putting her everything into being a cop.

I darted another glance over in his direction. I couldn't help it. He hadn't moved, though he'd drained his drink. I tore my gaze away. "I'm sure it happens all the time," I told Jaye, trying to sound reassuring. "Just because you and Boston don't normally disagree, doesn't mean that other partners are as in sync, right? Your chief is probably used to sorting out things like this."

The waitress came over, and Jaye ordered more cocktails for Tori and me, and a bourbon over ice for herself. The same drink Heath was probably having. Just another reason why the two of them should have been good together.

"I suppose you're right. It's just frustrating that Boston and I can't get on the same page." Jaye watched our waitress walk back to the bar with her drink order, her gaze sliding slightly to the left as the woman put down her empty tray.

I knew the exact moment she spotted Heath. Her entire body stiffened up, and she slunk down, trying to make herself smaller. "Is that Heath?" she hissed. "Fuck. I'm going to hide under the table."

Tori giggled. "It's him. He's been there since we got in. I don't think he's noticed us, though, if you want to make a run for it."

I laughed.

Jayela shot me an apologetic cringe. "Actually, I do."

I stopped laughing. "You aren't serious?"

"I'm dead serious. I can't deal with him tonight. I can't handle the puppy dog eyes, and the sad, 'You broke my heart' expression on his face."

I blinked, trying to figure out exactly how she'd come to the conclusion that Heath was still cut up about their breakup when the man hadn't even turned around. I parroted the lines that Tori had said to me earlier. "It's been four years. And the two of you only dated for a few months. I'm sure he's fine now."

Jaye just shook her head. "You weren't there when I broke up with him. It was horrific."

The waitress chose that moment to deliver our drinks, setting a tray down on the table and placing our glasses in front of us. I used the distraction to glance over at Heath again, my view blocked when Jayela pushed to her feet, after swallowing her drink in a couple of rapid gulps. I peered around her. Sure, the man was drinking alone at a bar, looking a *little* like a heartbroken loser with no friends. But that didn't mean he was sad still about their breakup. Maybe he'd been stood up? Maybe he just liked their nachos? Maybe his dog had farted so badly it drove him out of his apartment to seek refuge in a bar until it subsided? Point was, Heath drinking alone didn't mean he was still as broken as she seemed to think he was. Jaye was beautiful and smart and athletic. But she had flaws, just like everyone else. Did she really expect him to still be hung up on her after all this time?

It kind of bugged me.

Of course he's still hung up on her, the voice inside me that sounded just like my father, chanted in my ear.

Jaye threw a few dollar bills on the table, then pushed to her feet. "You coming?" She paused, waiting for me to answer her.

My cocktail was huge. I'd barely made a dent in it. And if I was being honest, I was still basking in the glow that being in Heath's presence seemed to cast over me. I wasn't ready for that to end. "No, I think I'll stay. I'm not in the mood to go home yet."

Jaye shrugged. "Suit yourself. I think I'll go back to work, anyway. I just can't let this thing go so easily. I want to go over some paperwork. I'll catch you at home later, okay? But don't wait up. I'll probably be late."

I nodded, picking up my drink again and taking a swallow.

Tori tilted her head, watching me for a second. Then she sprang to her feet. "Jaye? Can I get a ride?"

My mouth dropped open. "Wait. You're ditching me, too?"

Tori gave me a pointed stare, her gaze flickering toward where Heath sat. "Baby at home, remember? And a husband who is probably freaking out that I've been gone this long already."

"We've only been here an hour. What happened to girls' night?"

Tori ignored my feeble protests, seeing through them easily. "I think you'll be fine. Strong, independent woman and all that."

I would kill her later. I opened my mouth to answer, but Jaye beat me to it. "Heath is here. If you have any problems, just give him the signal. He's got that savior gene. He'd probably love to swoop in and rescue you." She rolled her eyes.

Tori giggled, but I didn't say anything. From where I'd been sitting, throughout their entire, disastrous relationship, Heath had been nothing but good to Jaye. They were just mismatched as a couple. Yeah, sure, he had a protector gene. But was there anything wrong with wanting to protect the ones you love? Was there anything wrong with wanting to keep your woman safe?

Sounded kind of romantic to me. And a hell of a lot better than my exes, who definitely seemed to be missing even the most basic of human decency genes.

But I did suspect it was this incompatibility that was the straw that broke the relationship camel's back, though my tight-lipped sister would have never admitted it. He had stifled her. She had that urge to protect, too. But hers had been syphoned into her career. She'd taken an oath to protect lives and property, to help people when they were at their most vulnerable.

Heath had nowhere for his to go but onto her.

"I don't need Heath to protect me." Which was one-hundred-percent true. On the outside, I might have been the sweet elementary school teacher, who wore flowery dresses and braided her long blonde hair into Elsa-style twists, just because the little girls I taught loved it. But that wasn't the only side of me. No, I didn't need a man's protection.

Though I probably wouldn't mind if Heath wanted to scoop me up in his muscled arms and whisk me away.

I wasn't going to tell my sister that, though. "I'll be fine. I just want to have a drink and unwind a little bit. I had a hectic week. End of the school year and all."

I don't know if Jaye didn't hear me or if she just was too preoccupied glancing over at Heath again, but she let out a low groan instead of answering. "Yeah, okay. He's seen me. Time to leave. Tori, if you want a lift, I'm going now. See you later, Mae."

Tori gave me a final pointed look, and I knew exactly what she was saying with her eyes.

You've had a crush on that man for four years. You're single. You're both alone in a bar. Make something happen.

The two of them weaved around the crowd at the bar and exited out the main doors. Through the glass windows, I watched them walk across the darkened parking lot with their arms linked, Tori laughing about something Jaye said, and then the two of them disappeared into her car.

A shadow fell across me.

"Hey, Mae."

My heart rate went haywire at the sound of my name on his lips.

I swallowed hard. "Hi, Heath."

2

MAE

"Jaye's avoiding me, huh?"

The tiny hairs on the back of my neck stood on end at the deep growl in his tone. God. Had his voice gotten deeper since the last time I'd heard it? It was so incredibly masculine.

Slowly I lifted my gaze, letting it trail up his mountain of a body until I reached his face. His gorgeous face that had frequented my dreams, even after he'd stopped being a regular presence in my life. Dark stubble covered his strong jawline, a new development since the last time I'd seen him. Jaye had always liked him clean-shaven, so I'd never seen him with any sort of beard. But I liked the scruff he wore now.

Nothing had changed about his eyes, though. Their blue was still the palest shade I'd ever seen. Every time I looked into them, I was reminded of snow and ice, of stormy days in a winter landscape. The cold color gave him a standoffish appearance, as did the tattoos, and the leather jacket that fit snugly across his shoulders. It all screamed, "Bad boy. Run."

But I knew I wasn't the only woman in this bar thinking she'd rather run right into his arms than from him.

Shit. I needed to get my hormones in check before I started dry humping the man's leg.

I gave him a tiny smile. "I should probably lie for her and say she just had work stuff to do, but yeah. She's avoiding you."

"She didn't have to. I could have left. It didn't need to be awkward."

"I know."

Heath's gaze ran over me for the tiniest of seconds, starting at my head, sweeping over my hair, lingering on my face and lips. "It's been a while, huh? You look good."

The breath punched out of me, and a distinct rush of attraction had me tingly all over. Had that been a flicker of heat in his eyes? I tried to come up with a response, something sexy and light and flirty. But my brain was short-circuiting, and I was pretty sure I was just gaping at him like a bug-eyed insect. Distinctly *not* sexy.

Silence descended over us, or as much silence as there could be in a bar blaring soft rock and multiple sports games showing on big-screen TVs.

The moment slipped away.

When Heath smiled at me, it was a kind tilt of his mouth, like he'd just remembered I was the kid sister of his ex. I was twenty-seven and hardly a child, but even his completely platonic smiles stirred feelings in me. Ones I shouldn't be harboring for someone who had once dated my sister.

Oh, this was a bad idea. Very bad. I shouldn't have stayed. I should have left with the others.

But he seemed completely unaffected by me, and I

started second-guessing if it had actually been anything at all. Maybe it had just been my wishful thinking.

He motioned back to his seat with a jerk of his thumb over his shoulder. "I guess I'll go back to the game."

I gathered up my lightweight jacket. "I was just leaving anyway. Enjoy your night." Something deep and low inside me whined like a disgruntled cat who hadn't been fed on time, and heat crept up the back of my neck. Was it really a whiny cat, or a needy pussy? Oh boy. I needed to leave, stat. My alcohol-tainted thoughts were on a one-way trip to the gutter.

The pussy could be silenced in other, more solo ways. She didn't need a man who was wholly off limits.

Heath squinted through the windows to the darkness beyond. "You still driving that old Beemer?"

Of course he remembered what sort of car I drove. Because he was thoughtful and kind beneath that bad boy exterior. "Yes. But it's not out there in the parking lot. Tori and I were planning a big girls' night. We walked here from my place."

Heath's dark eyebrows drove together. "So you're walking home alone?"

There was that protector gene Jayela had been talking about.

"It's not far."

"Can I walk you?"

I laughed it off, a little squeaky. "No, no, I'll be fine. I don't want to ruin your night."

"I won't be able to concentrate if I'm wondering if you made it home okay. The game is a dud, anyway."

I started to protest again, but he cut me off. "Just let me be a gentleman, Mae."

He said it so earnestly my words shriveled on my tongue.

He was basically the perfect man. Hot as sin, with a look that screamed of motorcycles, and back alleys, and slam-you-up-against-a-wall sex. But beneath that, he was the guy who would play peekaboo with a baby just to make her smile, or walk a little old lady across the road, before saving her kitten from a tree.

I bit my lip and nodded slowly, all while my heart fluttered about my chest. How did Jaye not like this? I was ready to swoon and faint like some historical lady with her corset too tight.

"Thank you," I agreed quickly, before I could change my mind.

We were walking home together. Old friends. Nothing more than that.

Except for the fact you find him incredibly attractive, that you've always had a crush on him, and you've spent years wishing you'd had the good fortune to meet him first.

Yeah. Except for all of that.

We walked side by side toward the door, and I managed not to self-combust when my fingers brushed his. Jolts of electricity lit up at my fingertips, sparking their way up my arm.

Again, he didn't seem to notice.

As soon as we were out the door, I put a little space between us and sucked in a lungful of fresh, head-clearing night air. There was silence for a minute or two, with no need to give him directions to my apartment, since he'd been there a zillion times. I kind of wished he hadn't known, though, because it would have given me something to fill the silence with. Instead, I skittered along mounting panic because I couldn't think of anything remotely interesting to say.

I needed more alcohol in order to converse at all effectively with this man.

Heath strolled casually, much more at ease than I was, hands shoved in his pockets. Thank God it was dark, the night lit only by intermittent streetlights, because his jeans hung so low on his hips that I might have seen a sliver of his abs if his jacket happened to move in the right direction. I was busily forcing my gaze to remain on the road when he filled the silence instead.

"So. Friday night. How was your week?"

The question took me a little bit by surprise. I didn't often find myself speaking much about myself. Now that Tori was married with a baby, I spent most of my time with Jaye, just hanging out in the apartment we'd shared for years. Her job was exciting. She always had new stories full of near-death experiences. So her conversation tended to dominate. I was a teacher in the local private school. My stories were full of seven-year-olds' drama and parent-teacher conferences. When Jaye came home and started talking about stakeouts and murder investigations, my stories about how little Zach had improved so much that I'd moved him up a reading group, seemed to fall away as not particularly exciting dinner conversation.

"Just the same old stuff, really. Teacher life and all that. Parent meetings, trying to keep kids engaged with their schoolwork, other teacher politics. You know how it is." I kicked myself internally, because how would he know how it is? He wasn't a teacher. And last I'd heard, he wasn't a parent of a school-aged child. *Stupid, Mae. Stupid.* "How was yours?"

He shrugged as we turned down the sidewalk to my apartment building. Jayela's car was missing from her parking space, and I breathed a sigh of relief, even though I really wasn't doing anything wrong. This was just one old friend walking another home.

Liar.

That voice in my head really needed to shut up.

"Same old shit, too. Landscaping for rich snobs isn't exactly exciting." Then he glanced over at me. "No offence."

I shoved him in the arm. "Firstly, are you calling me a rich snob? Because I earn a teacher's salary and share a tiny two-bed condo on the edge of Saint View with my sister."

He punched in the security code and held the glass door open for me. "You *own* the condo. It may be on the border, but it still has a Providence zip code. My apartment is in the slums by comparison. And no bank would give me a mortgage, even if I begged them."

I frowned as I passed him, not because he was holding the lobby door open for me and seemed intent on walking me literally *all* the way home, but how long had it been since that code had been changed? Obviously at least four years. I glanced up at the single security camera in the corner and cringed at the fact it pointed straight at the cheap carpet and a wilted indoor plant. Though it was true that Jaye and I had bought our place outright, and it technically was in the more expensive Providence area. "Fine. But I'm not a snob."

He grinned. "I'll give you that."

That boyish smile nearly made me forget that I had a second point. "And what do you mean you're still working as a landscaper?"

He hit the button on the wall, and it lit up, signaling for the elevator. "What else would I do?"

I peered up at him. "I thought you'd be working in some flashy kitchen somewhere by now. Creating menus and wowing food critics with your recipes. I still remember that gnocchi you made from scratch, and that sauce..." The memory of the best meal I'd ever eaten in my life replayed regularly in my head, often on nights I got home from work late and ate a frozen meal for dinner. "You told me that night you wanted to have your own restaurant one day." It hadn't seemed like an out-of-reach dream because I could eat Heath's cooking every day for the rest of my life and never get sick of it.

The elevator doors binged and opened. We both put a hand out to keep the doors from closing, but neither of us moved to enter it.

He ran his teeth over his bottom lip. "I forgot I told you about that. I've never told anyone else that I once wanted to be a chef, you know? Not even Jayela."

"You didn't?" I searched back through my memories and realized he was right. Jayela hadn't been in the room when he'd confessed his ambitions. She'd worked a graveyard shift and had gone to bed early, leaving Heath and me with the cleanup. But it seemed odd he hadn't told her at any point throughout their relationship.

"That's a story for when I'm more drunk than I am right now."

There was a sudden vulnerableness in his expression that ate away at me. Like I'd picked at a wound that had never quite closed and it was now verging on spurting blood again. I didn't want to open up something painful for him, but there was also a burning desire inside me that wondered why I, of all people, was the one he'd once chosen to open up to. And if I was being honest, I was enjoying his company. This was the end of the road, and I didn't want him to leave yet. I sucked in a deep breath and blurted out the words before I could really think them through. "If it's alcohol you need, I've got tequila upstairs..."

3

MAE

Heath eyed me with an easygoing grin. "You trying to get me drunk so I'll spill my secrets?"

Trying to get him drunk so he'll get you naked, more like it.

Good Lord.

I stepped inside the elevator and raised a challenging eyebrow. "You're a big guy. I'm sure you can hold your liquor. Unless you actually do want to spill your secrets, I'm pretty sure they're safe. But my first graders tell me I'm a good listener and secret keeper. I still haven't told anyone that Layla James held hands with Ryan Slade at recess on Wednesday." I wiggled my eyebrows playfully at him.

"Wow. Elementary school scandal, huh?" He chuckled as he stepped inside the elevator with me and let the doors slide shut.

I took a deep, steadying breath, trying to control the nerves at being enclosed in such a small space with him. Just the two of us. Alone. An emergency stop button just inches from my fingers... What would happen if I just hit it and trapped the two of us inside? Maybe he'd look at me the way he had in the bar, before he'd caught himself and jumped the line back into the friend zone.

I hit the button for my floor and watched the numbers flash as we rose from the lobby. "Oh, you don't even know the half of it. Seven-year-olds have some very intense boy problems."

The doors flung themselves open when we reached our destination, and I pulled my keys from my purse. Heath leaned against the doorjamb, watching me, which only made me more nervous, because he was so damn close. His aftershave swirled around my nose tantalizingly and did weird things to my chest. He smelled so good, it was all I could do to stop myself from leaning in and licking him.

These were not sober girl thoughts. I was acutely aware of that, but my imagination, or maybe my libido, was having a field day with this situation.

Eventually, I got the lock to turn and scurried inside my condo, dropping my jacket on the back of a kitchen chair. My heart rate picked up as he followed me in, my pulse thumping hard. I made a beeline for the refrigerator. "Drink? Beer? Wine?" My fingers trembled slightly, and I changed my mind. I needed something harder. "How about that tequila?"

"I could go for tequila."

"Great!" The word came out too high and too fast. Was I even breathing properly? Panting would not be a good look. I tried to remind myself that he was only up in my home for a friendly drink. A catch-up with an old acquaintance. We were not here to quench any sort of thirst except the one in my throat.

Oh my God. Heath. My throat. Parts of Heath inside my mouth, heading for my throat... I shot a panicked glance in his direction, as if he could read my mind and the dirty things I was suddenly imagining doing with him.

He was closer than I'd expected. Standing right behind me.

My throat was drier than ever.

"Can I help?"

"Limes," I blurted out, thrusting a bag of them into his hands. "We need limes. And salt!"

I edged away from him and practically skittered to the pantry, grabbing the saltshaker from its spot on the top shelf.

"You still keep your cutting boards in this cupboard?"

I slammed my eyes closed as he bent over to grab a board from the cupboard beneath the countertop. There was no way my hormones could handle the sight of Heath's ass, without me doing something embarrassing like smacking him on it.

By the time I opened my eyes, he'd already found a knife and had sliced a lime into easily suckable wedges. He watched me curiously. "Are you okay?"

I took the tequila and a couple of shot glasses from another cupboard and put them down on the countertop beside him. "Yeah, I just...sorry. It's just...is it weird you're here? With me, I mean?"

His gaze met mine and drifted slowly over my face once more, and this time, when he lingered on my lips, there was no doubt in my mind I was seeing things. I wasn't. There was something between us that hadn't been there—at least not on his side—the last time I'd seen him. It sparked between us now that we were alone, an almost tangible force that demanded attention.

"No weirder than any other guy you've brought home from a bar, is it?" He stepped in closer, and my skin tingled at the nearness of him. "You've done that before, right?"

"Once or twice," I admitted. I swallowed hard, frozen to the spot while I waited for his touch.

But he just reached for the tequila bottle and poured a hefty shot into each glass, then pushed one in my direction.

"Then it's not weird, because I know you a whole lot better than some random stranger does. At least you know I'm not going to search through your bathroom cupboards or steal your spare change. You ready to do this?"

I imagined the burn of the tequila rolling down my throat. I wasn't sure whether I was excited for it or dreading it. But I did know that the warmth would loosen the awkward tongue-tie I currently found myself locked in with Heath standing so close to me. I licked the back of my hand and picked up the saltshaker from the center of the table. "I don't think I've done one of these since college."

"Me neither. Not that I went to college, but I went to the parties." Heath took the salt from me, our fingers brushing in the process. He licked the inside of his wrist and sprinkled the salt over it, making sure a generous amount stuck to his skin.

I watched, mesmerized, and then tried to get a handle on my brain that was currently fritzing out and drunk yelling ridiculous things like, "Imagine it wasn't his skin he just licked. Imagine if it were yours!" That tingle that had shot through my arm at the tiniest of touches, turned into a full-body tremble that I tried to play off as the result of a cool gust from the air-conditioning.

"On three?" I held my hand up to my mouth and waited for his okay.

He grinned. "Three."

I hesitated for a tiny second, just long enough to watch

him lick the salt from his wrist, before I did the same, licking it from the back of my hand. In near unison, we both picked up our shot glasses and tossed back the clear liquid. It burned. Just like I remembered from back in my college days, it traced a fiery path straight down my throat and lower, warming as it went. We both grabbed lime wedges from the cutting board, and I stuck mine in my mouth, squeezing it between my teeth, sucking it hard, easing the burn of the alcohol.

Heath pulled the wedge away from his lips before I did. "Green smiles suit you."

I couldn't help the grin that tugged at the corners of my mouth. He was referring to the lime still clamped between my teeth. I let it go, dropping it to the countertop. The beginnings of a blush built behind my cheeks, and not wanting to show that his slightly odd compliment affected me, I held up the second of our shots and offered it to him. "Shall we do the other one?"

He raised a thick, perfect, naturally formed eyebrow, and his forehead wrinkled. "Back-to-back shots? Don't you know how old I am?"

I relaxed a little at his teasing tone and screwed up my face at him. "Not that crap again. I remember having this conversation years ago. You aren't that much older than me."

"Thirty-two this year."

"Oh, you're such an old man," I teased. Wait, was I actually flirting with this guy somewhat successfully? It kind of felt like I was, but hey, maybe that was the tequila and cocktails. Probably best I get this next shot down before I started doubting myself again, even though my head was already spinning.

"Five years on you." But he picked up his second shot

anyway, not bothering with the salt this time. "It kind of felt like a lifetime when I was with Jayela."

At the mention of my sister's name, I threw back my shot quicker than I had intended, and a cough spluttered up my throat. Though I tried to force it down, it was a losing battle. I choked, bringing my arm up to cough into my elbow. My eyes watered.

Heath held out a wedge of lime after downing his own shot much more successfully than I had, but when I continued coughing, unable to even take the wedge from his hand, his amusement turned into concern. "Are you okay?"

I forced myself to nod as I coughed. "Fine," I choked out. Well, this was embarrassing.

Heath scooted closer, and before I could protest, his big hand landed between my shoulder blades, alternating between patting and smoothing his palm down my back.

Even through my clothes, his touch was warm and delicious. If I died in that moment, choked to death by an overeager tequila shot, I wouldn't have cared. I would have died happy.

Maybe it was that touch that made me lose my mind. Or maybe it was the tequila. Maybe it was Tori hyping me up, or maybe the glue fumes from the art project I'd had my class do that afternoon had killed a few brain cells. But something made me brave. Something made me want more of those touches. Something made me want to shoot my shot.

My coughing fit subsided. "Are you still in love with my sister?"

Heath's icy-blue eyes turned up at the corner in amusement. "Seriously? We're going there?"

I nodded, completely serious. "Yeah, apparently. Are you?"

He snorted, his lips curving into a grin. “Is that why she left tonight? Because she thinks I’m still in love with her?”

I lifted one shoulder. “She thinks you’re still hung up on her, yeah.”

He shook his head with a chuckle. “She was never short of confidence, was she?”

I could agree with that. But he still hadn’t answered my question. I gazed down at my hands.

He put one finger beneath my chin and lifted it so I was forced to face him. “Hey. I’m not in love with your sister. I haven’t been in love with her for a long time.”

Relief crashed through me, but he was still touching me, staring at me with those eyes, freezing me to the spot. I couldn’t speak. Except I needed to. Because it wasn’t enough that he just wasn’t in love with my sister. “You’re dating someone then?”

He dropped his hand and tilted his head to one side curiously. His gaze raked slowly over me. “Not right now.”

I don’t know why, but I found that hard to believe. If he wasn’t in love with my sister, then what the hell was his problem? He could have had any woman in the bar on her back in less than thirty seconds, if he’d wanted to. I narrowed my eyes, suddenly suspicious he wasn’t telling the truth about being over Jaye. “You have dated, though? Since Jaye?”

He ran his finger around the edge of his empty shot glass, looking like he was battling back laughter. “You wondering if I’m a born-again virgin, Mae?”

A blush heated my cheeks. “Oh my God. No. That’s not what I meant!”

He chuckled. “Then why the sudden interest in my dating life?”

He was right. Those questions had been totally over the

line and inappropriate. It wasn't my business. "Blame the old crush I had on you." The words slipped out my mouth as if they had a mind of their own and echoed in the empty condo around us. I slapped a hand over my mouth then groaned. "And you can blame that on the tequila. How strong is that stuff? Let's have another." Anything to ease the embarrassment. If I drank enough tonight, perhaps I'd wake up in the morning and not remember any of it. I downed another shot quickly, and then poured two more, letting him take one.

Heath raised one eyebrow as he picked up his shot glass and downed the liquid inside. His throat had to be burning, but a chuckle formed on his lips. "Crush, huh?"

The pure amusement on his face put me at ease instantly. I'd already put my foot in it, may as well dig my grave a little deeper. By the time we got to the bottom of that bottle, this conversation would be a long-lost memory. "Yeah. A crush. You know, the embarrassing kind, that makes you say really stupid things when you've had too much to drink? Like telling your sister's ex-boyfriend that you think he's cute."

I cringed. Did I just say cute? Heath was not cute. Babies were cute. Puppies were cute. Heath was gorgeous, all man, and sexy as fuck. I threw my hands up in the air in defeat, tequila storming around my body now, fighting for full control. "Oh boy, I just keep going and going, don't I? Kill me now."

"Mae?"

I lifted my gaze to meet his, surprised it was suddenly a little on the hazy side. Or maybe it was *my* gaze that was hazy. I blinked to clear it, but it didn't do much to help. I tried not to let him notice, though. "Yeah?" I forced the word to sound more sober than I felt.

He hesitated, like he wanted to say something but was suddenly thinking better of it. He held a finger up, in a halt motion. "Wait." He threw back another tequila shot, stared at me once more, swore low under his breath, and threw back another. "I don't think you're cute."

Well, okay then! Nothing like a rejection straight to your face without any sort of beating around the bush. "Of course. Sorry. I'm drunk. Just ignore me." Disappointment crushed down on me like a ton of bricks piling up on my chest. I didn't think I was that bad to look at, but he'd dated Jayela, so I probably wasn't his type. Despite the fact she and I were sisters, we were nothing alike. She was all hard lines, abs, and '*I run five miles every day*.' While I was more soft curves, a tummy roll, and '*Maybe sometimes I do yoga, but mostly because there's a great bakery next door.*'

My breath hitched when he stepped in closer. His fingers skated down the side of my face and tilted my chin once more. "You didn't let me finish." He grinned, his words a little slurred. "You're not cute, anymore. You were, but now you're not. You're smoking fucking hot, Mae."

I just stared at him, then when the silence was almost awkward, I burst into laughter. "You are so drunk."

He shrugged. "Yeah, but I still meant what I said. And I mean this, too." He paused, his gaze on my lips again. "I want to kiss you. But I don't want to scare you off. Or do something you'll regret."

My eyes widened. I almost asked him to repeat himself but instead I picked up the tequila bottle and took a slug straight from the opening. It didn't even burn anymore.

Then I offered it to him because this was crazy talk. He swallowed straight from the bottle, too, his gaze never leaving mine.

"We can't be talking like this," I said, but I didn't move back, just watched his Adam's apple bob.

He shifted the tequila to his left hand and twirled a lock of my hair around his finger, the blonde strands falling back around my shoulders. "We're both consenting adults..." He ran his thumb over my lip. "Tell me to stop, and I'll stop."

He was insane if he thought I was going to tell him to stop. I couldn't now, even if I'd wanted to. The throbbing between my thighs had taken over and was talking for me.

"Jayela can't see you here."

"I'm not hers."

I shook my head but stopped quickly when it made the world spin. "That's not how sisters work. You were hers once. That makes you...forbidden fruit."

He laughed, and the sound curled my toes pleasantly. "Forbidden fruit? I'm just a guy, Mae. Nothing special. I'm single. You're single. We aren't hurting anyone, standing here like this." He leaned in, lowering his lips to my ear, brushing my hair aside as he went. "We wouldn't be hurting anyone, if while we were standing here, I pushed these straps down and kissed your shoulder."

I still wasn't saying no. I didn't want to. Not for a second. What I really wanted to do was scream, "Yes! Dear God, yes!"

His lips skated over the skin of my shoulder, dragging up toward my neck.

"We wouldn't be hurting anyone if I hiked that dress up, gripped your hips, and wrapped your thighs around my waist..."

My eyes fluttered closed, and a breathy noise escaped my throat.

I waited for him to do it, a pulse pounding between my legs.

The rattle of the doorknob turning had my eyes flying open in panic. All good feelings smashed into smithereens when I imagined my sister walking in and finding me standing in the kitchen with her ex talking dirty in my ear, and my nipples so hard they stood out through even a padded bra. I spun away, ready to intercept, but Heath's fingers wrapped around my wrist and hauled me toward my open bedroom door. My feet didn't move well after copious amounts of alcohol, and Heath caught me as I stumbled, shutting us into my room. I let out a nervous giggle, wrapped in his arms, and he pressed a finger to my lips.

"Shh. She'll hear."

I giggled again. "You shh."

His grin was devastating. He tightened his grip on me, and we both froze, listening to Jayela's footsteps pass my bedroom. Her door closed with a soft click.

His quiet laughter subsided. "I really do want to kiss you."

"I really want you to as well."

"But..."

With a sigh, I stepped away to the wall, sliding down it to sit on my carpet. "This isn't the right time, is it?"

"We're really drunk."

I snorted because that was the understatement of the year. "There's two of you. You'd be really hot as a twin, you know that? Like, two Heaths! Hotttttt."

We both laughed, shushing each other.

Heath stared down at me. "What now? You want me to sneak out once she's asleep?"

Maybe I'd regret it in the cold light of dawn, but right now, I just wanted him to stay, even if kissing was off the table. I tugged at the leg of his jeans and held up the bottle of tequila still clutched in my fingers. "You gotta be gone by the time she wakes up. But…we've still got tequila. You can't go yet."

He slid down the wall beside me, then took the bottle from my hand.

When I passed out, it was with Heath's arm wrapped tightly around my shoulders, my head on his chest, and a sense of rightness I'd never felt before.

4

HEATH

A thousand spears stabbed into my brain; tequila salt shoved into the wounds. I squeezed my eyes shut tight against the single blinding sunbeam shining in around the edge of the blackout curtain and racked my fuzzy brain for where I was and why I was so horrifically hungover. My stomach churned, and bile rose in my throat, threatening to erupt, but I went perfectly still, forcing the nauseous feeling away so I could think.

Mae.

Talking to her at the bar. Walking her home. Going inside and kissing her neck, and then... Shit. Then what? I squeezed my eyes tighter. She was five years younger than me and Jayela's little sister. What the hell had I been thinking?

My dick stiffened at the barely-there memory. I remembered standing in the kitchen wanting to kiss her. Wanting to run my hands up her thighs and over the curve of her hips and tits. But after that everything was black. Had we done more? The uncomfortable, stiff denim of my jeans still chaffed around my thighs, so I didn't think so, but my brain could neither confirm nor deny.

I cracked open one eye, expecting to see Mae's waterfall of blonde hair spread out across her pillow.

The hair spread out across the pillow wasn't blonde.

It was dark. Almost jet-black. And entirely too familiar. My eyes widened as I took in the decorations of the room around me. It was not the mint walls I remembered from Mae's bedroom. These were a more familiar navy blue and decorated with symbols from the police force. There was a certificate, received the day she finished at the Academy. And a medal for outstanding excellence she'd accepted at an awards night I'd accompanied her to. I scrubbed a hand over my face, the realization sinking in.

I wasn't in Mae's bed.

I was in Jayela's.

Shit. I was fucked and without any clue of how I'd gotten there. I'd been flirting with Mae while we did shots. We'd made it to her bedroom at some point, though now I wasn't exactly sure why, if it hadn't been to hook up. Ugh, fucking tequila. All those memories were surrounded in intense feelings of desire and need. They were good feelings. But after that it was a complete black hole of nothing. Maybe I'd gotten up in the middle of the night and gotten confused? I'd spent hundreds of nights here. Had it just been habit that had me waking up in the wrong bed? And how was it that Jayela hadn't woken up and kicked me out? Fuck! This was all seriously messed up, and I needed to get the hell out.

Jayela's back was to me so I couldn't see her face, blankets tucked tightly around her. She always had slept like the dead; maybe if I was lucky, I could sneak out of here without her even noticing.

I pulled the covers back on my side, only far enough that I could carefully slip out without disturbing her. I blinked a few times in the still dark room, my gaze fuzzy with sleep and the aftereffects of alcohol, and then stumbled for the door.

At the doorway, so close to freedom, a sudden sinking feeling swamped me so hard it stopped me in my tracks.

Something wasn't right.

An odd smell permeated the room, finally cutting through my groggy senses.

My eyes narrowed on Jayela's silent form, the only noise in the room my stilted breathing.

Jayela was entirely too still.

I stared at her for a long moment. Waiting for her shoulders to rise and fall with her breaths, but there was no noticeable movement. Concern seeped in, and my desire to escape disintegrated. I went back to the bed and reached out a hand to touch her back. "Jayela?" I whispered. When she didn't respond, I shook her shoulder a little harder until she flopped onto her back.

The breath punched from my lungs, and my knees went weak.

Her eyes stared emptily at the ceiling. Fixed and unmoving.

A red gash slashed across her milky-white throat.

I couldn't even identify the sound that ripped from my chest. It was something between a shout and a stifled, "No!"

A sudden rush of energy filled my body. The headache disappeared. The nausea disintegrated. The bile rising up my throat doubled, trying to choke me around a horrified scream that couldn't escape. But my body went into action. On autopilot I launched myself onto the bed, shaking her harder even though my logical brain was already screaming words I didn't want to hear. I yanked the blanket back and recoiled from the sight before me.

Blood. So much blood. It was everywhere.

The bile rose up my throat again as I tried to yell for Mae, but my voice wouldn't work. I tried again. My hands went into autopilot, one trying to stem the blood from her throat, the other blindly finding the center of Jayela's chest to start CPR.

Blood covered that, too.

But I pushed on anyway. I had no idea if I was doing it right, leaning on her chest, her body flopping and bouncing on the mattress beneath my weight, while her blood coated my hands.

"Mae!" I yelled, voice finally working.

From down the hall, the click of a door opening sounded. "Heath? Where are you?"

"Here." I pumped Jayela's chest, trying not to look at the unseeing expression on her face, trying not to see the blue around her lips, trying not to see how utterly lifeless she remained, no matter what I did. I choked on my words. "Call an ambulance."

Mae's footsteps in the hallway turned into a run at my command, and she threw the door open. I glanced up at her.

The expression of pure horror on her face gutted me from the inside out. She didn't even scream. The blood just drained from her face.

"Call an ambulance," I repeated.

She didn't move.

In that moment, Mae was as lifeless as her sister.

"Mae! Move!" I snapped. "Do it now."

She finally rushed across the room, grabbing her sister's phone from the charger and stabbing at it with trembling fingers. I couldn't pay attention to her any longer. I stared down at Jayela, down at my hands covered in her blood, and my heart broke open.

Her eyes didn't flicker. Her waxy flesh was freezing. Her wounds had stopped bleeding, her heart long given out.

There was no saving her. What I'd said to Mae last night had been the truth. I didn't love Jayela anymore. I hadn't loved her for a long time. But she'd been such a big part of my life once upon a time, and seeing her now, seeing her like this, seeing what some monster had done to her while I was passed out in the very same condo was impossible. It was futile trying to comprehend any of it. None of it made sense. I would have heard. I should have seen. How could I have let myself get so drunk that someone could do this and I wouldn't even know? Guilt swamped me hard and fast, an avalanche of remorse burying me deep.

I didn't notice when Mae dropped the phone to the floor. All I noticed was her tiny, shaking voice when she finally spoke to me once more. "What did you do?"

The tremble in her voice was like a tremor before the volcano erupted. Her words hadn't even sunk through my head before she was screaming. "What did you do, Heath?"

I froze. "What?"

She stared at the savage slit across her sister's throat. "You're covered in blood!"

I glanced up, into the mirror on the wall, and recoiled at my reflection. The blood wasn't just on my hands. It was splattered across my face. And when I stopped to look down at myself, it soaked my shirt and jeans.

"I didn't..."

But Mae's face said that I did. Said that I had. She stared at me with an expression I'd never seen before and one I hoped I never would again.

She stared at me with pure fear.

I'd been here before. With blood on my hands and people staring at me in shock. The screams echoed through my ears once more, as loud and clear as if I were right back there. The body beneath me morphed and became a face that had haunted my dreams for the past fifteen years. A face I knew I would never forget as long as I lived.

Mae launched herself across the room, hitting and pushing at me, her fists beating at my face. "Get away from her!"

I backed right off and stopped trying to be the hero who brought Jayela back. The logical side of my brain told me that it wouldn't make any difference anyway. She was gone. She'd been gone as I lay there by her side. I took in what Mae saw from across the room. The white shirt I'd worn to the bar last night was still stretched across my chest, but now instead of white, it was decorated a sickly crimson.

So was the knife that lay discarded on the floor at the end of the bed.

I hadn't even noticed it before...but now it was all I could see.

I staggered away until my back hit the wall, shock pumping through my veins. My brain yelled accusations. *You've been here before. You have a temper. You don't know when to stop. Look what you've done. Look what you've done. Look what you've done!*

"No."

I'd heard that voice before. For years it had taunted me, and I'd silenced it in so many different ways. Alcohol. Women. Therapy. I wasn't going back there.

I knew who I was. I knew what I'd done. And what I hadn't.

I might have grown up on the wrong side of the tracks. I might have been dealt with a shitty hand, over and over.

Jayela might have taken the one thing I'd desperately wanted from me. But I knew who I was. And killing an innocent woman—a woman I'd once loved—I was not that man.

But Mae's reaction was like the knife covered in Jayela's blood, stabbing through my own heart. Her screams and the fear in her eyes as she yelled for help sent me spiraling out of control, and the nightmare that was my past reared up like some evil beast, coating the room in its black smoke, swirling it around me, chuckling darkly as it went.

"Oh God, please." She clutched her sister's limp hand. "What have you done, Heath?"

There was no point trying to explain. I knew how bad this looked. My chest constricted. She wouldn't listen. And I couldn't breathe. I was literally suffocating in a room full of air.

I ran from the room, from the building, into the cold light of dawn, so the darkness couldn't take me under like it had once before.

5

MAE

I couldn't move. Even when Boston, my sister's work partner, kneeled at my feet and shook me by the shoulders, I didn't budge. I just held tight to my legs pulled up to my chest, while my brain locked itself away, too stunned to function properly.

I was dimly aware of the conversation around me, but it was little more than a buzz, a constant drone of white noise that I couldn't seem to isolate into individual words. I just stared with unseeing eyes at the blood soaking into my sister's sheets. I'd bought her the plain white Egyptian cotton set for her birthday just a few months ago. They'd been so pure, so soft, so blindingly white they'd almost hurt my eyes. But they'd gone perfectly with her navy walls.

The ugly deep red her blood had stained them didn't match the room at all. That color didn't belong here. None of this was right.

Strong arms came around me, trying to gather me up. I balked at the contact, thrashing, throwing out my arms and legs, and screamed, "No! Don't touch me!"

"Mae," a quiet voice said in my ear. "It's me. It's Will."

I peered up at my best friend's husband in a daze, taking in his familiar face and his concerned eyes. "Will? What are you doing here?"

Tori nudged into my line of view, steadfastly not looking in the direction of my sister's bed. Her eyes were wild, and filled with tears, but she spoke to me in the same way she spoke to her son when he was upset. "Hey. It's us. Let us help you, okay? We need to get you out of here. It's the only reason they let us in." Her cheeks were stained with tears, and her voice sounded hoarse. "The police couldn't get you to move without you lashing out. They were talking about sedating you, but we talked Boston into breaking the rules and letting us try first."

I glanced up at Will again and this time surrendered to being scooped up from the floor and carried out into the living room. Tori trailed after us, and when her husband placed me down on the couch, she was quick to put a blanket over me. I was grateful for it. My skin pebbled with goosebumps, and a chill sank right through my skin and deep into my bones.

"You need to leave," Boston's gruff yet familiar voice said. "We need to question her."

Tori, though tiny in stature, was like a bulldog. She drew herself up to her full five feet, two inches, and stared down the big police officer. "We aren't leaving. You can question her all you want when she's had medical attention. Can't you see that she's not in any state to do anything right now?" The anger in her eyes was belied by the crack in her voice. "God, Boston. What's wrong with you?" A sob cut off the last of her words, and her husband wrapped his arms around her small frame, drawing her into his chest and murmuring quiet words of comfort in her ear. Will, big into his church and faith, was normally the sort of guy who would frown if you swore in his presence. I knew he was really rattled, because he didn't even flinch when Tori took the Lord's name in vain.

"It's okay. I can do it." Out here, away from the sight of my sister's body, I could think better. I knew I'd have to talk, and I didn't want medical attention. It wasn't me who needed it. My sister... My throat went dry. My sister didn't need medical attention now either. She'd been gone from the moment I walked into her bedroom and seen... I didn't even know what I'd seen. I was still trying to work it out. I gazed up into Boston's hazel eyes and found them hard. Surprise hit me at the cold expression there. That wasn't like him. His eyes were normally warm and twinkling with mischief and laughter.

"I need you to get it together and talk to me," he urged.

His lips pinched together in frustration. How long had he been trying to talk to me?

"Do you want whoever did this to get away with it? Come on, Mae. I need you to tell me everything. Any little detail, and I need you to tell me now. There's no sign of forced entry, so this is probably someone you know. The longer you take, the bigger the chance we never catch this guy."

I bristled a little at the tone, and the insinuation that I was deliberately trying to hold up an investigation. I only let it go because despite the fact Boston currently appeared to be in full work mode, I knew he had to be in pieces on the inside. He loved Jayela like a sister.

"I don't know what happened," I admitted honestly. "We got drunk last night, and when I woke up this morning it was to Heath yelling my name—"

Boston glanced up sharply. "We? Who's Heath? There was someone else here?" He paused for a moment, as if wondering why that name sounded familiar. I could see the moment it dawned on him. "Heath? As in Jayela's ex-boyfriend Heath?" His eyes narrowed when I nodded. "What the hell were you doing with him?"

I didn't need to be able to read his mind to know what he was thinking. I could see the judgment all over his face. Guilt swamped me. "Yes. That Heath. I met up with him in a bar last night, and we came back here afterward."

Tori's eyes went wide.

"We had drinks. A lot of them." I glanced over toward my bedroom, the door still open, the near empty bottle of tequila discarded when Heath and I had finished it off and crawled into bed.

Boston looked over the messy sheets and the comforter spilling onto the carpet. "You had sex with your sister's boyfriend?" His tone was ice cold, like razor wire cutting through my skin.

"What? No!" I racked my brain, trying to remember, but nothing was clear. "I mean, I don't think so. We had some shots and we flirted. But then Jayela came home. We passed out. Or at least I did. I don't know what happened after that. All I know is when I woke up this morning, Heath was in Jaye's room, covered in blood..."

I stared up into Boston's eyes, and it was like looking straight into his head.

A fire raged, hot and angry, and ready for vengeance.

I suddenly realized the picture I was painting. And despite my own accusations, I'd had time to process the things I'd seen while I'd waited for the police to show up. "He was trying to save her, Boston. He had his hand on her throat, trying to stop the blood..."

"You think that means anything? He wouldn't be the first jealous lover who had instant regret. You're going to have to give me more. Tell me his full name. Quick, Mae. If I can get a team out over to his house now, before he does a runner, we might actually be able to nail him."

"Wait. Nail him? You don't know he did anything." I turned to Tori and Will for some sort of backup, unsure of what to do, but both of them were nodding. Confusion swirled in my brain. None of this made sense. "Michaelson," I told Boston. "Heath Michaelson. He has an apartment in Saint View. But I—"

Boston ignored my protests, launching to his feet, his heavy boots stomping across the floor as he paced. He pulled a walkie-talkie from the loop on his belt and spat out a series of commands into it. "Somebody find this guy's apartment and get a team over there now. Restrain him, but you do not talk to him until I get there. Is that clear?"

A garbled response crackled across his radio.

Boston stopped in front of me, his gaze never letting up for even a second. "Did you hear anything during the night?"

"No, I swear. Heath and I... And then nothing. Nothing until this morning when I woke up and heard him yelling for me."

"Did you see him with the knife?"

I blinked up at him in surprise. "What knife?"

He motioned to one of the officers leaning against my living room wall, and they moved into Jayela's bedroom, emerging a second later with a knife in an evidence bag. The officer passed it to Boston, and Boston held it up in front of me.

I cringed away, my sister's blood still coating the stainless steel of the blade. But I recognized it.

I had seen Heath with it. I hesitated, knowing it wouldn't

sound good to admit it. But I couldn't lie "I did see him with that knife but—"

"Son of a bitch," Boston muttered.

"That's all I saw, though." I grabbed his hand. "He used it to cut up limes for tequila shots last night. That's all."

He shook me off. "What do you know about him? Is he violent?"

"Heath? No, never."

"Has he got a temper?"

"I've never even heard him raise his voice. And he dated Jayela. You know how she is, she loves to argue. Loved... Oh God." A sudden wave of nausea swamped me, sending me jumping off the couch and running for the bathroom. I slunk down onto the cold porcelain tiles, desperate to be sick, desperate to rid my body of the turmoil of emotions coursing through it, but I couldn't. I just gagged, dry heaving until my chest ached.

"It's okay." Tori rubbed a hand down my back, lifting my hair out of the way.

"It's not okay! I don't understand any of this. Heath and I were great last night. And then I wake up this morning and my sister is dead and he's covered in blood. I don't know what happened in between. I can't remember anything. There's just nothing but darkness. I didn't hear anything, didn't see anything, and Boston is acting like I should have all the answers." I blinked up at Tori, tears blurring my vision, then darted a look over my shoulder. Boston talked with two other officers. They both watched me, suspicion etched into their calculated stares. "I blamed Heath," I hissed at her. "I asked him what he'd done! He was covered in blood, but... But it can't have been him. Why would he kill her then stick around to try to save her in the morning? It doesn't make any sense."

Tori dropped to her knees beside me and wrapped me in a tight hug. "I don't know."

I sobbed in her arms, trying to make sense of any of it. But the more I thought about it, the more none of it fit together. Heath wasn't a violent man. He didn't have a temper that I'd ever seen. I knew who he was. He'd loved my sister. And I believed him when he'd said last night that he was over her. What reason would he have to do something like this?

"Tori." She pulled back so she could see my face. "I've made a horrible mistake. This couldn't have been Heath. I just... I can't believe that."

"Okay, shh. I believe you. It's going to be okay. Boston is a good cop. He's just angry right now and searching for someone to blame. He'll talk to Heath and get it sorted out. You don't need to be worrying about it. Come on." She helped me up from the floor, put her arm around my shoulders, and guided me to where Boston stood.

"Is there any news about Heath?" I asked him.

He narrowed his eyes. "Why are you so concerned about him?"

I blinked at the hostility in his voice. "Because he's my friend!"

"Your friend? Are you kidding me right now? You said yourself that the man was covered in your sister's blood. She's lying dead in there, and you're worried about your 'friend'? Your friend probably killed his ex in a jealous rage, Mae! Don't fucking ask me how he is!"

I recoiled, stumbling back a few steps. "He was trying to save her! What reason would he have to kill her now, four years after they broke up?"

"Opportunity?" Boston spat, voice filled with venom. "You opened the door to your home when you opened your legs for him, and let the man back in. You admitted yourself that you were passed out, too drunk to hear a thing. You gave him the opportunity."

My mouth dropped open, my cheeks flaming hot.

Tori gasped, "Boston!"

Will stepped in front of her, his anger clear in the pinched tone of his voice. "I know you're hurting right now, man. But you're out of line. You're too close to this. Back off."

Boston rose to his feet, going chest to chest with Will.

I yelped, pushing between the two of them. "Stop it!" I whirled on Will. "Thank you, but you don't need to defend my honor."

I spun back to Boston and cracked my palm across his cheek.

A roar went up from the other officers, one launching himself across the room and grabbing me by the arm. It wasn't going to stop me saying my piece. Because I didn't care how close he was to my sister, or how much he was hurting right now. "How dare you," I seethed at him. "How dare you imply, even for a second, that I am in any way involved in what happened to Jayela. You can go to Hell, Boston."

The officer yanked me tighter and withdrew a set of handcuffs from a holder on the side of his pants. "You're under arrest for the assault of a police officer—"

Boston shook his head. "Stop. Let her go."

The officer glanced up in surprise. "But she—"

"I don't fucking care what she did!" Boston roared. "I said let her go!"

Both the officer and I took a step back, and the cuff disappeared from my wrist, as did the officer's grip. He scuttled out and hightailed it down the hallway.

"Sorry," Boston muttered, running a hand through his dark-brown hair. "I was out of line."

A little of my anger cooled, but I couldn't forget that quickly. His accusations had opened up a whole new well of guilt for me, that I knew I'd be drowning in just as soon as the anger dissipated. I stared him down. "I don't believe Heath did this, Boston. I don't. You need to listen to me. It looks bad, I know. I thought that, too. But now that I've had a minute to think about it—"

Boston's phone binged with an incoming message, and he edged away from me to read it. When he looked back up, his eyes were as good as dead. "It doesn't matter what you think. Or what I think. Heath Michaelson just admitted to murder."

6

HEATH

I don't know how I made it back to the bar parking lot. I ran blindly, barely noticing that the rough pavement tore at the bare soles of my feet. A woman stood at the door to the building, locking up in the early morning light after what had to be a long shift. Dark tendrils of sweaty hair stuck to the back of her neck, and a quick glance at her face revealed her to be the waitress I'd ordered my drinks from the night before. Her gaze fixed on mine.

Last night she'd smiled at me. Maybe even flirted a little, though I hadn't flirted back.

This morning her gaze flickered with recognition. But then it raked down my body, taking in my unkempt clothes, now covered in Jayela's blood.

I didn't need the woman to voice her thoughts. They were written all over her face. A gasp fell from her lips as she dropped her keys. A sob burst forth, and she scuttled to pick them up, frantically stabbing at the door, trying to get it open once more.

Trying to get away from me.

I didn't have it in me to try to reassure her that I was no threat. There was no convincing anyone of that in the state I was in. She was just as scared of me as Mae had been. Instead, I yanked my car key from the pocket of my jacket and popped the lock on my beat-up truck. The woman's choking cries followed me inside, and I slammed the door behind me, desperate to block them out.

I gulped in air for what felt like the first time since I'd started running. My lungs burned, trying to pull in the oxygen I so desperately needed. I turned the truck on and jerked the gearshift down into reverse.

It was a force of habit to look into the rearview mirror. But I immediately wished I hadn't. Blood droplets speckled my face, and a smear spread across my cheek. Dried blood stiffened the neck of my T-shirt.

I slammed on the brakes, suddenly overcome with nausea, and only just managed to open the truck door before I was sick. Pain pierced through my gut, my stomach muscles clenching and releasing as I hurled.

When I straightened, wiping my mouth, the woman from the bar was gone. Probably holed up somewhere inside, the doors locked behind her, her cell phone pressed to her ear while she frantically reported my license plate to the police.

There was little need, since they'd already be at Mae's house by now. Jayela was a cop. Mae would be telling them everything she'd seen, and they'd be wanting to arrest someone hard and fast for this. Fuck. The evidence stacked up in front of my eyes. I was from the wrong side of the tracks, born and bred in Saint View, with not even a high school diploma to my name. And with a record of violent crime to boot, even if it had been a long time ago. I'd been there at Mae and Jayela's condo all night. My DNA would be all over Jayela's bed, and then there'd be Mae's testimony that she found me, covered in her sister's blood. All it would take to put me away would be a motive, and even a first day lawyer would come up with some reason why an ex would have wanted to hurt her. An argument. Jealousy. This list would be long, they'd just pick their favorite.

I hadn't done it. I didn't care how bad it seemed or how blank my memories were of the night before. No matter how drunk I was, I hadn't done this. But no matter which way I turned, walls rose, huge unmountable objects that stood between me and anybody believing my innocence.

I drove home slowly, winding my car through the familiar streets of Saint View, trying to come up with a plan that didn't end with a lethal injection in my arm. With every mile that passed, it became more and more obvious I had no options. By the time I reached my street, I realized that all I could do was go to the police, tell my side of the story, and pray someone believed me.

Or run.

Fuck that. I wasn't going down for something I didn't do. They'd believe me. They had to.

It wasn't a surprise to find two police cruisers parked outside my shitty apartment complex. Although that wasn't an entirely uncommon sight around here, this time, I knew they were here for me. I trudged to my door, startling the officer stationed outside. His eyes widened as he took in my appearance, and he yelped, fumbling for his gun with nervous fingers. "Stop!"

I did as I was told, giving the young cop time to get his gun out and point it at me. "Take it easy. I'm not going to do anything."

"Get on your knees. And uh...put your hands up!"

I wondered if this was the first time he'd ever actually arrested anyone.

I dropped and lowered my gaze to the dirty ground beneath my knees.

"What the fuck?" Another voice, this one older and deeper, questioned as he came out of my apartment.

The weight of the rookie's gun trained on my chest was practically palpable. Even though I wasn't looking at him, I knew his finger trembled over the trigger. One tiny movement, and he'd send a bullet through my heart.

It already felt like he had. I was as dead inside as if my heart had stopped beating the moment I'd realized Jayela was gone. I might not have been in love with her, but I never wanted to see anyone like that. Especially not someone I'd once cared about.

I could only imagine what this was doing to Mae.

"Fucking hell, it's him. You son of a bitch. Get him in here before all the neighbors see and someone calls the news for a quick payout."

Rough hands wrapped around my wrists, yanking my arms down and securing them behind my back with cold metal cuffs. The older officer hauled me to my feet and shoved me toward the door. My chest touched the barrel of the rookie's gun, that he seemed unable to lower, frozen into position by shock or maybe fear.

The man behind me pressed in closer, his burly chest pushing against my back and shoving me further into the gun barrel. "He should put one of those right through your chest for what you've done," he snarled. "Move, cop killer."

The rookie, slightly more composed now that I was in cuffs and his older partner had taken over, watched me walk by him, his earlier bewilderment morphing into something stronger. "Fucking piece of scum," he taunted.

Obviously not his first day on the job, then. He'd been around long enough for his partner to teach him how cops rolled around here.

I didn't say anything. This wasn't anything I hadn't seen before. The police treated anyone with a Saint View address like they were barely better than dogshit on their shoe. We all knew to just shut up and go along with it. Mouthing off only made things worse. So I followed them into my apartment, noting the kicked-in door. I doubted they'd bothered with a warrant. When one of their own was the victim, I had a pretty strong feeling that all rules went out the window.

That theory proved correct just seconds after making it through the doorway. The older man shoved me into a kitchen chair so roughly it nearly toppled backward. The two front legs lifted off the floor, and it was only my own sense of self-preservation that had me leaning forward enough to counterbalance and keep the chair upright.

The older cop paced the floor in front of me, his fingers clenched into fists at his side. Barely concealed rage poured off him in waves. "Why'd you do it?" he finally managed to spit out. He stopped pacing and stared at me. "Fucking tell me why? Why her?"

"I didn't." I knew it to my core. I couldn't have. It didn't matter what I'd done in the past. I wasn't that man anymore. And I would have never hurt a woman. *Never.*

The older officer bent down, so his gaze was level with mine. And then he spat in my face. "Bullshit. Her fucking blood is all over you."

I had no way of wiping the spit from between my eyes with my hands cuffed behind my back, so I had no choice but to ignore it. I tried to remain calm and only tell the officer the things I knew for sure. "I woke up in bed with her this morning—"

"Shut up. We all know what you did. You charmed your way into her sister's pants, waited for Jayela to fall asleep, and then took your opportunity for revenge."

I blinked. "Revenge? For what?"

"She broke up with you a few years back. I remember wondering why, because the two of you seemed like the perfect couple." He reared back and laughed, the sound hard and cruel. "It's always the perfect-looking ones who hide the deepest sins, isn't it? She knew. She knew you were fucking rotten."

I studied his face again, and recognition flickered in the back of my mind. I'd met this man before. Maybe more than once. We'd shared a big round table at a police ball, the night Jaye had received her medal. Jayela had introduced us, and I'd shaken the man's hand. But I didn't remember his name. Johns? Johnson?

I did remember the way he'd looked at Jayela. It had been with barely concealed lust, though when I'd pointed it out on the way home, she'd laughed it off as ridiculous. I hadn't pushed it because I was used to other men wanting her. She was fucking beautiful, of course they stared. Did I like it? No. But in the scheme of things, a middle-aged man with a wife was no threat to me.

Until now.

"I want a lawyer."

The rookie cop snorted.

The older man reared back. "You'll get a lawyer when I say you get a lawyer."

Fuck this guy. He'd been waiting to take a shot at me for years, his jealousy written all over his face.

"I know my rights."

He spun on me, getting in my face. "You have no rights,

you piece of shit. You lost all rights when you murdered one of our own."

I battled to stay calm, but the anger I'd learned how to keep a handle on ignited inside me. "I told you, I didn't do it."

The man roared in frustration. Despite knowing how the police treated anyone from this side of the Saint View/Providence border, the punch to my midsection still came as a surprise. His meaty fist drove deep into my already tender gut, knocking the wind out of me. I grunted but gnashed my teeth together to keep from saying anything.

"Do you even know what sort of cop she was?" he ranted. "She was the best. Smart and talented and beau—" The man clammed up and threw another punch into my unprotected gut for good measure.

His unrequited crush wasn't lost on me. And that anger inside me picked up, swirling higher.

"Beautiful," I wheezed. "She was beautiful." The anger took hold of my tongue, even though my brain screamed for it to shut up. "And she didn't know you were fucking alive, that sound about right? Jealous, much? She loved me, and she never gave you a second glance. Maybe it was you who killed her."

The next punch cracked across my cheekbone, followed up by two more in quick succession. My head snapped to one side as the blows kept coming.

There wasn't a thing I could do to protect myself.

From the corner of my swelling eye, I saw the rookie cop grin and pull out his phone.

But it was his partner who was the real problem. The man's eyes were wild, spit balling at the corners of his mouth. "Admit what you did, you prick. Give her the respect she deserves."

I wouldn't. "I didn't do it." I could barely form the words around my swelling lips.

"You're covered in her blood. They found the murder weapon. How long do you think it'll be before they find your fingerprints on it?"

If I had any patience left, it disintegrated. "They won't because I didn't fucking do—"

The knife. The knife on the floor beside the bed had been the large silver knife I'd pulled from the block to cut up limes. They would find my prints on it. Whether I'd killed Jayela or not, my prints were all over it.

I froze. I might have had a chance when the evidence was all circumstantial. But my prints on the knife would be the nail in my coffin. Any flicker of hope was extinguished as if this cop had just taken a piss all over it.

"They will," the cop taunted, getting so close to me his coffee-tainted breath mingled with my own. "They will. So admit it. Open your mouth and let the words free. Maybe it'll ease some of that guilt sitting on your soul." He threw two quick punches to my temple that made my head spin.

I gave up biting my tongue. What the hell did it matter now? I could already see how this would play out, in full terrifying color. It didn't matter what I said or what I did. My prints on that knife, my history with Jayela, and Mae's testimony. It was an open-and-shut case. My heart ached for everything I was suddenly sure I would lose. And yet that was too hard to process. I let my anger swirl and rise instead, the feeling like a hug from an old friend I hadn't seen in years. It welcomed me back into its embrace and whispered seductively that I was home. "Ease my guilt? Or ease your guilt over your fucking hard-on for her? Ease your guilt that you wanted in her panties, but she wouldn't look twice at a man like you? Your jealousy reeks. You're the one who should feel guilty. Did you tell your wife that while you fuck her with your tiny dick, you're thinking of some hot piece of ass from the station?"

The man lunged, and his fingers closed around my throat. I threw myself backward, pushing off with my feet and sending the chair crashing to the cracked tiled floor. My arms twisted painfully behind me at the impact, and pain shot through my shoulder.

I ached to throw a punch. To feel my fist smash into this guy's mouth, just so the anger had somewhere to go.

But the cop followed me down with a force I hadn't reckoned on. And once he had me on the floor, I realized instantly how screwed I was. I kicked out with my legs, but the rookie was quick to jump on them, his phone scattering across the tiles in the process.

The older cop's ruddy face loomed over me, the downward pressure of his weight on my neck cutting off my oxygen. "Admit what you did to her. Admit what you took from me." His blows rained down, smashing against my head until the world swam around me.

The guy was completely unhinged. I couldn't breathe. I thrashed harder, fighting to get out from beneath him, but I couldn't budge his weight. Darkness flickered at the corners of my vision, panic coursing through my system. Fuzziness clouded my thoughts, making them slow and sluggish. Time ceased to exist, seconds morphing into days. The week becoming a year, the year becoming a decade, confusion scrambling my thoughts until I didn't know up from down.

But there, in the budding darkness, my memories took hold.

Admit what you did.

They taunted me, faceless shapes that swirled with malice. The bad things I'd done. The people I'd hurt.

The one time I'd lost control and let my temper get the better of me.

Admit it. Admit it!

I saw his face. The face of the life I *had* taken all those years ago.

I let the guilt and the shame in. All those feelings I'd held at bay with the help of a therapist, I let them flood. I let them consume me in a way there'd be no coming back from. They dragged me under, merging the present with the past. A past I could never outrun, no matter how hard I tried. Remorse clogged my throat, but I forced the words past it. I had to let them out. Had to say them out loud.

They demanded it. They'd never leave me alone if I didn't.

"I did it," I screamed.

The memories laughed, like it wasn't enough.

It was never enough.

I let them end me. "Is that what you want to hear? I did it. You fucking happy?"

Air suddenly rushed my lungs. I blinked as the present flowed back in, pushing out the memories once more, banishing them to the darkness. Light blinded me, and then came the pain, flooding my system while I choked and coughed.

The cop smiled a vicious grin, getting off my windpipe, leaving me beaten and broken on the floor. "Yeah. I'm happy."

Horror dawned as I put two and two together. This cop's smug expression. The fact he'd let me go.

He thought I'd confessed to Jayela's murder.

Before I could choke out a word, he stamped a boot into

the side of my head, and darkness covered everything once more.

I was glad for it. Because the darkness was what I knew. And it's where I should have stayed.

Maybe if I had, Jayela would have still been alive.

7

HEATH

The slam of a jail cell door ricocheted around my skull. I tried to stifle my automatic reaction to jump and instead forced myself to remain still. My ass was numb from sitting in the exact same spot for hours on end, but I had no desire to move. I stared at the flaking paint on the cell wall and tried not to replay the memories. But it was a losing battle. I'd let them back in, and now they consumed me. I deserved it. I deserved the pain.

I slowly peeled my fingers from my palms, straightening them out, and stared down at my now clean hands. But it didn't matter that the blood had been washed away. It was still there. I could still see it, smell it. And my gut instinct told me over and over that they were the hands of a murderer. Not Jayela's murderer, but a murderer nonetheless.

"You're both really fucking boring, you know?"

Two other men shared this intake cell, waiting alongside me to be processed and moved deeper into the prison itself. One was a young, quiet guy who was so silent I couldn't even hear him breathe. His long dark hair fell across his face, shielding him from the rest of the room. He'd been here when I arrived, and he hadn't uttered a word since, other than to say his name was Vincent when I'd asked. He answered without making eye contact, his gaze trained firmly on his lap, his hands tucked beneath his thighs. The kid was probably terrified, but I hadn't had it in me to try to reassure him in any way. His silence had been a blessing to the war raging inside me.

But the other guy...

I slowly raised my gaze to glance over at him. I'd heard him come in, heard him mouthing off to the guards, but I hadn't cared to make conversation with him. But now apparently, he was sick of waiting for someone to make polite chitchat. I met his gaze with a solid one of my own. "Not here to entertain you."

The man gave a throaty chuckle. He was a big guy, taller than me and a good few inches wider. Mouthing off was probably not my smartest idea, but I wasn't in the mood for anyone's shit. I just wanted to be left alone.

"What are you in for?"

I ground my molars together and ignored him.

"Going to make me guess then, are you? Car theft?"

I didn't respond.

"No?" He rubbed his thick hands together. "Okay, okay. Robbery. No! Armed robbery. You seem the type. Muscles and tats and all that."

I folded my arms and leaned back on the cement block wall. I let my gaze rest on him again, allowing my expression to show exactly what I thought of this little game he was playing.

Apparently, that wasn't clear enough. Because he continued on like nothing had happened.

"Not armed robbery, huh? Domestic violence? Oooh, hit-and-run? No? Tax evasion?"

My patience was wearing thin, and he obviously wasn't stopping. "Murder."

The kid glanced up, peeking at me through his wall of hair, but dropped his gaze once more when I looked in his direction.

The man let out a hoot of amusement. "Hoo boy, wouldn't have picked that in a million years. You're so pretty. I wouldn't have thought you'd know how to get your hands dirty."

I'd told him my charges in the hopes of shutting him up, but knowing my crimes only made him chattier.

"Did you do it?"

I raised one eyebrow in disgust. But hell, what was the point in staying silent? I'd already admitted to the police that I had. I'd be dead right now if I hadn't. That cop wouldn't have stopped until he got what he wanted. Didn't matter that this time I hadn't done it. Didn't matter I'd been so starved of oxygen that I'd had no idea what I was even admitting to.

All the evidence was stacked against me. They might have forced the confession into my mouth, but my old guilt had taken the wheel and finished me off. I could practically feel the cool steel of the knife in my hand, and in my head, I drew a picture of some warped reality where I took that knife and ran it across Jayela's throat. It sent chills down my spine, and I fought to get the images out, but the memories knew. They knew I had that inside me. That cold-hearted darkness that made me capable of taking a life. My temper, my lack of control, my anger, they were all things I'd spent almost fifteen years trying to get under control. I thought I'd done it. I thought all the years of counseling had changed the man I was.

But leopards couldn't change their spots, and neither could I. I couldn't admit to killing Jayela, because I hadn't. But I could admit to killing another. "Yeah. I did it."

The man grinned, showing off a mouthful of yellowed teeth. "Who was it?"

I wasn't about to tell him that.

"Cat got your tongue?"

"Fuck off."

The man's eyes narrowed, becoming beady in his oversized face. "Now, now, you talk to your woman with a mouth like that?"

Every muscle in my body stiffened. Mae's face flashed in my mind, taking me by surprise, because she wasn't my woman, and I didn't have any sort of claim over her. But she'd awoken something new inside me last night. Something that had felt full of promise for a tiny moment. Something that had been cruelly ripped away before I could even do anything about it. Anger rolled through my body like a tidal wave.

"Oh, so you're a girlfriend killer then? What'd she do? Not put out enough? Nah, that couldn't be the problem with you, being so good-looking and all. She cheat? She put her plump lips around another man's dick?" His hand slid over his crotch, and he grabbed himself through his orange prison-issue jumpsuit and groaned. "Fuck, I'd love some of that right now." He glanced over at Vincent. "Your mouth is almost as pretty as a woman's, you know. And you've got all that long, dark hair..."

The kid stiffened, and I saw red. Fuck that. I'd never been one to stand around watching the strong try to lord it over the weak. Especially not like that. Men who made sexual threats were the worst kind of scum. The kid couldn't have been more than twenty and was clearly terrified. He could have been one of my younger siblings. And if I was being completely honest? I was fucking itching for a fight. I was desperate for a way to unleash some of the pain inside me.

I exploded up from the bench and grabbed fistfuls of the man's shirt, slamming him back against the wall, so his head cracked off the cinderblock. "Shut. The. Fuck. Up." Anger seeped from my every pore, that wheeling rage inside me that was never too far from exploding threatening to burst my tentative hold on it. Would it even matter if I rammed my fist into this man's flabby cheek? Would it even matter if I pummeled him until my knuckles bled and his face was barely recognizable? Wasn't that what I did? Wasn't that who I was? I'd spend the rest of my life paying for it.

I let the man go and slumped back on my side of the cell.

A muscle ticked in his jaw. "You have no idea who I am, do you?"

"Don't fucking care either."

"You'll regret that."

I regretted a whole lot of things. But slamming his head against the cinderblock wall? That was the least of my concerns.

The small sliding window in the door of our cell opened, and a guard's voice filtered through. "Michaelson. You've got a phone call."

"Who is it?"

"Mae Donovan. Said she's with your legal team?"

What the hell?

He paused when I didn't move. Then sighed. "You taking it or what?"

My heart thumped erratically at the mention of Mae's

name. And for the tiniest of seconds, I entertained the idea of taking her call. Because there was nothing I wanted to hear more than the sound of her voice in this godforsaken hellhole I'd just put myself in for the rest of my life. But I couldn't face her. Not after what I'd done. I couldn't even imagine what she could possibly want to say to me, unless it was to tell me how evil I was. I didn't need her to tell me that. I already knew.

I eyed the guard through the slit in the door. "I'm not taking it. Go away."

8

MAE

Rain hit the church windows, fat droplets sliding down the glass windowpanes like the tears I'd spent five days crying. It had taken me an hour to get ready for Jayela's funeral, painstakingly applying copious amounts of foundation and eyeliner, trying to cover my red-rimmed eyes and blotchy complexion. But now that we were here at the church, I was almost grateful for the days holed up in my bed, buried beneath the covers, crying for everything I'd lost. It meant that now, in the presence of hundreds of people I knew, I was bone dry.

"There's a lot of people here," Tori whispered loudly.

Will glanced across at her and frowned disapprovingly.

She rolled her eyes at me and whispered a little quieter, "If I can't talk in church on the day we bury your sister, then when can I?"

I stifled a smile. Will really was a bit of a stick in the mud about church behavior. Tori normally was, too, having grown up in a strict Catholic family, but she seemed willing to make exceptions for me today. "I can't believe how many people have turned up for this. I haven't seen some of these people in years."

Tori snuck a look over her shoulder from our spot in the front pew. "It's almost like a high school reunion. And just like in high school, the jocks are all in the back row."

I followed her line of sight, to the back of the room, and found she wasn't wrong. Through the sea of faces, I spotted some slightly older but familiar profiles, mostly people I hadn't spoken to since the day we graduated high school. Tori, Jaye, and I had all gone to Providence School for Girls, but the back row was full of the grown-up version of the boys from Edgely Academy, the boys' school that had been linked to ours. Mentally, I ticked off their names in my head. Bradley Thomson, captain of the football team. Ryan Ranson, quarterback. My gaze narrowed on the third man; his cocky grin more familiar than I would have liked. Liam Banks, star baseball player. He laughed and joked with his friends, as if this was some sort of frat party rather than my sister's funeral. "Ugh. I always hated that guy."

Not entirely true, but it was the half-truth I preferred to focus on.

"Liam?"

"Yeah. He was always such an arrogant asshole. And judging by that suit he's wearing? Nothing has changed. I wonder if his parents are still paying for his love of Armani."

Tori cocked her head to one side, studying the man chatting with his friends. "I don't think so. I heard he's some big shot lawyer. Made partner at some crazy young age like twenty-five. Super accomplished in his field and well-respected."

I glanced over my shoulder at him again, and of course, had the unfortunate luck of my gaze slamming right into his. I froze, then quickly looked down, embarrassed to have been caught watching him.

"He's still really hot, though." Tori grinned.

Will groaned quietly beside her, and she patted him on the leg. "Not as handsome as you, my love."

She winked as she turned back to me. I had to stifle a giggle.

But then the guilt rushed in hard. Just like it had every time I'd even thought about smiling or laughing for the last few days. I sobered completely and faced the front. The priest was getting ready to start the ceremony, and I reminded myself that this was why we were here. It didn't matter if Liam Banks and his all-star friends were in the back row. We were here to pay respects to my sister.

The priest took a few steps toward me and asked quietly if I was ready to begin. I nodded, giving him permission to go ahead. I was ready. My sister needed to be laid to rest.

Father Brian opened by welcoming the congregation, expressing his sympathy to all of us on the loss of our sister, our friend, our daughter. I stiffened, knowing my father would be here somewhere, and grateful that I'd so far been able to avoid him. I just didn't have it in me today to think about him. Though I knew Tori had called him on my behalf and made sure he would attend. Jaye would have wanted that, even if I wanted nothing to do with the man.

My mind drifted, the service dragging on. I was too tired, too wrung out to keep my mind on Father Brian's droning monotone. For days now, in amongst the grief, in amongst the silence that surrounded my place now that Jayela was gone, there was one thing my mind kept returning to.

Heath.

Boston claimed Heath had admitted to Jayela's murder. But something didn't feel right about that. I replayed over and over the look on Heath's face when I'd found him that morning, covered in Jayela's blood. The pure shock, the confusion, the horror. He'd been trying to save her. His actions weren't those of a man who had brutally murdered a woman.

At least not until I'd accused him of the worst.

"What are you thinking about? Your face is weird," Tori whispered, her hand on my thigh, squeezing gently.

"Heath," I admitted.

"Here?" Tori shot me a worried glance. "Babe. You have to stop this. He admitted to it."

"I know, I know. I was there. I heard what Boston said. But I just can't believe that." I glanced guiltily at my best friend and admitted something I hadn't had the guts to tell her yet. Here seemed like a good place, where she couldn't yell at me. "I tried to call him."

Tori's fingers dug into my thigh. "How?"

"I called him at the jail, pretending to be someone from his legal team."

"Have you completely lost your mind?"

I was pretty sure I had. I was pretty sure the fact I was sitting at my sister's funeral, obsessing over the man who had admitted to killing her, meant that I was certifiably crazy. "It doesn't fit, Tori. None of it fits."

"So what? You think the man admitted to a murder he didn't commit?" She shook her head. "If you honestly believe that, you're as crazy as he is."

I knew what she was saying. To anyone else, my certainty that Heath wasn't guilty didn't make any sense. But they hadn't known him like I had. You learn a lot about someone when they date your sibling who you share a living space with. And nobody had been there on Friday night to see that he was still that same guy. They hadn't seen the way he was such a gentleman. He was kind, and caring. Jayela herself had admitted he had that protector gene inside him. She'd never been afraid of him. Hell, I was the most important thing in the world to her, and she'd happily left me at that bar on Friday night, because Heath had been there, and she knew that no harm would come to me while he was around. I trusted my sister. I trusted her judgment. She was an amazing cop, and she'd never once cast a shadow of a doubt over Heath's character. There was just no way that he could insist on walking me home, then treat me with such gentlemanly manners, with the sole intention of getting me drunk, just to murder my sister. That was the truly insane part about it all. Heath was a big guy, and he'd had four years of opportunity to kill my sister if that was what he really wanted to do. He could have broken into our home at any time. He'd proven he still knew the code to our security door.

But he hadn't. He'd just been a guy drinking at a bar, who I'd brought home to my condo because I thought he was cute.

I couldn't let it go. If I had to be a dog with a bone, then I would be. I needed to see Heath. I had to talk to him and find out what had really happened that night. I needed to be able to put this whole thing to rest, so I could get some peace.

9

MAE

I stood outside the church after the ceremony, making small talk with what seemed like a constant barrage of people who wanted to extend their sympathies. I was patted on the hand, the arm, the cheek, so many times that after a while, I really craved solitude. Couldn't these people see I wasn't in the right frame of mind for chitchat? Couldn't they all just move on to the wake, eat some tiny sandwiches, have a few drinks, and tell stories about what an amazing woman my sister was? I wanted them to talk amongst themselves, while I disappeared into the crowd, no longer the center of attention. I got it. They were sorry for my loss. There was only so many times I could hear it before I just wanted to crumble. And I didn't want to cry in front of all these people. I wanted to save that for when I was alone, for when there was nobody around to see me break down. These people, who I had barely seen in years, didn't get to see me be weak like that. So I suffered through the line of people, just trying to keep myself together by forcing smiles.

The line finally dwindled, and I was in the light at the end of the tunnel when one voice froze me to the spot.

"Hello, Mae. This isn't really how I wanted to see you again."

My skin crawled. Tori sidled in beside me and grabbed my hand, squeezing it tight.

My father's shrewd gaze slid from me to my best friend, and down to our joined hands. "Could we have a moment, please?" He gave Tori a pointed look.

"I don't think—"

I'd known this moment would come. I'd known I'd have to face him today. I was prepared for it. "It's okay. I'm fine. Go on ahead to the wake with Will. I'll see you guys there."

Tori grimaced, but she nodded and walked to Will's side, taking the baby from his arms. He shot a worried glance in my direction, too, raising one eyebrow in question, but I gave him a small shake of my head, signaling he should go on. I appreciated their friendship, but this was something I needed to do by myself.

"I didn't really want to see you at all," I said to my father, picking up his conversation. "To be honest, I don't even know why you're here."

"She was my daughter."

A frustrated laugh bubbled out of my chest. "Oh. That's right. The daughter you didn't hate. Or at least hated a little bit less than me."

My father shot a look around us, making sure nobody else had heard my accusations.

"Don't worry, Dad. I know how to keep my voice down. I'm not here to air any dirty laundry. But don't come to me now, acting like we're long-lost family. We aren't family at all."

"Why do you have to be like this? Today of all days?"

I widened my eyes. "Why do I have to be like this? What did you think was going to happen by coming here? Did you think I would be so grief-stricken, so desperate for a family now that Jaye's gone, that I would just fall into your arms and call you Daddy?"

The older man bristled. "I'm trying."

"Trying?" I hissed. "It's too little, too late. There is no trying. Not after what you did."

"There are things we need to discuss. Things of a financial nature, if not a personal one."

"Then you can talk to my lawyer. Because as far as I'm concerned? Jayela was the only reason I could possibly have for needing to speak to you again. Now that she's gone, there's no need for us to communicate at all."

Embarrassment flushed the old man's cheeks. "I see nothing has changed with you. Still as willful and ignorant as you always were."

"Yeah. Great, Dad. Thanks a lot. Always good to catch up with you, too."

I spun on my heel and stalked toward the parking lot, storming past cars and the line waiting to exit the church parking lot onto the main road. It was only as I got to my car and searched for the car keys that I realized my purse was in the bottom of Tori's stroller. I spun around, searching for their car, but it had already disappeared. Frustration roared through me, mixing with the emotions I'd been trying to keep a hold on all day. Tears pricked the backs of my eyes, and I slammed my closed fist into the side of my old BMW.

"You okay?"

I glanced up at the voice, surprised to find it belonged to Liam Banks. He stood leaning on the car parked beside mine, his iPhone in hand, thumb hovering over the screen as if I'd interrupted him in the middle of a text message.

I tried to breathe out some of my frustration and anger before I answered him. "Yeah. Fine. Just locked out of my car, apparently."

Liam bent and peered through the driver's side window. "Did you lock your keys in there?" He looked up at me with a ruggedly handsome grin that was tinged with a hint of mischief. The exact same grin I remembered from high school. "Want me to smash the window for you?"

I couldn't help but smile at the extreme overreaction. That was such a seventeen-year-old Liam thing to say. All action, with little thought to the consequences. Despite how smart and committed to his studies he'd been, he'd also been impulsive and a little wild. "No. My keys are with my friends. I'll just have to call and get them to come back."

Liam eyed my hands, and at the same time, I realized I didn't have my phone either. I sighed. "Well, shit."

He chuckled, holding his phone out to me. "You can use mine."

I shook my head, pushing it back toward him. "No good. I don't know either of their numbers by heart."

He pulled his navy suit jacket aside, placing his phone back in the pocket of his white dress shirt. "Sounds like you need a lift, then."

Before I could even think about it, I screwed my face up.

Liam raised one eyebrow. "Wow. Is it my car that disgusts you so much? My suit? It couldn't be my cologne because this stuff cost me five hundred dollars and smells damn good." He winked.

"It's not your cologne." His cologne did smell damn good. Though he was probably wearing too much of it if I could smell it from several footsteps away. "And your car is nice. If a tad flashy."

He clutched his heart playfully. "That cuts, Mae. That

cuts deep. This car is my baby." He straightened and went back to leaning on the side of it. "But if the car only mildly offends you, why the face?"

"Do you really want to know? Because it's already been a long day, and my polite chitchat allowance has all but run out."

He folded his arms across his chest, and I couldn't help noticing the way his jacket pulled tighter. Did he still play ball? I had a sneaking suspicion that beneath his fancy clothes, he was still hiding the same ripped body he'd had at eighteen.

"I'm a lawyer. Anything you say to me, I've already heard. My skin is thick, trust me."

"Fair enough. It was an automatic reaction. I had a throwback moment to high school Mae."

He seemed amused by that. "Did high school Mae have a severe case of gastro? Because that face you made just before looked like you had some bad stomach cramps."

"Did you just ask me if I need the bathroom? We're at a church, Liam."

He chuckled. "Fine. Explain the face then."

"It was just an automatic reaction to my internalized dislike for you." I held my breath, waiting for his reaction to my blatant honesty. I wasn't normally like this. Any other day I would have made nice and hid any old feelings I might have had for the man. But I just didn't have it in me today.

"Oh." He actually seemed relieved. "Is that all?"

It was my turn to raise an eyebrow. "I just told you I don't like you, and you're relieved by that."

"Nobody likes me. Like I said, I'm a lawyer." He grinned, and for a moment I thought about changing my perceptions of him. But then he went and opened his mouth again.

"But my money and my flashy car keep me warm at night."

I rolled my eyes. "Of course they do."

He opened the door and motioned for me to get in. "Come on. I'll drive you to the wake."

I considered my options. Then determined I didn't have any. "Fine. But this doesn't mean I like you. You've just proven again that you're still the same arrogant asshole you were in high school." I slid onto the leather passenger seat, while he ran around to the other side of the car and got behind the steering wheel.

He threw me a sidelong glance across the center console. "I am still the arrogant asshole from high school. Just ten years older. And hey. For the record, I didn't like you in high school either."

My jaw dropped open. "What do you mean you didn't like me? Everybody liked me."

"*What do you mean you didn't like me? Everybody liked me,*" he mimicked in a high-pitched voice that didn't sound anything like me. But was so nasally and childish we both sniggered, before he continued, "You were such a goody two-shoes. I bet you still are. It cracks me up that you're offended by the thought someone might not have considered you their best friend."

"I wasn't a goody two-shoes. I just like learning, okay?"

"If I can admit to being arrogant, I think you can admit to being a teacher's pet."

He was probably right. At least he owned it. In one short conversation, I knew exactly where I stood with Liam Banks. He didn't pussyfoot around me, offering hollow words.

And even if I didn't like him, at least knowing where I stood wouldn't keep me awake at night.

10

LIAM

I was no stranger to the country club. I parked my car in a member only spot, got out, and jogged around to Mae's door to open it for her.

She beat me to it, opening it up for herself when I was a few steps away.

I frowned.

"What?" she asked.

"Nothing."

She threw me an odd look, then gazed up at the country club entrance with a heavy sigh. "Well, thanks for the lift. I'll see you around." She didn't make a move to go inside, though.

Soft, loose tendrils of blonde hair framed her pretty face, and her blue eyes shone in the midday sun. I tried to keep focus, but the curves of her body, hugged tight by a black dress, demanded my attention.

Ten years had done nothing to stifle the attraction I'd once felt for this woman. It picked right back up where it had left off and dragged me close enough that my arm brushed hers.

She glanced over at me in surprise, like she'd forgotten I was even there.

Story of my life when it came to her.

"Hey," I said quietly. "If this all gets too much for you, just give me the signal. I'll smuggle you out of here."

She gave me a stiff smile. "I don't think I can skip out on my sister's wake, somehow."

"You can if it's causing you pain."

Surprise flickered in her gaze, and the vulnerability behind it hit me in the gut. She put on a good front, but behind it, she was in a world of hurt.

That didn't sit well with me.

But in the next instant, it was gone. Her walls went back up, and her gaze hardened. "I'll be fine. Thanks again for the ride." Without another glance at me, she strode into the club, leaving me behind to watch her walk away.

I sighed and followed her slowly up the stairs, only to be accosted by Ryan and Bradley who were waiting for me at the doorway. I hadn't seen either of them in years. We'd been good friends in high school but had drifted apart soon after.

Ryan let out a low wolf whistle. "Nice car, Banks."

"Forget the car," Bradley interrupted. "Watching Mae Donovan get out of it was a thing of beauty. When did she get so hot? You going there, or am I?"

I squinted at him, irritation prickling at the back of my neck at his tone. "Don't be a dick. We're at a funeral. And aren't you married?"

He shrugged, twisting the gold wedding band on his left hand. His gaze roved over the parking lot, like a panther stalking prey. A lot of the people leaving their cars and heading inside were old classmates I recognized from high school. Jayela Donovan had only been a year older than me and had gone to all the same parties we had. Everyone had known her. She'd been outgoing and popular.

I'd caught up with her a few times over the years when our paths had crossed. With her being a cop, and me being a lawyer, it happened.

But she'd never drawn my eye the way her sister had.

I went inside without another word to Bradley and Ryan, hoping they wouldn't follow. They might have been wanting to rehash their high school glory days, where we'd been the kings of the school with girls falling all over us, but I had other things on my mind. I pushed my way through the crowded room, smiling and nodding at people I recognized as I went, but always seeking out the one person who had always dominated my interest. The one person who had never fallen all over me, even though I'd wanted her to.

I found her at the back of the room, deep in conversation with Tori, who I remembered from school as well, and a few other people I didn't recognize. I paused, not wanting to interrupt, even though I desperately wanted to talk to her again. A waiter walked by and offered me a glass of wine, which I took gratefully, swallowing down a gulp even though I wasn't much of a drinker.

"What are you doing here?"

I glanced over and grinned when I recognized Rowe. It was a true smile; unlike the ones I'd shared with my old high school acquaintances. I slapped his hand and drew him into a half hug. "Just paying my respects. I went to high school with her. You know her through work?"

Rowe shoved his hands in his pockets. He was still dressed in his uniform, an ugly brown with the Saint View Prison logo on the shirt pocket. "Yeah. Just got off shift. I didn't make the church, came straight here. I need to go home and sleep but I heard this was happening today. Fucking awful."

I nodded. "I liked her."

"Yeah, me, too. She got family?"

"A sister." I pointed in Mae's direction. "And her dad. Not sure if there was anyone else."

Rowe glanced in Mae's direction, his gaze lingering for a moment. "Never met her. There's a lot of people waiting to talk to her."

There was. The crowd around Mae thickened with every passing minute. I shifted my weight from side to side, peering around the people between us. That tiny glimpse of vulnerability she'd shown me outside had me worried about her. She had no escape route without her car here, and I was more than willing to be her getaway driver if she needed one. But she seemed okay for the minute, and Tori was firmly fixed at her side, so I focused back on Rowe, who seemed tired enough that he might just take a nap on the floor at my feet. Dark circles shaded the skin beneath his eyes, and he slumped on the wall behind him, like he didn't have the energy to hold himself up.

"You look done, bro. Going to be good for training this week? Want to do the batting cages one night? We have games coming up."

Rowe nodded. "Yeah, for sure. I'll be fine once I sleep off the twelve-hour shift."

"You work longer hours than I do."

He shrugged. "All the more reason for us to go to the cages this week, then, huh? I don't want to lose our next game because you strike out again."

Rowe and I had played on the same baseball team for the past two years. It was just a social thing, a weekend competition that was mostly filled with guys like the two of us—single, no kids or other tie downs, and missing the ball games we'd had in high school. None of us were good enough to go further in the sport, but we still all loved to play. And we liked to win.

My phone buzzed in my shirt pocket, and I pulled it out, glancing at the name on the screen. I slapped Rowe on the chest and edged away. "Gotta take this. But I'll text you about the cages, yeah?"

Rowe nodded. "All good. I think I'm going to get out of here anyway. I'm going to fall asleep at the wheel otherwise. See you later."

I already had the phone to my ear, so I just nodded and waved as he moved toward the exit, my mind already on the call. "Barclay," I said to my boss, without saying hello. "What's up? I'm off work today."

"I know, I know," he answered. "But something's come up, and I need you to come in."

I spun around to face the window overlooking an eighteen-hole golf course. I barely noticed the rolling greens. "Is it urgent? I've wrapped up everything on the Simpson case—"

"Exactly. And word has gotten around about it. I need you to take another one. Jonas Borden wants us to take him on."

I closed my eyes. "That's a really high-profile case. Didn't he hit someone with his car and then leave them for dead on the side of the road?"

"Damn straight. And he's guilty as fuck. So I need you on it. If anyone is going to get him off, it's you."

I paused.

"Problem?"

Yeah, there was just the small problem of the fact the man was a disgusting human being. Everybody knew Jonas

Borden. He was a playboy hotel mogul, well known for his party lifestyle. He was a regular in the tabloids, and his antics were all over social media. The way he treated others, women in particular, made me want to throat punch the guy. And after my last case, I was really fucking sick of defending scumbags and getting them off when they deserved to be behind bars.

"This is a big case, Banks. Huge. It'll put your name, and this firm, on the map. And a nice big paycheck, too."

I turned back to face the room, pressing my back against the glass windows. My gaze snagged on Mae's, but she quickly looked away.

I sighed.

"I need an answer, Liam."

This case would take up all my time. And it would chisel away another little piece of my soul. But what else did I have? A room full of old high school friends I could no longer stand to be around? A cold and empty apartment to come home to at night? Mae's soft floral scent was still engraved in the back of my nose. There was certainly no woman to come home to. No family.

My job was my baby. My life. And other than a bit of baseball, there was very little else in it. This was what I'd signed up for. It was what was expected of me. So I shoved all of that back down, burying it deep. It did me no good to dwell on the things I'd lost, and the things I couldn't have. I'd made my bed and now I had to sleep in it. "Sure, Barclay. I'll take the case. No problem."

11

MAE

I'd never been to a prison before, but Saint View Prison looked much the way I would have expected from my limited knowledge that came from movies and TV shows. A huge imposing building, the ugly cinderblock gray of a stormy day, loomed in front of me.

I had to pass solid black gates to get to the main reception building, but once there, I found a buzzer on the wall with a little sign that said to press for assistance. I put my finger to it, jumping at the shrill noise, but recovered quickly, smoothing my hands down my dress, trying to hide the sweat building on my palms. Nobody spoke through the intercom, but the door in front of me popped open an inch. I took that as a sign I could enter and pushed my way through the heavy doors.

I cautiously approached the reception window, covered by a thick plastic with only a narrow gap at the bottom which allowed communication with the staff members on the other side. A man sat at a desk in the small room, his back to me, typing furiously on his computer.

I cleared my throat.

"Wait." He raised one hand but in the next second continued typing.

I frowned, wondering what sort of customer service training they had in place here. I would have been fired on the spot if I'd spoken to a parent or another staff member like that.

Eventually the man turned around and pushed to his feet, closing the distance to stand behind the plastic window. He paused, without even saying hello, his eyebrows knitting together in a frown. "I know you from somewhere, don't I?"

I blinked and tried to find an answer to the question I hadn't been expecting. From the bark and the rude way he'd acted, I'd expected an older man in his forties or fifties. Perhaps someone approaching retirement age who was just riding out the days until he could claim a pension check. But the man who stood in front of me now was none of those things. His short dark hair and deep-brown eyes were the same color as chocolate. His skin was a deep olive, and he was taller than I'd expected, too. Not quite as tall as Heath, I found myself noticing, but well taller than I was. Broad shoulders filled out his ugly brown guard uniform. He watched me with an arrogant impatience, as if his time were more important than mine, and I was wasting it. But I didn't recognize him. "I don't think so."

He lifted one shoulder in a shrug. "Fair enough. If you're just here to sell us shit, we aren't interested. We've already got suppliers for whatever it is." Seeming bored, he swiveled on his heel and went back to his computer.

I finally got my lips to work. "No, sorry. Wait. Not selling anything. I'd like to visit a prisoner, please."

The man turned back around to face me, and I found myself drowning in the depths of his eyes. It should have been illegal to be that good-looking. He was entirely out of place in such a drab environment. His face was so perfectly symmetrical it was impossible to comprehend how he'd found himself working in a prison instead of on a catwalk somewhere.

"You sure you're in the right spot? This is maximum security. For the men's prison. Minimum-security and the women's prison are on the other side."

I frowned at the fact he thought I couldn't follow the clearly marked signs that had led me here. "I'm in the right spot. I want to see Heath Michaelson, please."

The man raised one eyebrow, then grudgingly pulled paperwork from a folder and passed it through the gap in the shield. I glanced down at them.

"Goddamn prison groupies," he muttered, probably assuming that the plastic would muffle the sounds.

It didn't.

"Excuse me? Did you just call me a *prison groupie*?" I'd never heard the term before, but it was obvious what it meant. I fought to tamp down my annoyance.

He glanced up from pushing a pen beneath the shield. "Aren't you?"

I ignored his rudeness, deciding dignifying him with a response wasn't worth it. Instead, I picked up the pen and the sheaf of papers and began filling them out. The man watched me; his gaze shrewd like I might be trying to smuggle a shiv in under my summer dress. When I finished filling out my details, I handed them back beneath the gap and waited.

He read over my neat, elementary school teacher's handwriting, until he got to the bottom of the page. "What's your relationship to the prisoner?"

"What does that matter? That wasn't one of the questions."

His eyes narrowed, as if he was annoyed I'd dared to question him. "Might not be on the forms, but I still need to enter it into the computer. You won't be laying eyes on anyone unless we know what the nature of your visit is."

The nature of my visit? "That's personal."

"Nothing is personal here."

"Fine. He's my friend. I just want to see how he's doing."

The man rolled his eyes. "Friend. Okay then."

I wasn't a particularly confrontational person. But something about this man's tone reeked of judgment. And I was a little bit short on patience lately. "What's that supposed to mean?"

His gaze raked over me, taking in the soft floral fabric of the dress I'd picked out. It cut deep between my breasts, showing off a healthy but not inappropriate amount of cleavage. Though now I thought about it, any cleavage at all in a men's prison was maybe not my best choice.

"We see women like you all the time. Women claiming to be these men's '*friends*'." He made air quotes with his fingers.

"And that personally insults you?" Because he certainly looked irritated, with his jaw locked tight. I imagined his teeth might be hurting quite a bit right now, with the way he had them ground together.

"Actually, yes. It does bother me. It wastes my time. You women who romanticize these men? You're ridiculous."

"And you're rude."

"Yeah. *I'm rude.* And lover boy over there in his cell? He's a murderer. You do know that's what he's in for, don't you? Or did he play your heart to get in your panties, and tell you all about how innocent he is?"

I bristled at his tone, and at the insinuation I was a stupid woman who raved online about how handsome some random criminal was. That wasn't what this was. Heath wasn't some psycho I'd decided to take a fancy to. I knew him. He *was* my friend. And this guy could just fuck right off.

"You don't know anything about me. About my situation. Or Heath's for that matter."

"I read his rap sheet, lady. I know exactly who he is. And I know exactly who you are."

I threw my hands up in the air. "And who's that? Please, enlighten me since you seem to know so much from your box over there."

"You do realize that there are no conjugal visits here? Right?"

This guy was the biggest asshole I'd ever met. Or had a bee in his bonnet about something that didn't relate to me, and I was just on the receiving end of his bad mood. Either way, I was done trying to explain myself. "Just do your job. I'm here to see Heath. Make it happen." I spun on my heel before he could say anything else and sat myself down in one of the hard plastic waiting room chairs. My gaze bounced around the barren room while the muffled click of his keyboard filled the air.

Cheap linoleum lined the floor, dirty and scuffed and worn right through in one section so the cement floor beneath showed. The seats around me were identical hard plastic, spaced evenly along the walls, and bolted to the floor. I idly wondered if that was so people couldn't throw them. Did that happen in a place like this? Did the friends and relatives of the men behind these security walls act like that? Was that partly why the guy behind the desk was such a dick-knob? I really hadn't thought this through very well.

If I'd realized there was a chance just being in this waiting room was actually dangerous, I might not have come.

Yeah, you would have. Because you're riddled with guilt and will probably never sleep again if you don't get some answers.

I let out an involuntary yawn as proof of how little I'd slept lately.

A cheap clock on the wall ticked in the silence, counting the minutes that passed. Eventually I grew bored of waiting, and nervous impatience forced me to my feet. I crossed the small space to a bulletin board full of pinned announcements and advertisements. One tattered piece of yellowing paper caught my attention with its big black lettering, and I removed the pin, taking it down so I could get a better look at it.

Position Available - Education Administrator

I let my gaze roll over the job description. Monday through Friday evenings. Two hours per night, teaching groups of prisoners wanting to get their GED. Full security provided. My eyes bugged out when I saw the salary figure. With some quick mental math, I worked out the per hour rate was barely minimum wage.

I didn't particularly want to talk to the guard, but my curiosity got the better of me. I took the job ad to his booth and pressed it against the clear plastic. "Has this job been filled? The ad appears old."

He swiveled on his chair lazily and cast an eye over the piece of paper. "No. Teachers don't last long around here. It's been months since we had one."

"So who's teaching the men right now?"

"No one."

I frowned at the thought there might be men behind those walls who wanted to better themselves but couldn't because of a lack of resources. At my core, I wholeheartedly believed in education. And that it should be free and readily available to everyone. Guilt niggled at me. I wasn't helping the problem by taking a position at a very exclusive primary school. I'd let myself be swayed by the dollars, and I didn't feel good about that.

"Your visit is denied by the way."

That snapped me back to the real reason I was here. "Excuse me? What do you mean denied?"

"Do you need a dictionary to look it up?"

Oh my God, this man was such a douchebag! "I know what it means, but why was it denied? I gave you everything you asked for. I'm a frigging elementary school teacher, for Christ's sakes. What do you think I'm trying to do? Smuggle in drugs and weapons?"

His gaze narrowed. "Are you?"

I threw my hands up. "I made it through the metal detectors at the gate, didn't I?"

He ran his tongue over his teeth as he studied me. "You aren't on Michaelson's approved visitor list."

"So put me on it."

"Can't."

"Because…." Honestly, the man was infuriating, and drawing information out of him was like getting blood out of a stone.

"It's up to the prisoners who's on their list. I can't force him to put your name on it, lady."

"But you could ask him nicely. Or is that not in your wheelhouse? To do something nicely?"

A smile flickered at the corner of his mouth, like he found my frustration amusing.

That only pissed me off more.

"I did ask him. I buzzed down to his section while you were busy romanticizing that teacher's job in your head. He doesn't want to see you. In fact, I think his exact message was, tell her not to come back."

I ground my teeth, annoyed with Heath that he'd declined to talk to me for a second time. And annoyed with this jerk, because, well, he was a jerk. "I wasn't romanticizing it. I just believe in education."

He raised one eyebrow. "That's what all the prison groupies say."

I was suddenly glad he was on the other side of a protective barrier, because in that moment, I was seriously contemplating violence. Those chairs were lucky they were bolted down because I very well might have turned into one of those people who threw them. I clutched the job ad tighter in my fist, and with a huff, I stomped out of the waiting room.

I was pretty sure the man was laughing as I did so.

12

MAE

I did a thing. And whenever I did a thing, the first person I told was Tori. For as long as I could remember, I'd never kept a secret from her. I knew she wouldn't be happy about the one I was currently harboring, so I spent the rest of my day trying to distract myself from the urge to ring her and spill my guts. I cleaned my condo, avoiding Jayela's bedroom again. The room had been thoroughly cleaned by a professional service, though I still couldn't bring myself to step foot in her bedroom. So I cleaned around it. I scrubbed the bathroom, including the grout in the tiles, mopped the floors, and baked an extravagant lasagne for my dinner. I only had one week left of the school year, not that they'd let me come back just yet, so I didn't have any planning to do. The rest of my night was spent on the couch watching Netflix with my fingers twitching above my phone every few minutes.

I really wanted to tell her.

By the time I went to bed and spent hours tossing and turning, I knew it was a losing battle. I'd already been sleeping like crap. And keeping this secret from Tori was going to mean no sleep again tonight. I was tired. I really wanted a proper night's rest. I yanked my sheet up over my head and pressed my phone to my ear while it rang.

"Mae? What's wrong? I'm getting dressed. I'm on my way."

"Shit. No. Sorry. Get back into bed. Just listen to me. There's nothing wrong, I just... I did something. And I feel really guilty for not telling you about it."

Tori's mattress squeaked as she got up, and Will asked a quiet question in the background. She explained it was just me, and then came the quiet click of her door closing.

"Okay. I'm in the living room. It's been a while since I had a midnight call from you, so this better be good."

I made a face in the darkness. I had a feeling she wouldn't think this was good at all. "I went to the jail today."

"You what? Mae! You're so stubborn! I told you at the funeral, you have to let this go."

Oh boy. If she was already upset with me, she wasn't going to like what was coming.

"You know I can't. So I went there, and the guard was so hot but such a douche, and he took forever, so I started reading the bulletin board full of prison jobs available—"

"Stop, you're rambling things I can't take in at this hour. Get to the point. What did Heath say?"

"He wouldn't see me."

Tori breathed an audible sigh of relief. "Sorry, babe. I know that must have been frustrating for you, but I can't say that I'm upset. I hate the idea of you being in that place at all. Obviously, Heath does, too. He doesn't want to talk to you. You have to let this go."

"I can't. It's eating me alive. I just keep replaying it over and over. I just keep coming back to the same thought. That he didn't do it. And if that's true, then the real killer is still out there, and the police aren't even doing anything about it. I need him to look me in the eye and tell me it was him."

Tori gave a long-suffering sigh. She was used to me getting fixated on things to the point of obsession. She was good at being my voice of reason, just like I was for her. "He's not going to give you that, though. You'll get more answers at the trial. You just have to be patient. Have you spoken to that therapist who I gave you the number for? He'll help."

"A therapist can't give me the answers I need. And Heath's case can't go to trial. By that point it will be too late. We both know that a jury is going to find him guilty."

"Because he is guilty! Honestly, Mae. For a smart woman, you're not acting like one."

I couldn't even be upset by the accusation. Because I knew she was right. I would have been saying the exact same thing to her if the shoe had been on the other foot. But my mind kept going back to that night Heath and I had spent together. I kept thinking back to the way he'd protected me, insisting on walking me all the way home, right to my door. I kept remembering the way his lips had felt on my neck, and the sense of rightness as I'd fallen asleep against his chest. I was a smart, well-educated woman. I was a good judge of character. And I was willing to back my gut instinct right to the very end, even if nobody else was.

"I know it looks like I'm romanticizing all of this, the guard even called me a prison groupie today—"

"He's right! You're totally being an inmate groupie right now. What proof do you have he didn't do it? Proof, babe. PROOF."

"I don't have any," I admitted. "But I feel—"

"You feel with your vagina."

I frowned at that. "That was below the belt. Literally and figuratively."

Tori made a sad sound. "You're right. I'm sorry. But you're acting crazy. Next you'll be saying you're going to apply for the job at the prison."

The silence between us drew out.

"Mae. No."

There was another silence.

"Mae, seriously. No. You didn't."

"I applied online tonight."

Tori blew out a long breath. "You need help."

"Just think of it as a summer job."

"Summer jobs are lifeguarding at a pool or serving sundaes at the ice cream parlour! You're talking about teaching violent criminals their ABCs."

"Don't be insulting. It's high school education, and I'll be the teacher at the women's prison, too."

"Wait. What?"

"I might have done more than just apply. I start on Tuesday."

There was a cracking noise from her end of the phone line that I couldn't identify. "What was that?"

"The seal on a bottle of vodka. I'm drinking."

"It's nearly midnight."

"I know."

"Please get on board with this. It's safe. I promise."

Tori's voice became choked. "I know you don't believe that. I don't believe that for a second. What if it's not safe? I already lost one best friend this month, Mae. I can't lose you, too."

I knew where she was coming from. And normally the guilt over how she was feeling would have been enough to stop me. I never wanted to make my best friend worry about me the way she was now. But I couldn't shake the feeling that Jayela's killer was still wandering the streets, while an innocent man, one who meant something to me, one who meant something to my sister, was sitting in a jail cell, waiting for a trial that wouldn't be fair.

We both knew it wasn't safe. But it was the only way I was going to get to talk to Heath. So I was going to do it, at least until Heath gave me the explanation I needed.

13

MAE

Nerves fluttered around my belly as I drove into Saint View for my first shift at the prison. As per the list of guidelines I'd been given by the warden who'd interviewed me, I'd dressed conservatively. The floral skirts and hoop earrings I preferred while teaching my seven-year-olds were replaced with serious black pants and no jewelry at all. Apparently even a necklace could be used to choke someone, so that was out. I'd added a button-down shirt and blazer despite the warm evening. I would probably be boiling hot by the time I got there, but it covered me up and appeared professional.

At the prison gates, I showed a security pass to the guard and was allowed to drive through to a second lot marked as staff parking. The prison seemed a little less intimidating with a gorgeous sunset behind it. The pinks and purples washed over the dull gray concrete, softening the sharp edges. I got out of the car and pulled my shoulders back, taking the gorgeous sunset as a sign I was doing the right thing. This was just a teaching job. I'd had many of them, and I had to think of this one in the same way. This was a chance for me to make a difference in somebody's life. I wholeheartedly believed that education was life-altering. It was a game changer for disadvantaged kids, and that's who most of these prisoners were once. Maybe it wasn't too late to make a difference in their lives, too.

This couldn't just be about Heath. But I did want my answers.

"Now or never, Mae," I murmured to myself. "You doing this or what?"

I was doing it.

This time, I didn't have to buzz the intercom to be let inside. My security pass did the job of popping the lock and I pushed my way in, looking for the guard who was supposed to meet me for my first shift.

"You're fucking kidding me."

I ground my molars together. Sitting on a bolted-down table was the impossibly gorgeous guard I'd argued with the last time I'd been here.

He shook his head as if he was as disgusted to see me and folded his arms across his chest. "This is some bullshit."

I tried to rein in my temper. "Well, hello to you, too. Want to tell me what your problem is today?" The words came out sickly sweet, taunting him. I didn't care if I was being rude. It had been one thing to put up with his attitude when I was just here as a visitor. I certainly wasn't going to take his shit now he was my colleague.

He stood and crossed the gap between us to stand in front of me. "Boss didn't tell me the new teacher was a woman." He swore low under his breath. "Probably because I would have told him I wasn't doing it."

"Doing what? As far as I know, I'm the one who's here to teach. Not you. All you need to do is show me where my classroom is. Then you can screw off to whichever bridge you crawled out from underneath."

A muscle ticked in his jaw. "Of course you think it's that simple. Because you're so green you're practically Kermit."

I might have laughed if I hadn't also been contemplating punching him. "Well then, I guess that makes you Miss Piggy. Can we go?"

He shook his head, eyes rolling toward the ceiling. But he motioned toward the security door. "Don't say I didn't warn you."

After giving me a locker where I could put my things, he punched a code into the security panel by the door that would allow us entry into the belly of the prison. I grabbed the door before he could, opening it for myself. I took a deep breath, trying to remain calm. I was going to have to work with this man. We'd gotten off on the wrong foot for sure, but I didn't want this to be the way we went on. This workplace would be hostile enough as it was. I didn't need my colleagues adding to it.

Though it went against every instinct in my body, I was willing to try to be the bigger person. "I'm Mae, by the way."

He didn't bother glancing in my direction. "I know. I've seen your driver's license, remember?" The corner of his mouth flickered up. "Nice photo, by the way."

Oh. This guy. Screw being the bigger person. My driver's license picture looked like I'd spent the night before partying on a pirate ship with a parrot sitting in my hair. I had no idea how I had managed to take such a bad photo. I totally blamed the guys at the DMV for not telling me my sunglasses had snagged and completely ruined my ponytail. "And yours is perfect, I guess? Hand it over, then."

"Not a chance. But I will say that at least I know what a comb is."

Fine. Two could play at that game. I reached over and grabbed the little plastic ID tag hanging from his shirt pocket. It clipped off easily, and I stepped away from him so he couldn't snatch it back. "Rowe Pritchard." I glanced over at him, expecting him to be annoyed that I'd taken his ID, but he simply strolled along the corridor like nothing bothered him. And when I gazed down at his photo, I realized why. "Is this one of your modeling photos? Because this is not normal. Nobody looks this good in a passport photo."

He smirked and took the ID back from me, snapping it back onto his shirt. "I do."

I couldn't have rolled my eyes harder if I tried. "Well, at least I know your name now. *Rowe*."

"Pritchard to you."

Oooh. A twitch I could exploit. It was my turn to smirk. "No. I think I'll stick with Rowe." I started humming "Row, Row, Row your Boat" beneath my breath.

It was small, but the flash of annoyance that crossed his features gave me a sick sense of satisfaction. Annoying Rowe might just be my new favorite thing to do.

We reached the end of the corridor and turned left, stopping in front of a painted wooden door that had a space for a room name but was currently blank. I frowned. I'd change that. I'd label the room properly, and make it my own, just like I did in my elementary school. The learning environment was just as important as books and pencils were. And that started here, with the door, and with the men knowing from the minute they saw it, this was a place of learning. I took a deep breath and reached for the handle, ready to get on with the job.

Rowe's fingers circled my wrist, stopping me. His dark-brown gaze bored into mine. "Listen to me. Don't think I don't know why you're here. And don't think I won't be watching your every move. You don't look at the prisoners. You don't talk to the prisoners. You don't touch the prisoners. I don't care if lover boy is sitting on the other side of the door, waiting for you to run into his arms. You make one wrong move and you're out of here." He paused, but his gaze didn't shift from mine. "It's only a matter of time. You don't belong here, *Mae*."

My brain told me to pull my hand from his grasp. But there was something deep inside me that oddly liked the touch of his fingers over my pulse point. And maybe it was my imagination, but for a tiny second, I thought I felt his thumb smooth over the soft skin of my wrist. So I didn't move an inch.

But I also wasn't going to let him get away with speaking to me like that.

I wasn't his student. I wasn't his underling. I wasn't his anything. "What do you mean I don't belong here? I was hired to do a job, *Rowe*." I said his name like it tasted bad. "So get out of my way."

His fingers tightened around my wrist. "Of course you don't belong here," he hissed. "I don't know how you wormed your way in. You aren't even qualified."

"I have a teaching degree. I'm qualified."

"You're an elementary school teacher. So sure, if you're planning on teaching these guys how to count on their fingers, you're qualified."

"I can do a little more than that. Thank you for your vote of confidence, though." I wasn't about to tell him that the warden himself had admitted they were so desperate for a teacher they were willing to take anyone with any sort of education qualifications. "I'm here to help these men. So how about you let go of me and let me do my job?"

We stared each other down, neither of us willing to give the other an inch.

"She said let go of her."

Rowe and I both spun at a voice to our left.

My heart plummeted through the floor. "Heath."

But Heath's attention was firmly fixed on Rowe. He didn't even turn my way. Something flashed hot in his ice-blue gaze, and I desperately wished for it to land on me.

Rowe dropped my wrist and faced off with Heath. "Did you say something, prisoner?" His tone was so low and commanding that even I took a step backward.

It was only now that Heath looked at me. I gave a tiny shake of my head, trying to tell him that it wasn't worth going head-to-head with Rowe over. I was fine. Rowe didn't scare me. And though he'd held my wrist tightly, he hadn't been trying to hurt me. A flicker of guilt rose at the fact I'd actually liked his hands on me.

Heath got my message. "Nothing. I didn't say anything."

I could see exactly how much it hurt him to say that.

Rowe's gaze slid slowly from Heath to me. "Whatever you two are playing at, it won't last. I'll see to that. I know there's something going on. One wrong move and you're gone." He turned to Heath. "And you'll be put in solitary. Got it?"

Heath didn't answer. He just stared Rowe down, not giving him an inch.

Something passed between them, something hard, hot, and full of alpha male energy that was so tangible it practically crackled.

Heath's fingers clenched into fists at his sides, and I instinctively knew that if these two men had met each other outside this environment—at a bar or on a football field—they would have been throwing punches within minutes.

Or slamming each other up against the wall in a kiss that would have seared my eyeballs to watch.

That was the feeling that sucked the air from the room right now. A pure intenseness that could have gone either way.

But here in prison, with Rowe as guard and Heath as prisoner, there was only one way for that energy to flow.

It swelled and peaked and overflowed into a storm of hate.

A trickle of panic rolled down my spine. Heath didn't need to be making enemies in here. And neither did I. I knew I couldn't touch Heath, though my fingers burned with the need to. So instead, it was Rowe's wrist I reached for. "Come on. I'm late for my first day, and you already made it pretty clear I can't go anywhere in this prison without you. Let's go."

Rowe stared down at my fingers around his wrist, and then back up at me before pulling from my grasp. He pushed open the door, waiting for me to go ahead of him. "Get on with it then."

I couldn't help it. I glanced over my shoulder once more at Heath, but his expression had completely shut down. He spun on his heel and disappeared down the corridor.

14

HEATH

I stalked away down the hall, shock at seeing Mae here, of all places, coursing through my body. Every step of distance I put between us just felt wrong and unnatural. Leaving her behind, alone with that asshole guard, went against every fiber of my being. I couldn't stop seeing his fingers wrapped around her slim wrist.

I hated that he could touch her and I couldn't.

I hated that she could touch him but not me.

"Got a bee in your bloomers?"

I stopped in the doorway of the recreation room and looked over to see who had called out to me. DeWitt. The same big man who had been one of my cellmates on intake. He and I, along with the young kid, Vincent, had all been moved to the General Population area on a trial basis. If we were good, we'd get to stay there, where prisoners could mix more freely, at least at certain times. If we got ourselves into trouble, we'd be sent to the cells while we awaited our trials.

But while Vincent had been placed in a separate row, I now had the unfortunate displeasure of being DeWitt's neighbor. The two of us had been assigned side-by-side cubicles, each containing nothing more than a bed with a lumpy mattress and a small writing desk with a hard plastic chair.

Tonight, he sat at a circular table in the middle of the common area, surrounded by three other men, identical tattoos etched into the skin of their necks, marking them as members of the Saint View Sinners. Officially a motorcycle club, but in reality, they were a whole lot more than that, with connections rumored to run deep and right across the country.

That was what DeWitt had been talking about when he'd questioned if I knew who he was. I hadn't noticed his tattoo at the time, but even If I had, it wouldn't have mattered to me.

I had nothing to lose.

He'd regarded me cautiously ever since. Giving me a wide berth, just the way I liked it. Only now, he motioned me over.

I went because it wasn't like I had anything better to do. He pulled an empty chair up beside him and patted it. "Sit. Play a round with us."

"Pass."

A muscle ticked in his jaw, but he didn't insist. "Fine. Keep pacing the hallway like a caged rat." He dealt a fresh round of cards to his friends like I wasn't standing there watching them. A few guys across the other side of the room laughed at an *Everybody Loves Raymond* rerun on a tiny TV mounted on the wall.

"You seem to know everything that goes on in this place."

De Witt paused in his dealing and glanced up at me. "Maybe I do. Maybe I don't."

I hated the idea of asking him for anything. But I desperately needed to know why Mae was here. "What's going on in the room down by the bathrooms? That Officer Pritchard is down there with a woman."

DeWitt shrugged. "One of the guards from the women's prison? Who gives a shit?" He went back to his game.

"Not a guard. Civilian. She doesn't have anything to do with the prison system."

That got his attention. His grin turned mocking, and he started a little dance on his seat, rocking his shoulders, his hips thrusting like the complete perv he was. "A civilian, you say? Pritchard got himself a prison groupie? Lucky fucking prick. Those bitches must be willing to sit on anyone's dick."

One of DeWitt's friends sniggered. "You fucking blind? He's so fucking attractive, I'd sit on his dick."

They all burst into laughter. But it only grated on my nerves.

"She's not fucking him." I was sure of that. The thought of Mae being a prison groupie was completely absurd. She had to be here because I'd refused to take her phone calls or to see her when she tried to visit me. Shit. That was on me. I should have just taken the call and let her yell at me. Now she was putting herself in danger to do it, and that was the last thing I wanted. I had no idea how she'd gotten past the security walls. She was completely insane. This was no place for her, or any woman. The men here weren't just criminals. They were dangerous. A woman here, especially one as beautiful as Mae, was a recipe for disaster.

"Oh, wait." DeWitt swiveled in his seat, turning to look at me. "They in the schoolroom? The one at the end of the corridor? Damn. If they've hired a woman, maybe I'm suddenly in need of some education."

I put the pieces together and groaned, scrubbing a hand

over my face. My shoes squeaked on the floor as I paced back to the room Mae had disappeared into, and I paused on the outside, listening. Her voice filtered through the door, muffled, but still a balm to the aching in my chest.

I plastered myself to the wall and let the stifled sounds of her lesson sink into me like sunbeams on a cloudless day. She worked here now? How the hell had she swung that? Every word she uttered had me wanting to bust down the damn door and kneel at her feet to beg for a chance to explain myself. It was one thing to refuse her visits when I couldn't see or hear her. When her name was just a word on the lips of a guard. But now, knowing she was so close, holding myself back was an exercise in torture. I wanted in that room like I wanted my next breath.

But after our little showdown earlier, Pritchard would throw me out the second I tried. There had to be another way.

DeWitt came up behind me in the corridor, his voice interrupting my frantic thoughts. "She's your prison groupie, isn't she? The one you've been moping over ever since you got here."

"Don't fucking call her that."

"I know a way you can talk to her. Away from Pritchard. Because he ain't gonna give you an inch."

I already knew that. But I also knew that anything from DeWitt didn't come free. "I'm listening."

"You'll owe me."

I nodded, accepting the debt. Mae was worth it. Getting her out of here and away from these pieces of scum would be worth it.

"There's a women's bathroom, just down the hall. That's the only chance you've got of talking to her without

Pritchard up in your grill. It's keypad operated, can't get in there without the code. Not even a swipe key will help you."

"Not much good to me then, is it?"

DeWitt's grin widened. He folded his arms across his wide chest, his yellowing teeth making me nauseous. "Lucky I've got a soft spot for you, pretty boy. I know everything that happens in here. Including the code."

I was immediately suspicious. "How?"

He chuckled darkly. "You aren't the only one who wants some alone time in this place, you feel me?" He put one hand out at hip height and splayed open his fingers as if they were resting on the back of another inmate's head. And then pumped his hips as if he were thrusting into their mouth.

Bile rose in my throat. "If that's how you think I'm going to repay you, you've got another think coming."

"Nah, pretty boy. As much as I'd like your lips wrapped around my dick, I think you're saving that for someone else."

"What is that supposed to mean?"

"I saw the way you and Pritchard were eyeing each other earlier. You looked ready to rip each other's clothes off."

I shook my head sharply. "Don't mistake hate for lust."

DeWitt strutted like the cat who'd swallowed the canary. "Fine. If you say so. It's beside the point anyway. Now, about that debt. You'll owe me. And I'll claim it when I'm ready. Deal?"

I ground my teeth together, but Mae's voice still floated through the closed door, and I knew I couldn't just let it go. It was at least a half an hour drive from Saint View Prison back to her place. And if she was teaching here? She'd probably been here for a while. There was a good chance she would detour past the bathroom before she left. I had to at least try.

"Fine. Deal."

"Pin code is seven-nine-eight-three-eight-five. Probably how many hearts Pritchard has broken on the outside, don't you think?"

I didn't care. I was already striding for the bathroom.

15

MAE

Two students.

It wasn't much of a start, but it was something. And the upside of having such a tiny class? The two men both actually wanted to be there. They'd been polite and respectful learners for the entire time.

I bent over Vincent's desk and studied the simple math problems I'd first demonstrated, then left for him to solve solo. I put my hand on his shoulder to get his attention. "Hey, look at that. You did it. Well done."

The young man didn't glance up at me, but he had his shoulder-length black hair scraped back into a messy ponytail, so I saw the tiny flicker of a muscle in his cheek that made me think he might have wanted to smile.

That was what my job was all about. Watching it click for a student was exactly why I loved it.

Rowe cleared his throat, an obnoxious sound that he'd been making all night.

"What now?" I sighed in frustration at his umpteenth interruption.

He jerked his head in an overexaggerated fashion to stare at my hand on Vincent's shoulder.

"Oh, for Christ's sake." I removed my hand and waved it around in Rowe's face so he could see that I'd followed orders.

His expression didn't change. "Class is over. Go back to your cells."

The two men both stood immediately, their chairs scraping over the floor.

"Hey, hey, wait a minute. Class isn't over until I say it is."

But the two men were already filing past me for the door.

"Sorry, Miss," Vincent said beneath his breath as he passed. "I don't want to be disrespectful, but we gotta do as he says."

I softened and nodded at the younger man. "Of course. Go on. Thank you for your hard work tonight. I'll see you next class."

The man nodded and scurried away.

With the door closed behind my students, I glanced over at Rowe sitting behind a desk in the back, face screwed up like he'd just been given a lobotomy.

"Well, that was boring."

"So's your face, but I didn't comment on it," I snapped, still annoyed at his interruptions and for dismissing my class five minutes before it was supposed to end.

Rowe looked as if he was biting back laughter. "So, tell me. Do you feel some sense of purpose? Like you've done your bit to help humanity now that you've taught exactly two inmates what a fraction is?"

"Oh, so you were listening? I dumbed it down a little, just for you." I gave him a sickly sweet smile.

He pushed up out of his chair, straightening the desk.

"Like anybody actually has a need for fractions around here anyway."

"Doesn't mean you shouldn't want to learn them."

He headed for the door, and I scrambled to pick up the folder of paperwork I'd brought in. I followed him over, surprised when he actually held the door open for me without a smart-ass comment.

"Thank you."

He didn't say anything, just headed back down the corridor, toward the main reception area. We passed small signs marking two rooms to the left as male and female staff bathrooms. At the sight, my bladder reminded me that I'd been here for hours. I stopped. "Wait. Can I use the restroom, please?"

Rowe sighed like it was an extreme imposition but mumbled a string of numbers, giving me the code for the locked bathroom. "It's how many times I dozed off during your class."

I flipped him the bird and pushed open the door while he muttered about not taking too long because he had better things to do than babysit me any longer.

"Doubtful. You're not that important," I called, walking backward, letting my ample ass bump open the door. The interior darkened as the door closed, and I fumbled for the light switch, while simultaneously engaging the lock, sliding a latch from green to red to show the facility was in use. I didn't really think that Rowe would let anyone try to enter while I was in here, but I wasn't going to risk it.

A big body pressed against my back, a hand covering my mouth.

I was too shocked to try to scream. Panic forced the air to disintegrate from my lungs, keeping me silent. But my brain flashed bright-red warnings behind my eyes. Tori had been right. My very first night, and I was about to be attacked in the bathroom. I raised my fist to bang on the door and get Rowe's attention.

"Stop. It's me."

My arm fell limply to my side as I recognized the voice. I slumped back against Heath's chest, relief-filled tears pricking at the backs of my eyes. His arm wrapped around my middle, holding me tight against his chest, while my knees attempted to give out.

"Nod if you're okay and not going to scream."

I did as asked, trying to get my rapidly beating heart under control. It thumped for two reasons.

Leftover adrenaline from thinking I was about to be attacked.

And pure longing at Heath being this close.

He slowly peeled his fingers from my mouth, but he didn't let me go.

I turned, taking a step back so I could gaze up at his face. "You smell different."

He frowned. "Prison soap. It's not exactly the expensive stuff."

It didn't matter to me. He still smelled good. He still smelled like safety and comfort, and now that I was out of his arms, I just wanted back in them.

His gaze hardened. "What are you doing here?"

"You wouldn't see me."

"Because I didn't want you to see me here. Not like this." He sighed in frustration, then changed tactics, a hint of curiosity creeping into his voice. "Why would you even want to talk to me?"

"Because I don't believe you did it. That's what I've been trying to tell you all along."

He gave a harsh laugh. "Guess they didn't tell you I confessed."

I wasn't going to be swayed by that. "They did."

"And yet, you're here."

I eyed him critically. This wasn't the Heath I knew. He had defenses up, but I suspected they weren't to keep him safe. He'd never been one to care more about himself than others. This was just another attempt to push me away. To get me to leave this thing alone. But I couldn't. I had no idea why he'd confessed to the cops. Why he seemed intent on going down for something he didn't do. But I wasn't giving up that easily. "Say it then. Say it to my face."

Heath's expression was stony. Unreadable. "What?"

I stared him dead in the eye. "I want you to look me in the eye and tell me you did it. Tell me you killed my sister."

It was only in that moment that it occurred to me that if he said yes, he'd murdered Jayela in cold blood, I was in a very dangerous position. I was locked in a bathroom, and nobody knew he was here with me.

He didn't say anything.

I pushed at his chest. "Tell me you did it."

He shook his head. "I can't."

Relief flooded my system. I was sure for a moment that I would lose my legs out from underneath me again. A sob burst forth, and I clutched at the fabric of his jumpsuit, staring up at him, and words vomited from my mouth. "Then why? Why did you say you did? I'm so sorry. I'm so sorry for the things I said to you that morning. I was in shock. I had no idea what was going on. I shouldn't have said anything to them. This is all my fault. I told the police... But then I tried to tell them it wasn't you. I knew it wasn't. Something in my gut just said that it couldn't be."

A tear dripped down my face, and he pulled me tighter

against his chest. "Shh. It's okay. It's not your fault. They beat the shit out of me. They forced that confession into my mouth and gave me no choice but to say it. He would have killed me if I hadn't."

I pulled back and stared at him in horror. I hadn't noticed them in the dim light of the corridor earlier, but in the brighter fluorescent light of the bathroom, there were the tinges of old bruises, now nearly healed around his jaw and eyes. I traced them with my fingertips, sick that my words might have caused his pain. "What can I do?"

His gaze raked over my face as if he were drinking it in, committing it to memory. "I'm fucked. All the evidence points to me, even if that video of my confession doesn't stand up at trial. My public defender is useless. You know what he told me? He told me the best I could hope for was to not get the death penalty."

I couldn't breathe. "No."

He didn't say anything. His silence was the worst confirmation of all.

My fingers trembled. "There's got to be something we can do. I can't just leave you here."

His arms tightened around me, and he pressed his lips to the top of my head, inhaling. "Do you truly believe me?"

"Yes!"

He cupped my face and tilted it to look up at him. Whatever he saw there in my expression must have convinced him.

He nodded. "If you really want to help, find me a good lawyer. A really good one, Mae. Because I need a miracle."

A thumping on the door broke us apart, and I spun around, staring at the door with wide eyes.

"Did you fall in? Do you need a rope?" Rowe's annoyed tone filtered through.

"Fuck, I hate that guy," Heath muttered.

"Me, too."

"You've gotta go before he gets suspicious."

I didn't want to. I dug my fingers into Heath's biceps, not wanting to leave him behind. "Come to my class. I'm here three times a week, and at the women's prison the other two. I need to be able to see you."

There was more banging from the other side of the door.

"No. Don't come back. It's not safe."

"I don't care. I need to see you. I'm going to get you out. I'll get you the lawyer. The best one money can buy."

He shook his head like he couldn't believe that. He kissed my forehead, his soft lips against my skin, branding me. I wanted to push up onto my toes and kiss him properly. But he spoke before I could.

"Seriously, Mae. It's not safe. Don't come back." He reached across me and unlocked the door, yanking it open and giving me a little shove before I could respond.

I stumbled out into the corridor, an intense loneliness instantly pressing down on me.

"I'll bring matches next time, shall I? Seriously. Probably a good thing there's no other women employees in this place." Rowe smirked at me.

I didn't even have a witty comeback. All I could think about was getting him as far away from the bathroom as possible so Heath could leave it. I hurried toward the reception area, leaving Rowe to follow me.

16

ROWE

Mae power-walked to the main exit, like she was trying out for the Olympic Games. At the security doors, she fumbled with her pass, tapping it against the black reader attached to the wall. It didn't do anything except frustrate her. She whirled on me, irritation etched into the frown between her eyes.

I strolled casually after, not caring I was making her wait. I moved in close behind her, trying not to notice the delicate scent of her perfume. Shit. How long had it been since I was close enough to a woman to smell her scent?

Way too long.

No point dwelling on that, though.

"You have to put the exit code in first, and then tap your security pass." I leaned around her to punch in the code, but my fingers froze over the keypad.

"What? Don't tell me you forgot it."

"Of course I didn't forget it," I snapped. Fact was, tendrils of Mae's long blonde hair ghosted across my cheek, the delicate touch taking me by surprise. That, combined with how good she smelled? I was pretty sure my brain had short-circuited temporarily.

I got the door open for her and escorted her into the cool night air.

"Um, thanks for tonight, I guess?" She paused. We'd picked up her stupidly sized purse and other belongings from her security locker, and now she held them to her chest like they might keep her warm.

I resisted the urge to take off my jacket and offer it to her. "Why thank me? This isn't a date. I did my job. I sat through your boring lecture, I didn't fall asleep, I escorted you from the premises without anyone shanking you." Just like the warden had told me to. In hindsight, I should have realized the new employee was a woman. He'd never asked me to escort any other new employee to the door.

I could almost hear the grinding of her teeth as she bit back a retort. "Well, thank you anyway. I'll see you next shift. I'd attempt to make my class more interesting for you, but I suspect your favorite pastime is playing video games in your parents' basement. Right? I can't really cater for that level of intelligence in anyone over eighteen."

It was an effort not to laugh. I had to admit, I kind of liked her spunk. Her verbal sparring skills were on point. And it wasn't often somebody challenged me in that department. But that didn't mean that this—her working at the prison—would work out. It wouldn't. I already knew exactly how this would end, and it wasn't well. Better that she just leave now before any real damage was done.

Or before anyone got hurt. Because that was the real concern here.

"That is if you even come back," I mumbled under my breath.

Apparently, I didn't mumble quiet enough.

"Oh, I'll be back. See you tomorrow."

I stifled a groan of irritation and turned away as she strode across the darkened parking lot. At the small window, I watched her get inside an old BMW, put her bag on the passenger seat, check her hair or makeup in the rearview mirror, and then finally get the keys in the ignition. I cracked my knuckles when there was no sign that she'd locked the car around her. "For fuck's sake," I mumbled while she drove out of the security gates. Her taillights disappeared into the darkness.

"Who was that?"

I spun around at the question, instantly recognizing the other guard. "New schoolteacher," I told Colt. "Can you believe that? Warden is out of his mind hiring her."

"Why? She not qualified? Or you just being a sexist prick?"

I was a prick, but I wasn't sexist. Technically she wasn't qualified. But the board had been on the warden's back for months about supplying a teacher for the men. We had a state standards inspection coming up, and we'd be marked down for not having all the appropriate programs in place. He would have taken anybody. But I had a good reason for not wanting Mae here. Colt hadn't worked in the system long enough to know what could happen. What had happened in the past. But I knew all too well.

Because I'd paid the ultimate price. And so had she.

Never again.

"Both." It was easier to let him think I was pig, rather than explaining any further. I liked Colt and I wasn't in the mood to pile my burden on to him.

He didn't push it either; instead, he yawned, covering his mouth with his arm. "Sorry. Tired."

He looked it. Dark circles shadowed the skin beneath his eyes, and he yawned again as if to prove the point.

"Baby kept you up again?"

Despite how tired he appeared, his face lit up at the mention of his daughter. "Yeah. Lacey thinks its colic. But I don't know. All four of us were up all night, trying to get Luna comfortable enough to sleep."

"Why don't you just take turns? That's gotta be the upside to this weirdo relationship you're in." Colt was almost a decade younger than me, but he seemed older than his years, and we'd struck up a friendship in the last few months since he'd started working here. He had an odd relationship at home, though. He was totally obsessed with his woman but shared her with his two best friends from high school. Like, *shared* her. In all ways. And none of them seem to mind or get jealous. Six months after I first met him, I was still trying to understand exactly how that worked. But the four of them had a baby together and were battling through their first year of college as well. And somehow, even with all that on his plate, I don't think I'd ever seen anyone look as happy. I almost envied him. Except I'd been that happy once, too. And I knew how badly it hurt when it all went away.

"I know. We're ridiculous. But, Luna, man... If she is upset, we're all upset. There is no sleeping when she's screaming down the house in agony." He pulled out his phone from the pocket of his work shirt. "Seriously. I know it doesn't make any sense, but wait until you're a parent. You start doing things that once seemed crazy, just because you can't get enough of that kid's little face. You have to see this photo that I took of her yesterday. She's the cutest thing I've ever seen."

I played the diligent friend and watched over Colt's

shoulder as he scrolled through what had to be five hundred photos of a chubby-cheeked baby with the same dark eyes and dark hair he had.

"Anyway," Colt said, finally putting his phone away. "What's happening in this place tonight? Anything I need to know about? I only just got on, and you're the first person I've seen."

He followed me toward the security doors, and I scanned the two of us in.

"You missed the big excitement. Should just be the same old, same old now. But there is something I want to do. Come with me?"

"Sure. Where are we going? And why are you frowning like that? You look like you ate something sour."

We stomped through the halls, heavy boots on the solid floors, our similar heights making us evenly paced. "I need to check something."

Some of the prisoners moved about freely, on their way back to their bunks from the recreation room, which would be closed for the night in the next ten minutes when curfew was called. Colt eyeballed two prisoners acting shifty, but I didn't slow my pace to bother investigating whatever they were up to.

In the General Population housing area, a sea of small cubicles with the men's beds and personal belongings spread out in front of me. But there was only one I was interested in right now. I strode to row four, passing Mae's little protégé, Vincent, hard at work with a sheet of Mae's math problems as I went. My gaze caught his, but he lowered his eyes and went back to his task without comment.

Mae would be pleased he was doing his homework like a good prisoner.

In row four, I found who I was searching for. "Ah. Just the man I wanted to see."

Heath Michaelson raised his gaze at the same time his cubicle neighbor did.

"My lucky day then." Michaelson's neighbor ran his tongue over his fat lips. "The two most attractive guards in the prison. To what do I owe this extreme privilege?"

"Shut up, DeWitt," Colt said. "You know he didn't mean you. Quit being a suck-ass."

"I wouldn't mind sucking your a—"

Colt might have been young, and just doing this gig to bring in some extra money for his family, but he was an excellent guard. He silenced DeWitt with a single glare. Which was good, because the man wasn't my favorite, and I wasn't in the mood for his shit.

Michaelson remained quiet throughout the whole exchange, not moving from his spot on his bed.

"What's your relationship to Miss Donovan?"

"Miss who?" DeWitt looked confused, his gaze bouncing back and forth between me and Michaelson like he was at a tennis match.

"We have no relationship." Michaelson's icy-blue eyes darted up and to the right.

I shrugged like I believed him. But I was pretty sure he was lying. "You right-handed or left-handed?"

Michaelson gazed down at his hands, and then back up at me. "What's it matter?"

"Just making friendly conversation."

"Right-handed."

I thought as much. That eye dart up and to the right was a dead giveaway. It was something I'd been taught at my old job, a little hint that helped determine when prisoners were full of shit. If a person is right-handed, when they tell the truth they'll often look up and to the left. But when they lie? They look up and to the right. Left-handed people were the opposite.

I went on like Michaelson hadn't spoken. "She your girlfriend?"

A muscle ticked in Heath's jaw. "No. I told you. We have no relationship. I'm just not the sort of guy who walks by when another man has his hands on a woman he shouldn't have."

It was on the tip of my tongue to tell this asshole that the only reason I'd touched Mae earlier today was to keep her safe. I hadn't been joking when I'd called her green. She had no idea the sort of men who sat on the other side of that classroom door. I didn't want her just walking in, completely unprotected and unaware. There was a reason the warden had assigned her protection. She might not realize it yet, but she couldn't just go wandering around the prison, doing whatever she wanted. As much as it pissed me off, I was her babysitter when she was here. It wasn't a responsibility I would take lightly. If that annoyed her, or if it annoyed this dickhead, then that wasn't my problem.

DeWitt leaned forward, resting his elbows on top of his knees. "Ooh. The new teacher is your girl?" He scratched at his temple, attempting to appear confused, but his acting was awful. "I thought the bitch you killed was your girl?"

"Shut up, DeWitt," Michaelson and I snapped in unison.

I eyed the prisoner. "I don't like the idea you and her know each other somehow. And I don't like that you're lying to me. It's my job to keep her safe. And I can't do that if I don't know all the details." I leaned in closer, bending over and resting my hands on my thighs so we were closer to eye height. I was well aware of how patronizing the position was. It was how adults spoke to children. And it was a deliberate ploy on my behalf. I knew he wouldn't get up off his seat. Colt and I would have had him flat on his ass in seconds if he tried it. "You don't have to tell me, but I'm going to find out. And then I'm just gonna be annoyed that I had to do all the research for myself."

"Guess you're going to be annoyed then."

I shook my head slowly as I straightened. If he wanted to play it like that, then so be it.

"Pritchard. This her? You said her name was Donovan, right?"

I turned around and took the phone Colt offered.

"Yeah, Mae..." The words died on my lips when I read over the article that Colt had brought up. The headline shouted "Hero Cop Found Dead" in thick black letters. And beneath it, Mae's image appeared in a photograph taken with a familiar face.

Jayela.

She'd been a favorite around the prison.

I suddenly realized why Mae had looked familiar the first time I'd seen her. I'd seen her briefly at Jayela's funeral. Shock punched through my gut. And then I stared hard at the man. I was well used to being around the worst of the worst. Murderers. Rapists. Arsonists who had taken dozens of lives. But a man who murdered a woman, and a cop at that, had a special new level of dislike in my heart. "You're the cop killer?"

DeWitt's mouth dropped open, and he stared at Heath like the man had suddenly sprouted another head. "No fucking way. I heard about that. That was you?"

Nobody paid him any attention.

I'd known Michaelson was in on pending murder charges, but I hadn't looked into who the victim was. I saw hundreds of men's files every day, there was no point or way of remembering every detail of them. As sad as it was, the victims' names just didn't matter here. But Jayela mattered. She was one of the good ones. "What in the hell of twisted games are you two playing? You killed her sister? And yet she's still trying to visit, and taking a job in this shithole just so she can see you? You got golden fucking sperm or some shit?"

DeWitt chuckled. "I've seen him in the shower. His dick is pretty fucking golden. Good chance his sperm is, too."

I didn't even want to know what DeWitt had been doing or thinking about in the shower. It was Michaelson who was the real problem here. "You stay away from her. Got it?"

I didn't wait for Michaelson to answer me. I just walked away, wondering how the spunky, full-of-life woman I'd met earlier today, could be so under this guy's thumb.

17

HEATH

DeWitt waited until the guards were on the far side of the room, occupied by other prisoners, before he approached me again. He loitered around the foot of my bed, not entering my personal space, but hanging around the edges like a bad smell.

I stared up at the ceiling, my hands tucked behind my head, ignoring him. Whatever he wanted, I wasn't interested.

But DeWitt wasn't one to pick up on subtle body language. "*Psst*. Michaelson. We need to talk."

I lifted my head slightly, just enough to make eye contact. He glanced around, fidgeting, impatient for me to pay attention to him. I dropped my head back onto my hands. "Talk then." I'd already been here long enough to know that he would anyway. The man never shut up.

He came inside my space and perched on my desk chair. "I just came to say thanks."

"For what? If you think I did you a favor, you got the wrong guy. I didn't do anything for you."

"Nah. You did. I got the right guy. I just wanted to tell you thanks for taking the rap."

That got my attention. I sat up. "What are you talking about?"

"I know you didn't kill the cop."

Shock rippled through me. I knew I didn't kill her either, but there was no way for DeWitt to know it. Suspicion rose, thick and fast. But at least it was a productive emotion. De Witt might have liked to play the clown in here, but I'd been watching him for days. He was smarter than he appeared. And he had pull that made him either a very powerful ally or a very dangerous enemy. "Why do you say that?"

DeWitt leaned back on the chair, tucking his hands behind his head and grinning at me widely. "I put out that hit on the cop."

It took a moment for the words to even register through my thick head. But when they did, they flipped a switch inside me. The rage didn't start small, there was no kindling of a tiny fire that gradually builds in intensity. It came hot and fast. An instant explosion that fueled every muscle in my body.

I launched myself at DeWitt, only to find strong hands around my biceps that hauled me back down onto my ass. I blinked in surprise. I hadn't even seen DeWitt's guys moving in around me.

DeWitt chuckled and waggled a finger in my face. "Now, now. No fighting in here, remember? You want to get us all thrown in the hole? I get it. You're pissed off."

I glanced over at the guards, but none of them were looking in our direction. DeWitt's guys were huge. The rest of his gang subtly moved closer, pretending they were doing other things, and yet it was obvious to me that all of them were tense and ready to mobilize if their boss gave the word.

I was well and truly outnumbered.

But that did nothing to calm the rage inside me.

"Why?" I spat the word.

DeWitt shrugged, like he ordered hits every other day, and just for fun. "That bitch cop had been getting in my way for too long. I got her partner on the take, but she was all high and mighty, and full of morals." He rolled his eyes. "Bitch thought she was better than me. Smarter than me. She was making trouble, so she had to go."

DeWitt patted me on the knee, and I fought the urge to slap his hands away, my mind racing. Boston had been Jayela's partner for as long as I'd known her. DeWitt had him on the take? For how long? Had he known there was a hit out on Jayela? Boston had always been a good guy, and he and Jayela had made the perfect team. It was impossible to believe the man could have been dirty or had a hand in the murder of his partner.

But Boston was hardly my biggest concern right now.

DeWitt might be full of shit. Why on earth would he just announce what he'd done, if not to make himself look big in front of the other inmates? They all did it. Talking shit about the crimes they'd done, blowing them out of proportion until they were so ridiculous they could have been straight out of a telenovela. Anything for a bit of street cred.

But fuck... If it was true, DeWitt had just given me a way out of jail. And right now, I needed that hope. "You have to tell someone. Dammit, DeWitt. I could end up with an injection in my arm for this. You gotta testify. You gotta tell someone that this was your gang and not me."

DeWitt stroked his chin, mulling that over. The man was clean-shaven, and his fingers pulled over his flabby jowls. "I see your predicament. Truly. I do. I'm not unsympathetic. But here's my problem. I don't think I'm gonna be telling anyone that, because that'll shine a dirty old spotlight onto my guys on the outside. And even though I'm in here, I got a business to run. I don't need no media attention, or no cops at my house. I don't need none of that. So I'm not really seeing much appeal in testifying on your behalf."

"You son of a bitch—"

"Such language. Like I said, I'm not unsympathetic." He looked around, commanding the attention of the other men without even trying. "He's with us. You all hear that? He's under my protection. Nobody touches him. Nobody gives him a hard time. Michaelson here is my new best just buddy. Capiche?"

"Boss, but—"

DeWitt held up a hand, silencing his second-in-command, the tattooed guy who followed him around like a shadow. "Don't want to hear it. My word is law. We all know that, don't we?" He said it so sweetly, it was practically a song. And yet there was an undertone beneath it that almost dared him to argue. He backed down immediately.

Once again, I was awed by the power DeWitt commanded in here. And wondered who the hell this man was on the outside.

18

MAE

I tossed and turned all night, and by the time dawn arrived the next day, I was still thinking about Heath. I could still feel the warmth of his chest at my back, his arms tight around me, holding me close. But every time I thought of him, I thought of where he was. I thought of him sleeping on some shit-tastic prison mattress, in a bleak cell, with no hope he'd ever be released. By the time I got out of bed and showered, I knew what I had to do. I groaned, and it echoed off the tiles in my bathroom. "Of all the people."

The elementary school had signed me off for the rest of the school year on bereavement leave. So I had nowhere to be until my two-hour shift at the prison in the evening, and no reason not to drive into the city and park outside Simonson Lawyers and Partners. I stopped in the lobby, found the right floor from the listing on the wall, and took the elevator to level three.

The receptionist lifted her gaze when the elevator binged, announcing my arrival.

"Good morning. Do you have an appointment?"

"No. I don't. Is there any chance I can speak to Liam Banks, though, please? It's quite urgent."

The woman frowned, delicate lines creasing her forehead. "Mr. Banks has a full schedule for quite some time. His first available appointment is in six weeks on a Tuesday. Would that be suitable?"

I opened my mouth to tell her that no, it wouldn't be suitable, when Liam appeared from the office behind her. His gaze slammed into mine, and his eyes widened in surprise. "Mae? What are you doing here?"

I wanted to cringe. This was awkward. I didn't want to lead with, "I really need your help to get a confessed murderer off his charges." But since that was why I was here, I didn't have much else to open with.

The receptionist cut me off before I could even say anything. She bristled, spinning on her chair to face Liam. "I was just telling the young lady that you're completely booked up until the middle of summer."

Liam shook his head. "I think I've just had an opening become available." He held his office door open for me. "Come on in."

I smiled politely at the receptionist as I skirted her desk, and she scowled back at me.

Okay then. We obviously weren't going to be friends.

Liam's office had a floor-to-ceiling glass wall that overlooked the city. I wandered over to it, ignoring the chairs at his desk and the armchair and couch set to one side. "Tori wasn't wrong when she said that you were the best of the best then, huh? You don't get an office like this by being average."

There was a beat of silence, and I turned back to face him.

He perched on the edge of his desk, watching me, his

arms crossed over his chest in much the same way he'd stood leaning on his car after my sister's funeral. I wondered if there was a reason for it. Did crossing his arms like that give him some sort of sense of protection or was it just because his biceps looked really frigging good in that position? I tried to talk myself out of staring, but it was hard not to.

"It's not the nicest one in the practice. The senior partners have those. But it's not bad." He cocked his head to one side, not noticing my ogling, or at least not commenting on it.

"Not trying to be rude, Mae. But I am kind of wondering why you're here. Need to sue someone?" He grinned and cracked his knuckles. "I really hope you need to sue someone. Because I love that shit. It's not really what I do, but hey, for you, I'm willing to get my hands dirty."

If only it were as simple as suing someone. "Not exactly. Do you also by any chance love getting pending murder charges dropped? Kinda hoping you love that shit, too."

He raised one eyebrow. "I'm going to go out on a limb and assume it wasn't you who murdered someone?" He held his hand up in a stop motion. "Actually, just in case it was, don't tell me. Despite what the movies tell you, you really can't tell me you murdered someone if I'm going to defend you. Even I have more morals than that."

I couldn't help but smile at him. "Just out of interest, who do you think I would have murdered?"

"Well, I haven't seen you much over the past few years, so I can really only go off what you were like in high school. So...if we're working on that assumption, I probably would guess it was me you'd murdered. But since I'm still alive, there's a few holes in the theory."

"I didn't hate you enough to murder you. For the record."

"Good to know. I feel much safer now that I'm not wondering if you plan to stab me in the chest with a stapler." His tone was playful, but then the smile slowly fell, and he waited patiently for me to actually explain myself.

"It's Heath."

"Heath..." He picked up a yellow legal pad and scribbled something on it with an expensive pen.

"Michaelson? He is currently in prison, waiting on his trial. They wouldn't give him bail."

I could see the moment that Liam fit it all together. "Are you talking about the guy who admitted to murdering your sister?"

I cringed. "Yes?"

He moved across the room and took me by the arm, guiding me to sit on the couch. "Are you actually insane?"

"Why does everybody keep asking me that?"

He peered at me over the top of his black-rimmed glasses. "Because you talk the crazy talk! It's not very often I get somebody who walks in here and asks me to get their sister's murderer out of jail. In fact, it's normally quite the opposite." He peered around him, as if he were looking for someone. "Huh. I was semi-expecting a Jerry Springer set to rise out of the office floor. Or maybe Ashton Kutcher to jump out from the closet and start a *Punk'd* revival."

I pulled a face at him. "Hilarious. So can you help me or not?"

"Tell me more about this guy."

Liam pushed off the couch, moving by me to sit behind his desk. He was suddenly all business, and I followed him, dragging out the seat on the other side of his desk and sinking into it. I mimicked his posture, sitting up straight and folding my hands on my lap. I had his full attention, his gray gaze sweeping over me. There was nothing sexual about it, but I still found myself slipping back into that high school version of myself who had thought he was so cute. Ten years hadn't changed that. Just because I'd thought he was an arrogant prick back then didn't mean I'd been blind. And teenage hormones were no joke.

Apparently twenty-seven-year-old hormones were no joke either.

But mentally undressing him wasn't why I was here.

I racked my brain for information I could supply him about Heath. But I realized quickly that I didn't know much that would actually be of help. "I don't know what to tell you. He dated my sister for a few months about four years ago. He's a really good guy. Jayela wouldn't date someone who wasn't. He grew up in Saint View, he has an apartment there now."

Liam glanced up from scribbling on his legal pad. "Saint View? I don't do pro bono."

I bristled at his judgment. "Jesus Christ, could you be any more of a snob? Who asked you to do it pro bono?"

"I'm not a snob. Well, actually, that's a lie. I am. I'm sure your murderer friend is really nice and all, but if he lives in Saint View, he can't afford me. The best don't come cheap."

I couldn't help the snort. "You haven't changed a bit, have you? And this right here, is exactly why I didn't like you when we were at school."

"No. You didn't like me because I never asked you out."

My mouth dropped open. "Excuse me?" Heat rose up the back of my neck, and I prayed with all my might that it would stay there where he couldn't see it. Because if it traveled to my cheeks and let him know there was probably some truth in those words, I would be mortified. "I... Never... I don't even know what you're talking about."

Liam grinned at me. "Yeah, you do. You had a whopping big crush on me. It's okay. Everybody did." He winked.

I faked a gagging sound, while I clutched my fingers around my neck. "Seriously. I'm choking on the secondhand embarrassment. I can't breathe. Your ego is suffocating me."

He picked up his pen again. "Comes with the territory. You can't do this job without an ego. Just the way it is. And like I said. I don't do pro bono."

For a second I thought about walking away. I thought about telling him he could stick his ego where the sun didn't shine and that I'd find another lawyer. But I could already see he was right. A great lawyer wasn't going to do this job pro bono. And then where would I be? If I walked out of this office right now without securing Liam's services for Heath, I'd be right back where I started, only slightly more annoyed and slightly more turned on, than I had been when I arrived in the reception area.

Freaking Liam.

"I'll pay you."

"Don't want your money. That's a losing case if ever I saw one. Don't really want my name attached to it, you know? My name has value."

"Can you just take the job before I roll my eyes so hard I have a seizure? Seriously. I'm concerned for my health here."

He chuckled and ran his pearly white teeth over his bottom lip. Shit. Why was that so hot? Dammit. I bet he knew it, too. It was probably a ploy to see if I actually was harboring old feelings for him. Which I wasn't. Totally not at all.

Stupid Liam and his stupid cute face.

"Nope."

Worry had me clenching my fingers in the fabric of my dress. I really had no other plan if he didn't accept this proposal. I didn't know why, but I hadn't planned on him not wanting the job. I kept seeing Heath's desperate gaze in the back of my mind and knew I had to try harder. A gut feeling told me that if the shoe had been on the other foot, Heath would have done it for me. "Fine. You don't want my money. What do you want?"

"A date."

I blinked. "With me?"

"No. With Victoria Beckham. But since I suspect she'll turn me down, what with David being such a fox and all, I suppose I can settle for a date with you."

I frowned. "Isn't this completely inappropriate? Pretty sure you took some sort of oath that said you can't ask out your clients."

"You're not my client."

"I'm trying to be."

"No. You're trying to get Heath to be my client. I'm just trying to help you sweeten the deal."

"I think most people call that blackmail."

"Maybe so. Hey. Do you think that's why people hate me so much?" He chuckled as if the idea of people actually truly hating him was completely ridiculous. And it kind of was. He was annoyingly charming. And let's face it. That sixteen-year-old girl inside me? She was squealing loudly. She wanted a date with Liam Banks so bad.

"Fine. But it's not a date."

"Fine. Call it what you want. Call it a catch-up between two old friends."

"Have you already forgotten that I hated you in school? We weren't friends."

Liam threw his hands up in the air. "Fine. Let's just call it a catch-up with somebody I met at a super depressing funeral."

"Sorry my sister's funeral was such a downer for you."

"Apology accepted."

"So you'll do it? You'll take Heath's case?"

He sighed. "Yeah. I'll do it. But just so you know? In all seriousness. I don't think even I'm a good enough lawyer to get him off a murder he admitted to. And as you've already pointed out, I've got a pretty healthy ego."

I bit my lip as I left his office, hating that he was probably right.

19

HEATH

"Michaelson. Stick with me today. You've been in as long as I have, and you haven't properly met all the guys yet. Randall here is thinking you don't like us. But I keep telling him you're just shy." DeWitt leaned on the cinderblock wall of the corridor, eyeing my prison-issued workout clothes. Or more likely, imagining what was beneath them.

Randall sniffed in my direction, punctuating his leader's words.

I'd grown used to DeWitt's constant sexual innuendo, and I was even more bored with it now than I was in the beginning. He didn't intimidate me. I knew I could hold my own if it was just him and me. But I was well aware that inside this place, DeWitt was popular, and I had no one. He'd been reminding me of that as often as he could. He might have called a temporary truce between us for now, but I knew he could change his mind at any time.

It wasn't enough for me to want to hang out with him when I didn't have to, though.

"Pass. Need to run."

DeWitt's lips pressed together in a scowl.

Randall sneered in my direction. "He's got better things to do than talk to us. His loss."

I didn't care what Randall thought. They were all sheep. Lemmings, following each other over the cliff. Everybody in this place agreed with whatever DeWitt said. I still wasn't exactly sure why the man wielded as much power as he did, but it wasn't something I was losing any sleep over.

Mae on the other hand... I was losing all my sleep over her.

We had to line up at the exit in pairs, like a group of five-year-olds on their first day of school, but when the guards opened the doors, and the sunlight and fresh air rushed in, it actually was like being a kid again. The excitement was real. I wasn't the only one who hurried out, but where most of the others headed straight for the weight equipment or the picnic benches where they'd sit in groups chatting like eighty-year-old women at the hairdressers, I headed straight for the fence and started up a jog around the perimeter.

I'd never much liked jogging on the outside, but this was as close to alone time as I could get now. The sun was my one saving grace in the never-ending sea of ugly gray cement. There weren't enough windows inside the prison for my liking, and the lack of natural light to someone who normally spent all of his days working outside was a prison sentence in itself. The muscles in my legs sang with pleasure, and I twisted side to side, trying to get some movement through my torso again.

Across a wide walkway, the door to the women's prison opened, and straight lines of inmates filed into an identical courtyard to the one we were in. Randall, and a couple of the other guys on my side, young and white beneath their sleeves full of colored tattoos, lazily got up from the picnic bench, overstated swagger in their gaits as they made their way over to the fence.

"Hey, baby," one of the women called out. "Looking good today."

I tried to edge around the men, ignoring the fact that Randall stuck a foot out in an attempt to trip me. He and his friends sniggered, watching me as I passed.

The woman across the walkway pouted at the lack of attention. "Baby. You didn't even notice what I did with my hair."

Randall turned to his friends and raised one eyebrow, the two of them egging him on with taunts about his missus being high maintenance.

She shoved her hands on her hips, waiting for his reply. When it came, it obviously wasn't what she'd been expecting.

"Why the hell would I care? It's only good for hanging on to while you suck my dick."

I kept jogging, but the small size of the yard meant I still heard and saw every word of their shouted conversation.

The woman's mouth dropped open. "You don't talk to me like that. You wish I'd suck your puny cock." Some of the other women roared with laughter, a few of them making tiny dick gestures.

Randall stuck his middle finger up at her. "Whatever, bitch. Don't fucking need you anyway."

He'd picked the wrong woman to tangle with. That much was clear. She was faster and wittier than he was. "Nah, baby. You don't need me. You got your boys, right? They suck that dick real good?"

I fought back my amusement, keeping my head down, eyes glued to the cement while I pounded over it. I liked a woman who could put a moron in his place.

Her boy on this side was floundering, searching for a way to save face. "We got a hot new blonde bitch over here. The new teacher is fine, baby! Not a crusty old..."

I didn't even hear the rest of their argument. My fingers clenched into fists, and it was a struggle to keep my pace even. What I really wanted to do was put on a burst of speed, fly across the courtyard, and ram my fist straight into this guy's mouth for talking about Mae like that.

But that would only end with me making enemies or locked in solitary. Which would also mean not seeing Mae when she came in to teach. As it was, that guard Pritchard glanced in my direction from his position in the corner of the yard, talking to two other men in uniform. His gaze raked over me, hard and calculating, and I knew exactly what he was looking for. He hated the connection between me and Mae. Hated he didn't know exactly what it was. I knew his type. Complete control freaks who went into this line of work because they got off on telling grown men what to do.

I wouldn't give him what he wanted. So I let Randall run his mouth about Mae. I let him talk it up, let him make his prison wife jealous, all while letting it build inside me. Because the anger was easier than the guilt. Mae wouldn't have been here at all if not for me.

I'd thought of nothing but her for the past twenty-four hours and the feel of her against my chest when we'd been in that tiny bathroom together. I needed more of that. It was what I'd clung to as I'd lain awake in my bed last night, listening to the sounds of the other prisoners around me and trying to forget where I was.

It wasn't safe for her to be here. But at the same time, there was nothing I could do about it. I knew how determined she was. It was a miracle she was on my side at all. I doubted anybody else was. I'd called my mother to let her know where I was, and all she'd done was laugh. "Guess you aren't really all that much better than us after all."

I'd hung up without responding. I'd never thought I was better than them. My mom with her drinking and drug habit. My sister who'd been hell-bent on going down the same path. I'd just wanted to make something of myself. School was never my thing, but I'd wanted more than the life my mother had lived, crabby and aged well beyond her years by substance abuse. Beaten down and abused by the men in her life.

After dropping out of school, I'd looked for apprenticeships in a kitchen, but all I'd been able to find was dishwashing jobs. I'd been set to take one, ready and willing to work my way up from the bottom when the landscaping job had fallen in my lap. The father of a kid I'd gone to school with needed some grunt work done. He'd offered me more money than the dishwashing job, and so I'd taken it. Because to a kid from Saint View who didn't have a cent to his name, even a few dollars above minimum wage seemed like a better bet than chasing some stupid dream of being a world-famous chef.

So I'd let the dream go, never to mention it again.

Except to Mae.

I didn't know what it was about her. She'd just always been easy to talk to in a way that nobody else was. Jayela hadn't been one to ask about my hopes and dreams. She was too practical for that, focusing only on what was right in front of her. But Mae had asked. Mae had watched me with interest and listened when I spoke. She read between the lines, hearing the words I wasn't saying, and fought for more.

I'd been blinded by how hard I'd fallen for her sister,

even though in hindsight, Jayela had been right. The two of us didn't work. Had things been different, and we'd stayed together, we would have destroyed each other.

I'd never seen what was right there in front of me. I'd never noticed that Mae was nothing like Jayela. Not even a little bit.

I noticed now.

Jayela would have looked at the evidence and declared me guilty. Mae looked past that to the man I truly was.

She saw me. It was a heady feeling, that knowledge. One I wasn't sure I'd ever experienced in my life.

I ran past Pritchard and tried not to make eye contact with him, though he stared at me like he could read my thoughts. And even though I knew he couldn't, I pushed the thoughts of Mae away, wanting to save them for myself. Instead, I found myself wondering if the man had ever even been in a fight, because his nose was so impossibly straight, I doubted it had ever been broken.

He laughed at something one of the other guards said, ignoring the hollering from the female prisoners trying to get his attention. It was as if their catcalling was complete background noise to him. The man had to be used to it. He probably had women throwing themselves at him at all hours of the day, and a different woman in his bed every night.

I shook my head as I ran past, making sure he didn't see me watching him. I didn't need to be wondering about a guard. I shouldn't even be thinking about Mae. She wasn't mine to think of. All I needed to be doing was praying she had some way of getting me a good lawyer.

20

MAE

My first night at the women's prison went a little bit differently to my first night at the men's. For starters, there was no sinfully hot guard to greet me in the reception area. There was actually nobody to greet me at all, since it was after hours and anyone on a reception shift would have left at five. But my swipe card worked, as did the pin code Rowe had given me during my last shift. So I wandered along, looking for someone to help me or for a door marked as the schoolroom, butterflies rioting around my belly at the thought I may find the prisoners before I found the employees.

But a few steps farther down the hallway, a door to my left was marked with a single word: Infirmary. I breathed a sigh of relief, knowing that while there would be patients inside, there would also be staff who would hopefully be kind enough to point me in the right direction. I knocked timidly on the door, cringing at the sounds of a woman's moans of pain from the other side.

But the head that popped out from behind the blue surgical curtain was sunny, with the brightest smile I'd possibly ever seen. Her hair was the deepest of auburns, and freckles dusted her pale skin.

"Well, you aren't a sick prisoner, are you?" She pushed back on the bed frame, which sent the black stool she was sitting on rolling across the linoleum floor. Her maroon surgical scrubs hung loosely on her frame, and she pulled latex gloves from her hands, dropping them in a trash can to her left as she stood. "Should I be concerned, or do you come in peace?" She cocked her head to one side, studying me.

I shook my head. "I'm Mae. New teacher? I'm supposed to start here tonight, but I'm not really sure where I'm supposed to be."

The woman rolled her eyes. "And yet you managed to get all the way back here? Unbelievable. I'm sure Thad was supposed to meet you, but he's probably asleep in the guard's room. It's been a quiet night—"

The prisoner's moan of pain cut the nurse off, and we both looked over. The woman in the bed didn't wear the ugly orange jumpsuits the prisoners did. Her frail shoulders were covered by a flimsy hospital gown that slipped to one side, exposing her aged and wrinkled skin. Her lined face contorted in pain, but when it cleared, she focused on me. "Are you from the church?" she rasped. Hope lit up her gaze.

"Uh, no. Sorry. I'm the new teacher..." I glanced at the nurse beside me, but she gazed at her patient, her face somber.

A tear slipped from the old woman's eye. "Are they coming soon, Perry? They will come, won't they?"

Perry edged around the bed and took the woman's slender hand. It was clear even to me that this woman was at the end of her life. She seemed barely a shell, frail enough to fly away on the back of a gentle breeze should someone open a window. But it was the depth of sorrow in her watery blue eyes that made my heart ache. She didn't look like a woman who had committed crimes. She could have been someone's grandmother, wasting away in an infirmary bed.

I swallowed hard, a ball of emotion rising in my throat.

Perry squeezed the woman's fingers. But she didn't make her any promises. "Just try to rest, okay? You need sleep."

The patient closed her eyes, her lids as thin as rice paper. Perry stood and steered me out into the hallway with a heavy sigh.

"She's dying?" I asked quietly, walking slowly away.

Perry nodded. "Soon, I suspect. A week or two, maybe. Terminal cancer. Diagnosed a few months back."

"They don't release terminal inmates so they can be with family when they pass?" I was well aware that some of these women were truly bad people. But I suspected a lot weren't. They were just ordinary women who had made bad choices or been pushed into bad situations in order to survive. Nothing was ever as black-and-white as good and bad. Most people fell somewhere in the middle.

"Sometimes. But not this time." Perry's gaze hardened. "It makes me mad. Myra didn't even try for early parole. She knew it wouldn't be granted. She's tried many times in the past, and each one was denied. All she wants now is for a priest to come and bless her before she dies. To confess her sins and pass away, knowing that in the eyes of her church she's been forgiven." She gave me a sidelong glance. "Are you religious?"

I shook my head. "No. But my best friend and her family are. Strict Catholics."

Perry nodded. "You understand how important religion is to some people then."

I nodded. I did. And though I didn't share Tori and Will's

beliefs, I respected them. "There's no priest coming for Myra, is there?"

Perry shook her head. "No. The warden won't allow it."

"Surely that's her right?"

"I don't know. I believe so, but I also know there's a lot of things that should happen around here but don't." She straightened her shoulders and plastered on a smile that didn't quite reach her eyes. "But at least you're here now. We haven't had a teacher in so long, there was probably cobwebs and dust over every inch of your room. I know they cleaned it out for you already, though, because one of the prisoners ended up with me after cutting her arm in the process. Something about a loose metal frame on the chalkboard. Wound was completely gross, even for me. So watch out for that." The woman widened her eyes. "Oh!" She stuck her hand in my direction. "I'm Perry, by the way. Night nurse."

I already liked her. I took her hand, squeezing it. "Pleasure. Do you work every night?"

She turned down another corridor, and I fell in line beside her.

"Monday through Friday, same as you, right? Last teacher didn't work weekends anyway."

I nodded. "I'm only in the women's prison some nights, though. I'm teaching a high school GED class at the men's prison as well."

Perry looked me over and grimaced. "How did that go?"

I smiled, thinking about my two students, surprised I truly did see them that way. During the two hours I'd had with them, I hadn't treated them as prisoners. Just men wanting to better themselves. The same way Perry obviously saw her inmates simply as patients. "There's one student I like quite a lot. He worked hard last night. I can see potential in him. The other wasn't quite as diligent, but at least he showed up, right? There wasn't much other interest. That was a little disappointing."

"Wait until word gets around about how beautiful you are. I bet that class fills right up. I'm sure Pritchard will have a conniption about that."

I scrunched up my face involuntarily.

Perry laughed. "Girl, don't tell me you're one of those women who can't take a compliment?"

I grinned at her. "It's not one of my superpowers. But thank you." Even though compliment uncomfortableness wasn't really the reason for the face, it was better to let her think that than explain that the mention of Rowe had me feeling weird. A strange mixture of attraction, annoyance, and intrigue. I wasn't about to tell this woman that. She obviously knew him and had no alliances to me. I didn't want it getting back to Rowe that I'd been affected by the mere mention of his name.

Perry stopped outside a closed door. "Anyway. This is your classroom. Good luck."

"I survived the men. I'm sure this will be a walk in the park."

Even as I said it, I realized I was probably tempting fate. It was a rookie teacher error. If ever you looked at your new class list and thought, no sweat, great class! You could be sure that come the first day back, every one of those gorgeous students will have turned into complete monsters over the summer. You just didn't ever say something would be easy when it came to teaching.

Perry confirmed it when she patted me on the arm. "Don't underestimate them. They may not have the brawn the men do, but they're smarter. Some of them are downright wily. If they like you, they'll be your best friends. But if they don't..."

I sucked in a deep breath. "I better make them like me then, huh?"

The inside of the classroom was not much different to the classroom I had on the men's side. A mostly empty space, with a dozen or so scratched-up, old-school-style desks with the lids that lifted. There was none of the technology I was used to from teaching at a fancy private elementary school. All I had was a faded black chalkboard that had a 4-foot-high penis, complete with hairy balls, artfully drawn on it.

I sighed and picked up the eraser, readying to remove the image, when I remembered Perry's words. I needed to make them like me. So instead, I put the eraser down and retrieved a discarded stub of chalk. I poked my tongue out the corner of my mouth as I worked, adding to the rude picture, feeling pretty amused with myself.

"Is this part of the lesson? I didn't come prepared for drawing, I'm afraid."

I turned at the interruption and gazed upon the middle-aged woman who had just entered the room. She was slim beneath her prison-issue jumpsuit, her long hair pulled back in a simple low ponytail. She didn't move with confidence exactly, but her stride did have the determination of someone who knew exactly what she wanted. She took the seat closest to the teacher's desk in the front row and peered up at the huge penis drawing that I'd added a smiley face to, as well as arms holding a little sign that said, "Welcome to High School Ed."

"He's friendly-looking."

My gaze met hers, and we both burst into laughter.

Without really thinking about it, I held my hand out for her to shake. "I'm Mae."

She stared down at my hand and smiled before she took it, shaking it gently, her eyes going misty.

I ducked my head so I could see her face better. "Hey. Are you okay?"

She brushed at a welling tear with the back of her hand and gave a nervous little laugh. "Of course. I'm sorry. It's just been a while..."

"Since somebody shook your hand?"

"Since somebody showed kindness without expecting anything in return."

That hit me in the gut. And told me that I really had underestimated this place. If a handshake could bring this woman to tears, how awful was it in here? I shuddered to think.

I put a hand on her shoulder. "In my classroom? You're just the student. I don't care what you did on the outside. I just want to help make you a better person on the inside."

The woman gave me a watery smile. "I'm Selina by the way."

"It's lovely to meet you, Selina. I think we'll get on just fine." I peered at my watch, then over at the door. "Do you think anyone else is coming? It's only two minutes until I'm supposed to begin."

"Oh, I'm sure they'll all turn up at the last moment. But can I ask you something while we're alone?"

"Of course. About the curriculum?"

Selina bit her lip. "No. I was just wondering... I heard outside on the yard that you worked at the men's prison, too. My son-in-law works there."

I froze. "Rowe? I mean Pritchard?" He was the only one I'd met who was young enough to have a mother-in-law this age.

"Oh no. Colt McCaffrey?"

"I'm sorry. I haven't met him yet."

"Oh. Okay. It's just that it's his birthday tomorrow. I was kind of hoping you might pass on happy birthday message from me." She stared down at the desk and shrugged. "It's silly. I mean, he and my daughter and her other partners are really good about coming to visit me. I'll see them on the weekend. But I hate knowing he's just over there, and I can't even give him a hug."

The door crashed open, and a dozen rowdy women stormed the room, yelling and laughing, one skipping around the desks like she actually was one of my first graders. Another took one look at me and barked. Like she thought she was actually a dog, she barked at me some more before sitting on one of the desks in the back. Another let her gaze run over me, taking in my professional pantsuit, and made a loud joke about the new teacher being a fancy pants.

I tried to calm the racing of my heart. For some reason, this classroom full of women was twice as intimidating as the big men I'd had yesterday. But intimidated or not, I wouldn't let them get the better of me. I was here to get Heath out. But I was also here to do a job. And I intended to do it well.

Before taking my place at the front of the classroom, I squeezed Selina's shoulder. "I'll find him tomorrow. I'll give him that hug for you."

Selina's eyes lit up like I'd promised her a million dollars.

"So this the bitch all the guys want to fuck?"

My head snapped up. I had no idea who'd said it because the entire room was laughing and speculating over why the guys would be so interested in me.

"She is a bit rat-looking, don't you think?"

I took a deep breath before letting it out.

Selina gave me a small nod of encouragement. At least if nothing else, I might have won one prisoner over today.

21

MAE

I was completely and utterly drained by the time I made my way out into the parking lot after class. More than anything, I was yearning for a long soak in a hot tub, an overflowing bowl of ice cream all to myself, and an episode of *Bridgerton*.

But my visit to the infirmary haunted me. That woman, lying on her deathbed, frail in her old age, body riddled with cancer... She was hardly a danger to society anymore. And all she'd wanted was a priest. Someone from the church to treat her like a human being.

I didn't have the pull to get a priest. But I knew someone who did.

I got out my phone and called Tori's number.

"Hey, sunshine. Whatcha doing?"

I gripped my phone a little tighter. "Just finished a shift at the prison."

My best friend still wasn't happy about me taking a position there, but like the good friend she was, she'd said her piece and then let it go. "How was it?"

I sighed. “Good mostly. But there is something bothering me, and I wonder if you can help me...”

I filled her in on the situation in the infirmary, on what I’d seen, and how my heart had gone out to the woman.

Tori’s murmurs became increasingly louder, filled with sympathy, and then with outrage. “They can’t deny her access to a priest!”

“They have.”

“On what grounds?”

I shrugged. I leaned against the wall of the prison, staring at the back end of my car. “There’s a lot of problems here. The warden doesn’t seem to be very proactive in getting programs running. I don’t know if it’s a lack of budget or if he just doesn’t care...”

“That doesn’t mean they can just deny a woman her last rites.”

“I agree. Is there anything you can do on your end? Someone at the church who could help?”

There was fierce determination in her voice when she answered. “Leave it to me. I’ll fix this.”

I smiled into the darkness. This was why I loved her. She was such a determined little firecracker. I had no doubt in my mind she’d organize both a priest and the warden into anything she put her mind to.

She hung up on me to start organizing her new mission, and I put my phone away in my bag, pleased I’d known someone who could help. I headed again for my car, the junk food stashed in my kitchen, and Netflix calling my name.

When I was halfway across the lot, though, the skin prickled at the back of my neck, awareness crawling over me. I glanced around, but there wasn’t much to see. A few other cars parked beside mine, but no other people. I clutched my keys a little tighter anyway, unease creeping, even though I could see nothing to warrant it. I couldn't shake the feeling of being watched.

I'd use the keys as a weapon if I had to. I darted a peek over my shoulder, instantly realizing the source of the feeling.

Rowe's dark-brown gaze met mine through the prison window.

I breathed out a sigh of relief and raised a hand in greeting.

Rowe disappeared from the window completely.

"Well, hello to you, too, grump," I muttered.

"I thought I was in a pretty good mood, but I can be grumpy if you want me to be."

I shrieked at the voice behind me and spun around. "Liam!" My heart pounded against my rib cage. "Holy shit. Where the hell did you come from?"

He pointed to his car parked beside mine. "Just there. I was sitting in my car, waiting for you to finish your call."

I hadn't even recognized his Porsche. He was the last person I'd expected to see here after nine at night, so I hadn't exactly been looking for it. "What are you doing here? Stalker much?"

He was dressed more casually tonight than I'd seen him since high school. Blue jeans covered his long legs, and a short-sleeved button-up shirt clung to his chest in a way that was very pleasing to my eye indeed.

He shoved his hands in his pockets. "It's hardly stalking when you have an invite. And a security pass."

"Who invited you? Wasn't me."

"Do you not remember our conversation in my office? I agreed to represent your little murderer friend, and you agreed to go on a date with me."

"He's not a murderer."

"So you say. How about that date?"

"Bit late, don't you think?"

"Bit late if you're eighty, I suppose. Last I checked we weren't even close to that old. Come on. Leave your car here. I'm starving and I know this great place to get something to eat."

I opened my mouth to protest, but he cut me off.

"I promise, Grandma. I'll have you tucked up in your bed before midnight."

He gave me such a boyishly charming grin that I couldn't say no. If I was being honest, there was a little part of me that was kind of thrilled he was so impatient for this date that he'd turned up here tonight. I changed directions, heading for the passenger seat of his car. "Fine. You want to do this now, we do this now. Then I owe you nothing."

"Deal. But I bet by the end of the night I'll have you wishing you did owe me another date. Because I am the date master. I know you never got to experience it in high school, because you were too busy being a stick-in-the-mud, but my reputation was widely known."

I slid into the passenger seat and rolled my eyes. "Your reputation as a man whore was widely known. Your reputation for dating girls, on the other hand, was about as well-known as Whirlwinds of Aurora."

He paused with his hands on the wheel. "Who?"

"Exactly."

He frowned at that, turned his car on, then said, "Hey, Google. What is Whirlwinds of Aurora?"

I dropped my head into my hands, embarrassment already heating the back of my neck. "Dammit, Liam. You couldn't just let that one go?"

Google took that moment to pipe up with an answer.

"Whirlwinds of Aurora was a three-piece punk rock band out of Providence. It was formed by lead guitarist Simon Schuler, drummer Laura Burns, and vocalist Mae Donovan."

I dug a toe into the floor of his car, hoping for an escape hatch to appear.

Liam gawked at me. "You were in a punk rock band? Excuse me, I'm so confused right now. Maybe I need to play that again because I don't think I heard it right. There is no way that sweet little Mae Donovan, valedictorian and hall monitor, started a punk rock band. Hey, Google—"

I punched him in the shoulder. "Shut up. I wasn't that much of a nerd."

"Yes, you were. And part of the reason you didn't like me at school was because I scored better than you did." He paused and chuckled at himself. "Both in the classroom and out of it."

"Suffocating on your ego again." I pulled on the handle of the door, opening it up. "Here, some extra space for your massive head."

He grabbed my hand. "Hey. I'm only joking. Get back in."

His touch froze me to the spot. His fingers were soft and warm and felt distinctly nice wrapped around mine. I didn't tell him that I'd really had no plans on going anywhere. For a moment I thought about pretending to get out again, just so he'd keep holding my hand. But I shut the door and dealt with the disappointment when he let go.

Liam put his hand on the back of my chair as he looked over his shoulder, reversing out of the parking space. My hormones did a happy little dance, and I stole the opportunity to let my gaze wander along Liam's forearm, his biceps, and then finally his profile.

He dropped his hand to the gearshift, putting the car in drive and steered toward the big black gates that would let us out onto the roads of Saint View. "So tell me more about this band. What did you call it again? Windy Fedora?" He threw me a teasing grin.

"Whirlwinds of Aurora."

"Quite a mouthful."

"Yeah. But at the time we thought it sounded poetic. Teenage angst and all that."

"So, what happened to the band? Or are you still secretly the lead singer, strutting your stuff onstage for thousands of screaming emo fans after you finish teaching little kids how to count on their fingers each day?"

"Not so much. It was a very short-lived adventure. Band broke up when Simon asked Laura out and Laura turned him down."

"I would have thought that was a good reason for a new song?" He raised his voice a few octaves and sang in the worst, most off-key voice I'd ever heard. "Guitarist and a drummer! Should have been a stunner! But she said no. Oh, what woe."

I cringed. "Damn. I really wish I'd known back then about what an awful singer you are. Not to mention a shockingly bad lyricist. It would have made me feel a whole lot better that you scored higher than I did on the SATs."

"Ah, you admit you were jealous of me."

"I admitted no such thing." But we both knew I had been. I liked to win. So did Liam. Even though we hadn't attended the same schools, they'd been so intricately linked it sometimes felt like we had. My valedictorian certificate still hung in a corner of my bedroom. But I'd never forgotten that Liam had been a grade point or two ahead of me when he was announced valedictorian for Edgely Academy. That had irked me something fierce.

Liam steered through the streets of Saint View confidently, making turns, taking us deeper and deeper into what was essentially the ghetto. I stared out the window. I hadn't been this far in years. This area was really nothing like Providence. The further in we got, the more the houses on the streets outside fell into disrepair. They became smaller and smaller, the yards littered with rusted car shells and beat-up old bikes. Some houses were completely abandoned, windows smashed, graffiti decorating the walls, no sign of life from within.

Liam's stupidly expensive car would draw attention out here. An uncomfortable worry niggled at me over that. I couldn't imagine where he was taking me, though I instinctively knew not to be concerned about him. I might not have liked the guy, but I'd never felt unsafe in his company.

The streets outside were another story. They gave off a menacing vibe, shadows lurking, danger promised in dark alleys. "Do you know where we're going? Please tell me you aren't one of those guys who won't use the GPS because your sense of direction is just so great you couldn't possibly need it?"

Liam didn't answer me, distracted by slowing the car to a near crawl, almost stopping altogether outside one house. It was on a very poor street. Only every second or third house was lit from the inside with electricity, and I suspected that if there was anyone inside the others, they were squatters. But this house did have a glowing shine from behind tattered curtains. And the front lawn had been neatly mowed recently. The steps that led to the porch had broken boards, though, and the streetlight out the front lit up the night enough for me to see the peeling paint on the front door.

Liam stared at the house.

"Liam?"

He jerked like he'd forgotten I was there and put his foot down on the accelerator a little too hard. The car lurched forward, my head bouncing softly on the headrest behind me.

"You okay?" I asked.

And just like that he was back to being his cocky self. "Of course. And yes, to answer your question. I do know where I'm going. We're just about there."

He turned the car down a narrow driveway and parked at the back of the nondescript building. There were obviously people inside, judging from the light and soft music lilting through the warm evening, but there was no sign on the building that gave away what this place was.

I peered through the windows, slightly nervous. "What is this place? Do you really want to leave your car here?"

"Worried it might get stolen? You snob."

"I'm not a snob. But I am slightly worried that we may get back and find your car has no tires."

Liam laughed as he got out and walked around to my side, opening the door and escorting me out as well. "You're totally a snob. It's a friend's place. The car will be fine."

The music was louder outside the car, and I realized there was a live band playing inside. The woman's voice was deep and throaty, in a way mine had never been. But oh, had I ever wished it was. The tone was enticing, almost siren-like, and I found myself walking toward the door, pulling ahead of Liam.

"Hey. Wait for me."

I let him open the door for me and stepped inside the

brightly lit room. I blinked in the lights, my eyes adjusting from the darkness outside. It took them a moment, and my nose was quicker. A delicious aroma wafted past me, and my stomach grumbled in response, reminding me I hadn't eaten dinner. "Oh, wow. What's that smell?"

Liam came up behind me. "Smells good, huh?" He took my hand and led me around a couple of empty tables, to where the band was playing. They stopped when they saw us, the woman's eyes widening in surprise. She cut herself off mid lyric. "Well, well, well. Look what the cat dragged in, will you? What are you doing here? Shit, am I being sued again?"

Liam grinned. "I was in the neighborhood, and hungry. You know I won't eat anywhere else around here."

The woman stepped down off the small makeshift stage and crossed the space between us. She paused in front of Liam, not even glancing in my direction, and just shook her head at him.

He gave her one of his charming grins. "Please, Eve. Feed us. We don't want to go somewhere else and get food poisoning."

"Damn straight you don't. The only other place open at this time would be Ugly Joe's."

Eve made a face, and Liam made a gagging noise, then they both grinned.

The woman finally turned to me. She glanced over me, her gaze starting at the tip of my head and working its way down my body so slowly it might have been uncomfortable, except for the fact that her gaze was completely unsexual. "Who's this?"

I wasn't going to wait for Liam to introduce me. "Hey, I'm Mae."

"You here for a job?"

I frowned. "A job? No, no. I have one. Actually, I have two. Definitely don't need a job."

Eve shrugged. "Pity. You'd do well with that face and body. If you change your mind..."

I blinked. "Sorry?" I glanced around the room in confusion before my gaze came back to rest on Liam.

He was barely containing his laughter. He put his arm around my shoulder, his heavy biceps weighing me down deliciously. "Oh, Mae. Sweet, sweet innocent Mae. You really haven't changed all that much from high school."

Eve chuckled. "Stop being a jackass. She's obviously not from around here." She turned back to me. "You're at a strip club, sweetie. I actually thought that was why Liam had brought you here. It wouldn't be the first time he'd asked me for a job for a friend."

I gaped at her. And then elbowed Liam sharply. "That better not be why you brought me here." Then I realized how insensitive that probably sounded to Eve and rushed to clarify. "I'm sorry. I didn't mean to imply that wouldn't be a very, um, nice job. I'm sure you're a very good employer. But like I said, I'm pretty full up on the employment side." Heat flushed my cheeks.

I could honestly kill Liam.

Liam took my hand again and led me to one of the tables, pulling out a chair for me. I glared at him as I sat. "Don't think that gentlemanly manners are going to save you from this one, buddy."

"I swear, we're only here for the food. I happen to know that Eve makes the very best stew around, and that she always has a pot of it on the stove on Tuesdays when they're rehearsing. The club isn't open to the public Monday or Tuesday, though, so no strip show for you, unfortunately."

Eve piped up. "You're welcome to come back on Friday night, though. We go all out on the weekends."

"Um. Thanks. That sounds nice."

Eve nodded, seemingly happy with that response. "I'll bring you both stew, yes?"

"Yes, please. With bread?" Liam asked.

Eve ruffled his hair, like he was an annoying little brother. "Fine. Bread, too. But you owe me a free consultation next time someone tries to sue me, got it?"

Liam rolled his eyes at me. "She hasn't paid me for a single consultation yet. And she's been sued a lot."

"I heard that," Eve called from the kitchen.

My stomach rumbled again, impatient for the food that smelled so good. "Is that how you two know each other? She's one of your clients?"

"No."

He didn't elaborate. Okay then. "Ex-girlfriend?" The beautiful brunette woman had curves I would kill for. Her long dark hair tumbled around her shoulders in waves, and her tight-fitting dress showed off her killer legs and thighs. It was easy to imagine that she may have, at one point, had them wrapped around the man sitting across the table from me right now.

Liam snorted like the idea was ridiculous. "God, no. We've never... And never will."

But he still didn't elaborate any further on what the relationship between the two of them was. Instead, he changed the subject. "Any other night, this place would be full of people. It's super popular. Cheap drinks, sexy dancers. She's got a few more rooms that lead off of this one, for guys who dance for guys. Or guys who dance for girls. Some other things, too."

I widened my eyes. "What sort of other things?"

Liam gave me a wicked grin. "The sort of things that your sweet, innocent mind has never even thought about."

Despite his assumption that I was still the naïve nerd from high school, I was pretty sure I knew what he was getting at. It wasn't a huge jump to go from strip club to sex club. "The kind of thing that requires such a high level of familiarity with a lawyer?"

"Not so sweet and pure after all, are you? Exactly those sorts of things."

I glanced around the room again with a new eye. Right now, it just looked like a somewhat run-down commercial space. But on closer inspection, I noticed the lights pointed at the stage, and a DJ booth at the back of the room. The concrete floor sparkled in spots, and when I squinted, I realized it was glitter. If the house lights were off, it wasn't completely unimaginable that this room could be filled with people, with half-dressed dancers making their way through the crowd, making sure everybody had a good time.

Eve arrived with two bowls full of steaming stew and a plate of crusty bread. She set it down on the table between us, and then stood back, crossing her arms beneath her breasts.

I nearly groaned out loud just from the intense aroma. "Thank you."

"Welcome. Enjoy it. We're done with practice for the night. But Liam knows how to lock up. Wash your plates."

Liam stood and kissed her on the cheek. "Thanks. Catch you later?"

Eve nodded and strode out toward the door we'd come in, her two bandmates following after her.

Liam sat back in his seat and stabbed a fork into a thick chunk of sauce-covered meat.

"We going to talk about why the owner of a strip club in Saint View trusts you to lock up her business?"

"Nope. Eat your stew."

Fair enough. The food was calling my name. I dug in, my taste buds exploding at the delicious flavor. "What is this? It's amazing."

"Old recipe her mom taught her how to make. It's her specialty. And Eve will feed anyone who happens to be in the neighborhood. She probably had half her staff here earlier, and who knows who else. Seriously. Eat your food."

We ate in silence for a few minutes, Liam concentrating mostly on his bowl. I didn't mind. It gave me the chance to really study him. He ate slowly and carefully, like he was savoring every bite. He found napkins for the two of us, and after we both wiped our mouths, he leaned back in his chair. "Do you still sing?"

I shook my head. "No. Singing died when Whirlwinds of Aurora broke up. Laura and Simon went on to get married after all that drama, and I turned my angsty poetry writing into somewhat less angsty English classes for seven-year-olds."

"Were you good?"

There was a tiny edge of a competitive challenge in his voice. I remembered it from school. It wasn't really in my nature to brag on myself, but there was something about being in Liam's presence that made me competitive, too. And truth was, I was good. "Yep."

He jerked his head toward the stage, Eve's microphone still cradled in a stand. "Have a go."

"Not a chance."

"Come on. I think you want to. I saw the way you practically ran in here when you heard Eve singing. You're drawn to music."

"I am. So what? You want me to just put a show on for you?"

He bit his lip and raised one eyebrow. "Shows here generally involve nudity, you know. Just saying."

"You wish."

He pushed to his feet, striding over to the microphone and grabbing it from its cradle. He flicked a few buttons, and the speakers around the room crackled to life. "One song. It can even be a Whirlwinds of Aurora original if you want."

If looks could kill, he would be dead on the spot.

He chuckled and plugged his phone into a cord by the speakers. "Pick your poison, then. Taylor Swift?"

I stood and closed the distance between us, taking the microphone from his hand. "For the record, there's nothing wrong with Taylor Swift. She is gorgeous, rich, and insanely talented. So I resent the sarcasm in your tone. But no. Give me your phone."

I plucked it from his outstretched fingers. He already had his Spotify app open, and I went right for the search bar, knowing the song I was thinking of wouldn't be on any of his playlists.

I found the right listing and hit 'play', grinning as the opening riff to, "Sugar, We're Going Down" by Fall Out Boy, blasted into the room. I spun around in a happy little circle, the familiar song never failing to make me happy. "I love this song."

"I can see that. Sing it."

There was a challenge in his voice that he knew I couldn't back down from. And as the music rolled through me, I let my mind go blank and released the tension I'd been holding on to for the past few weeks. The stress of Heath being in prison, and my new job there. Rowe, and the way he seemed intent on running me out. And the biggest one of all... The fact I missed my sister so desperately I couldn't even stand to think about her. I'd spent weeks trying to block out the memories of her lifeless body, and I didn't want to let that back in. So instead, I sang. I let the entire first verse pour out of me, reliving the song I'd first learned when I was sixteen years old and the lead singer of a three-piece garage band who thought they were going to take over the world.

I opened my eyes for the chorus, and my gaze slammed into Liam's. There was something in his eyes that made my heart skip. Maybe it was because I'd suddenly been transported back to that teenage girl who had a huge crush on him. That girl would never believe that I was standing here right now, singing a punk rock song in the middle of an empty strip club, with Liam Banks as my only audience.

The words died on my lips. The lyrics completely flew from my brain while it went haywire over the sudden pull of the man who was no longer the teenage boy I remembered. He was something a whole lot more. Still cocky. Still arrogant. But not in a way that made me want to beat him anymore.

Now, I was pretty sure I just wanted to do a whole host of other things. Much more adult things.

The realization was startling.

Liam closed the space between us, his long legs eating up the distance with ease, his gaze never leaving mine. He stopped just a few inches from me, close enough I had to tilt my head.

My breath caught in my chest. Butterflies rippled around my belly. The hand that held the microphone to my lips dropped to my side, and Liam's fingers wrapped around mine, stopping it from clattering to the floor.

"Mae," he said softly, my name on his lips low and sexy.

I tried to make my mouth move, tried to get it to say something that made coherent sense, but the best I could manage was a strangled, "Mmm?"

His gaze dipped to my lips, and his fingers tightened around mine. "Did you forget the words?"

"Something like that," I whispered, my voice barely audible over the music.

"Why?"

I couldn't tell him that. I couldn't tell him it was because I was drowning in the depths of his eyes and thinking about what he'd look like naked.

He brought the microphone back up to my mouth. But my brain was still completely shut off, and any lyrics that I'd once memorized were now lost in a surge of hormones that had taken over with Liam this close to me.

He lowered his head another inch, and when his lips parted, I sucked in a deep breath.

Jesus Christ.

Liam Banks was going to kiss me and make all my teenage dreams come true. I closed my eyes, waiting for it. Yearning for it. Desperate to know how he tasted.

The screech of tires on the road outside broke us apart.

And a spray of bullets exploded through the room.

22

MAE

There was no mistaking the sound of bullets shattering glass and punching through drywall. A scream ripped from my throat, cut off only when Liam threw himself at me, knocking the two of us to the floor. My shoulder slammed into the hard concrete, the wind pushing from my chest, and pain shot through my arm and elbow. Liam's big body covered mine, my head cradled in the crook of his elbow, his face pressed into my neck.

I squeezed my eyes shut tight, protecting them against the clouds of debris floating from the puncture wounds the bullets made in the walls. I waited for one to pierce my skin.

It didn't come.

The debris settled, and the noise of gunshots disappeared in the distance, replaced once more by Fall Out Boy lyrics.

"Liam."

But he cupped a hand over my mouth and shook his head hard. His gaze raked over me, checking for injuries. "Are you okay?" he whispered. "Don't speak. Just nod."

I did a quick scan of my body and found that apart from

where we crash-landed on the floor, I was uninjured. I nodded and tried to speak from beneath his hand. "Are you—"

Liam cut me off. "Quick. Get up. Go lock yourself in the bathroom."

He rolled off me, and I instantly missed the safety his weight had provided. "What? Why?"

"They might be following up on foot. Seriously, Mae. Go."

But I wasn't about to do that. I wasn't going anywhere without him. I wasn't going to leave him out here for dead if some gang stormed the place. I wobbled, getting to my feet, and brushed the plaster dust off me. "I'm not leaving you. So unless you're coming, too, I'm staying right here."

With a sigh and a mumbled word that sounded an awful lot like "stubborn," he hurried to the doors, checking the locks, and peering through the peephole. He pulled his phone from his pocket, punched something into the keypad, then held it up to his ear. "It's okay," he said to me, while he waited for the person on the phone to answer. "I don't think there's anyone out there. Probably just a drive-by."

"Just a drive-by?" I squeaked.

He'd said it so casually, like it was a completely normal Tuesday occurrence. My heart still slammed against my chest so hard it was almost painful. "Are you calling the police?"

I trailed after him, not wanting to be alone, and not wanting him to be alone either.

"No. Eve. She's going to have a fit."

I blinked. "Somebody just sprayed this room with bullets, and you're not calling the police?" I pulled my phone out and tapped out the numbers nine-one-one.

Liam shot a hand out and grabbed my wrist. "No, don't."

I shook him off and hit the green button, connecting the call. "Why not?" I hissed.

"That's not what they do around here."

"That's ridiculous—hello? Yes. I need the police, please."

Liam groaned. He raked a hand through his normally neat hair. "Fuck." Then he turned away to fill Eve in on what had happened, while I did the same with the police. Even though the adrenaline was fading, nerves replaced it. It was hard to stand still while I answered the dispatcher's questions.

Liam and I both finished our calls at the same time. I went to move toward him, but his expression stopped me.

"Come on. I'll take you home. I'm an idiot. I shouldn't have brought you here," he said stiffly.

"Wait, what? We can't just leave. This is a crime scene. The police will want to interview us. And what do you mean you shouldn't have brought me here?" I bristled at the sudden assumption that I didn't belong here. I was still pissed off about Rowe telling me that. I didn't need it from Liam, too. I didn't need any man telling me where I did or didn't belong.

"I don't know what I was thinking," Liam went on vacantly, almost as if I wasn't even there. "I could have taken you anywhere. This wouldn't have happened in Providence. I should have just taken you to a nice restaurant. You could have been killed."

My annoyance dissipated instantly at the pure regret in his tone. I softened at the guilt he'd obviously piled straight on his own shoulders. "Well, I doubt you were thinking that somebody was going to shoot the place up. I know I don't normally walk into a business assuming the walls are about to become Swiss cheese." I said it with a tiny smile, but my attempt at humor fell sadly flat. I tried a different tack.

"Hey, I'm fine. And we were having a good time, weren't we?"

Liam didn't answer, his gray eyes stormy.

A hard knock came on the door, and Liam moved away so quickly it left me feeling like he was grateful for the interruption. I wrapped my arms around myself, the warmth in the room suddenly evaporating and turning cold. Liam opened the door, admitting two police officers, one familiar.

"Mae? What the hell?" Boston stormed over to my side and grabbed me by the tops of my arms. "What are you doing here? Were you here during the shooting?"

I nodded, the weight of Liam's gaze touching the side of my face.

"I was the one who called the police."

"Good. It's about time somebody around here did the right thing." Boston glared at Liam, something unsaid passing between the two of them.

Liam didn't get a chance to reply before Eve burst through the door, eyes wide and hair wild.

Gone was the sexy, tight-fitting dress she'd worn earlier. And in its place were fluffy slippers and a silky robe tied hastily around her waist. It was so short it barely covered her ass, and whatever she wore below it cut deep between her breasts, showing off her full cleavage. Her gaze darted around her damaged club, finally landing on the two cops. Her lip curled. "Get the hell out of my club, Boston. I've got this."

Boston's gaze flared hot as he took in Eve's outfit, but he shut it down in the space of a second. His eyes narrowed on her. "Your club is now a crime scene, *Evil*. So how about *you* get the hell out. You're holding up my investigation."

At the taunting nickname, Eve shot Boston a look that should have withered him to the spot, leaving his new partner to not only investigate the shooting, but Boston's sudden and instant death. Probably a violent one, too, if the fire and sparks shooting from Eve's gaze were anything to go by. "I have rights," she seethed.

"You do. Like the right to let me work out what the hell happened here tonight. Don't make me arrest you, Eve. Not again."

My eyes widened. I was suddenly beginning to understand why Liam hadn't wanted me to call the police. There was obviously no love lost between these two, and a whole lot of history.

I gave my statement to Boston, while Liam gave his to Boston's new partner. More police cars arrived while we talked, and they blocked off the scene with copious amounts of yellow-and-black crime scene tape.

Both of us refused medical attention, and then we were free to go. Eve stood on the other side of the tape, glaring at anyone who dared to meet her gaze. She didn't seem to give a shit that she was barely dressed. All she cared about was getting back inside her club, and maybe killing Boston in the process. Her gaze followed him around the room, watching his every move, like he was some petty criminal who might be considering shoplifting from her.

Liam's hand touched the small of my back. "Come on. Let's get out of here."

"What about Eve?"

He shook his head. "She'll be fine. She's Saint View born and bred. She knows how to handle it, and there'll be no getting her to leave anytime soon. The club is her baby. The true love of her life. As soon as the cops let her in, she'll go straight into damage control mode, cleaning up and fixing the walls. She'll have the place back together again before the show tomorrow."

I let myself be guided to the car and watched Eve through the windshield as I put my seat belt on. She didn't even glance our way, the club her entire focus.

Liam got behind the steering wheel, and we left the lot silently, nobody paying us any attention.

The silence in Liam's car was the complete opposite to how we'd driven here, laughing and joking with each other. Now it was tense and awkward. Neither of us even tried to turn the radio on. We moped in the tension, the silence becoming more and more unbearable as the miles rolled by.

Once we got into Providence, I directed him to my building in short, mostly one-word instructions until there was nothing left but for me to actually get out of the car.

But I didn't move. I didn't want to leave. Not like this.

Liam cleared his throat. "Listen. I'm sorry. I feel awful."

"I really wish you wouldn't. It was hardly your fault."

He nodded, but I could see that he was seriously beating himself up over it. All I wanted to do was make him feel better. He was so damn hard on himself. I hadn't been lying when I'd said I'd been having a good time. And I certainly hadn't forgotten the way it felt to have his hand wrapped around mine, his breath misting over my lips. I hadn't forgotten how much I'd wanted him to kiss me. "So you were right, by the way."

"About what?"

"You said by the end of the night I'd be wanting another date with you."

The edges of his lips turned up, and the cocky Liam I knew started edging his way back to the surface. He peered at me from the corner of his eye. "You asking me out, Mae Donovan?"

I lifted one shoulder. That hadn't exactly been my plan. But I was still a bit buzzed. It would have been easy to blame the adrenaline, except it wasn't only that. A large part of it was that I'd been standing there, anticipating his kiss. And feeling things I hadn't felt since...well, since Heath.

The reminder of Heath made me pause.

Liam let out a long breath. "Okay, well, I read that wrong..."

I put a hand on his knee. "No. You didn't. I was sort of asking you out. I was having a good time with you tonight, until...you know...our date turned into a Jason Bourne movie."

Liam didn't smile. His gaze was fixed on my hand on his leg.

Shit. The gesture was probably too intimate for how little we actually knew each other, and I went to pull it away.

But his hand clamped over mine, fingers threading and holding it to him.

"I like your hand there," he said quietly. He finally looked up, turning those stormy eyes on me. "But I feel like you're only half here."

I knew what he meant. Because half of me was here with Liam, reliving that moment in the club where he'd been so close to kissing me, I could practically taste it. But the other half of me was in my kitchen with Heath, with his lips on my neck and the promise of more on his tongue.

"I like my hand there, too," I whispered. "But..."

He squeezed his eyes shut tight. "I'm not going to like this, am I?"

I almost didn't want to say it, but I didn't want to be dishonest either. That wasn't in my nature. "I can't...I don't know. I'm not in a position to get into a relationship."

Liam nodded. "Okay, and..."

I blinked. "Well. And nothing, I guess. It's just, there's kind of someone else... God, I'm so sorry, that sounds awful after just sort of asking you out, not to mention almost letting you kiss me..."

He cocked his head to one side like he was truly confused. "I don't understand. You wanted me to kiss you, though, right?"

My cheeks had to be red. "Yes," I admitted.

"Because you think I'm hot." He grinned.

Arrogant shit. "I never said that."

"Your *kiss me, Liam* face said it."

"I do not have a *kiss me, Liam* face!"

"Oh, but you do. Looks a lot like that." He pointed one finger at me and made a circular motion, roughly the same size as my head. "You're making it right now."

I went to bat his finger away, but he caught my hand instead. His fingertips rested over the pulse point in my wrist, and I hoped he didn't notice how hard my heart was beating. Any argument I had died on my tongue. "You wanted to kiss me, too." It was a weak protest.

"Fuck yes, I did. I still do."

It was as if the air had been sucked from the car. I couldn't breathe.

Liam's fingertips stroked absently over the smooth skin at my wrist. "I get you have feelings for Heath."

I jerked back an inch. "How...?"

His fingers walked a path up my arm, tickling the soft skin. "Why else would you be asking me to help him? Most people wouldn't put themselves out on such a limb for just a random guy they barely know."

"We haven't even spoken about it," I admitted. "Heath and I. We aren't dating or anything."

"But you know it's there. You feel it." He pressed his fingers into my arm, demanding my attention. A tiny groan escaped him. "Fuck, Mae. I don't even care. I'm not asking for a relationship. I don't even think I'm in a place to give you that, either. I'm not a relationship sort of guy. But I want to kiss you. I've wanted to kiss you since the minute I saw you at the funeral."

"Weird thing to be thinking at a funeral, Liam."

He chuckled. "Couldn't help it. You're really cute when you've got running eye makeup and snot all over your face."

"Oh, shut up. I didn't even cry. My makeup was flawless. There was certainly no snot. God, you're annoying."

He grasped my chin between his fingers. "And you're still the most beautiful woman I've ever seen."

Oh, he was smooth. "How many women have you said that to?"

"Only you."

He was probably lying. He was a lawyer, for Christ's sakes. He lied for a living. "It's late. I should probably go inside."

He glanced at the clock. "Two minutes to midnight. I told you I'd have you home on time for your cup of tea and knitting." He laughed at his own, not even funny, joke.

"Did I really say I was thinking about asking you out again? I think I hit my head during the shooting." I tugged the handle on the door. "Bye, Liam."

"Bye, Mae."

I got out and strode down the path, trying to concentrate on how I'd have to get Tori to drive me to the prison tomorrow to pick up my car, and fumbling for my house keys in the deep pockets of my purse. Anything to distract myself until Liam drove away. I didn't want him to see that I was disappointed over my own inability to make a move.

I should have just kissed him.

"Mae!" A car door slammed behind me, then footsteps thumped against the path.

I spun around to find Liam chasing after me. "What? Did I forget something?"

He stopped in front of me, so close I had to crane my neck to look up at him.

"Yeah. You did."

He cupped my face with both hands and laid the softest, sweetest kiss on my mouth. It was barely a brush of lips, a mere taste of what he had to offer before he pulled back.

But something in that tiny kiss made my insides light up like the Fourth of July. Sparks flew through my body, igniting at my mouth and traveling all over.

Liam stared at me for a moment, then snaked his hand around to the back of my head. "Fuck, Mae," he muttered softly. "What the hell?"

He echoed my thoughts exactly. And this time when he leaned in again, he kissed me properly. His lips found mine, sweet and soft, his tongue immediately seeking entrance.

I opened for him, fingers finding his belt and hauling him in close. His body was big, his chest hard, and he crowded me in the best possible way. His other arm came around me, caging me as if I might try to walk away from him.

But I wasn't going anywhere. Any concerns or worries I might have had flew straight out of my mind, and I let myself get lost in Liam's touch. Everything around me disappeared, until it was just him and me, and the connection sparking between us.

It could have been minutes or hours that we stood there, kissing like we were drowning. He held me tight, a solid strength, until he finally moved away, reluctance clear in the slow, agonizing movement of parting.

His eyes were slightly unfocused, and he blinked once, clearing them.

My lips tingled, and something deep inside me yearned to pull him in again, and just stand out here for the rest of the night, kissing until we both collapsed. "That was..." I didn't even know how to describe it. Earth-shattering? Mind-numbing? The best kiss of my life? I'd had good kisses before. I'd had kisses that turned to more.

But I couldn't remember one ever being like that.

The way Liam kissed was like opening a portal to a different part of me, one I didn't even know existed. It was a heady feeling, just kissing someone and having that be enough because it was that damn good. It was experiencing your first love all over again, where you were too young to think about going further, and every kiss was a whole new experience.

He swallowed hard. "You're going to turn into a pumpkin. It's past midnight, Cinderella."

I loved the rasp to his voice. It was so freaking sexy. There was a matching one in mine. "Cinderella is in the mood to be a rebel."

He ran a finger down the side of my face, then over my lips. The longing in his eyes told me everything his words weren't. He wanted to kiss me again. "Tomorrow. Eleven."

I glanced up at him. "You asking me out again?"

He bit his lip, the longing clear on his face. But gave a tiny shake of his head. "Not exactly. I'm meeting with Heath. And he wants you there."

23

MAE

This time when I filled out the paperwork to visit Heath, my visit was approved instantly. As was Liam's, and I followed him through to the visitor's room. The big space had the same unpleasant smell of cheap disinfectant, and the floor-to-ceiling windows let in light but were marred by ugly security bars. There was no attempt at decoration, just a bunch of scuffed tables and chairs spread out haphazardly around the space.

Liam scrunched his nose up at the grubby table we were assigned and avoided touching it, like it was the seat of a public toilet.

I couldn't help laughing at him. "Don't want to get your Armani suit dirty?"

He glanced over at me. "Would you? This thing is worth thousands, and it's my favorite. I don't know what I was thinking, wearing it here. I forgot I'd have to do this interview in the visitor's room. That's your fault, you know? I'm totally sending you the dry-cleaning bill."

I gaped at him. "How is it my fault?"

"Normally I'd get an interview room. But since you're

tagging along, I can't get us in there. I tried pulling strings with one of the guards, but it was a no-go."

"Jesus," I grumbled. "And you called me Cinderella. Who's being a princess now?"

He grinned, inching closer to me, until his leg brushed mine beneath the table. "Speaking of last night..."

I didn't look at him. "What about it?"

"I can't stop thinking about it."

I tried to hide a grin. "Well, being in a drive-by shooting is quite a traumatic experience. It's understandable it might be on your mind."

His mouth moved close to my ear. "That's not what I spent all night thinking about."

A tiny shiver ran down my spine. "You didn't sleep?"

"Couldn't. I just kept thinking about what I could have been doing if I'd asked to go inside with you."

I glanced around the room. We'd been the first in the visitor's line, but now that we'd been in here a few minutes, the place was filling up. Other prisoners were already at tables with their families, but there was still no sign of Heath. I lowered my voice, hoping the buzz of the people around us would give us a tiny bit of privacy. "Did you want to knit, too?"

He sniggered. "Not exactly what I had in mind. Unless... do you do that naked? I could get on board if it's naked knitting."

I stifled a giggle right as a shadow fell over me.

Heath.

Guilt instantly swamped me, and I jumped up. "Hey!" I said it a little too loudly. My gaze fell to the cuffs around his wrists. On instinct, I moved in to hug him.

He sidestepped, right as a voice across the room barked, "Donovan! Keep your hands to yourself or you're out."

My mouth dropped open, my gaze sliding past Heath and straight onto Rowe.

He smirked at me.

Did the man ever take a day off? I smiled sweetly and flipped him the bird.

"Leave her alone, Rowe," Liam called out. "She's with me."

I gaped at him. "You know each other?"

"He's the guard I know. We play on the same baseball team."

"Seriously?"

"Seriously. He's pretty good, too. Not as good as me, but he does okay." He said it loud enough for Rowe to hear, with a big grin.

Rowe huffed something unintelligible and turned away.

But my gaze lingered on his back, and the way his broad shoulders narrowed down to his waist, and his ass that looked entirely too good in his uniform.

Someone cleared their throat, and when I tore my gaze away from Rowe, I found Heath and Liam already seated and staring up at me.

I slunk down in my seat. "Sorry," I murmured, embarrassment flushing my skin. Well, this wasn't awkward at all. I was just casually surrounded by one man who I was harboring some real feelings for, one man who I'd shared the best kiss of my life with last night, and a third who was just sinfully hot and kinda made me want to jump his bones, even if he was a complete and utter asshole.

All three in the same room. All three staring at me.

"Sorry, what?" I asked Liam and Heath, suddenly aware they were waiting on me to say something. How long had I been staring at Rowe for?

"I was just telling Heath about the information I have on his case."

I leaned forward, resting my elbows on the table. "Okay. And?"

"And honestly, it doesn't look great. I mean, the fact his prints are the only ones on the murder weapon is kind of a big problem."

"So the murderer wore gloves!" I huffed.

Liam waved a hand at me. "Settle down, Sherlock. There's also the fact there was no sign of forced entry."

"Maybe Jayela didn't lock the door when she came in?"

Liam frowned at me. "And there's audio of Heath confessing."

"They were beating the shit out of him! What was he supposed to do? Sing a tune from *Fiddler on the Roof*?"

"We'll try to recant his statement, but it probably won't do us much good."

"That's such bullshit!"

"Mae," Heath said quietly. "Stop. It's okay."

"No, it's not!"

Liam shushed me, which was fair enough because I was getting screechy enough that Rowe looked over in our direction again. I lowered my voice. "That's all circumstantial."

"Maybe so. But I've won prosecution cases with less evidence than this. A lot less. And you better believe they're going to put a lawyer as good as me on this case. When it's a cop, they aren't going to push this off to some first year. They're going to get the guys who go straight for the jugular." He offered Heath a sympathetic glance. "Sorry, bro. But you seriously have no case for me to argue. Like, nothing. Isn't there anything you can give me?" He turned to me. "Either of you? Anything. Nothing is too small at this point in time. A noise in the night? Something out of place in your building? Some *other* huge, jealous, handsome ex who would have a reason to do this?"

Heath rubbed a hand across the back of his neck. "Actually, I do have something. But the more I think about it, the more I suspect it's too good to be true."

Liam made a hurry-up motion, flicking his hand around. "Skip over the dramatic pause for effect and start talking."

"One of the guys in here, DeWitt. He's in with a gang. Seems to be a big shot from what I can tell. He said there was a hit out on Jayela. Actually, he said *he* was the one who put the hit out there."

Shock punched me in the gut, robbing me of breath. That was the last thing I'd expected him to say.

Heath shook his head slowly, his gaze focused on me now, instead of Liam. "He claims Boston was on the take. But Jayela wouldn't play the game so..."

"So he had her killed?" My head spun, nausea swirling in my stomach. "No." I shook my head. "No. I can't..."

Liam's hand landed on my back as I pushed my chair away from the table and rested my elbows on my thighs. I dropped my head while my mind spun and I tried to breathe around lungs that felt crushed. That couldn't be true. I knew my sister's job was dangerous. But not like this. And Boston was a good guy. A good cop! He would never be under some gang lord's thumb.

Liam rubbed soothing circles on my back, and when I finally felt like the band across my chest had loosened, I looked up and met Heath's gaze.

It was tortured.

"This is killing me," he choked out. He had to swallow hard before he could speak again. "I hate that I can't touch you. I'm so sorry, Mae." His fingers curled around the tabletop, clenching so hard they turned white.

I nodded, trying to get myself together. All I wanted to do was run into his arms as well, but I couldn't. And there was no point making this harder for both of us by needing it.

I turned to Liam. "We can use this, right?"

Liam scribbled something on his legal pad, but the frown etched into his forehead had me nibbling on a fingernail in worry.

He put his pen down. "I don't know. I hope so. I've got some contacts, and I'll put some feelers out. Try to get confirmation that this hit actually did exist. But unless this DeWitt is going to take the stand and testify..."

"He won't," Heath said stiffly.

My hope ebbed away at the finality of the statement.

"...then this is nothing but gossip. And we need proof if this is going to trump the evidence the cops already have."

Liam must have registered the dejection on both mine and Heath's faces. He picked up his pen again and forced some pep into his tone. "But that doesn't mean this is over. I don't give up that easily, and neither should the two of you. So, who else? Right now, we just have to look for viable suspects who we can cast reasonable doubt upon."

Heath nodded, pulling himself together quicker than I could. "The cop who beat me up. He had feelings for Jayela. I guess you didn't hear it on the tape?"

Liam pointed the pen at Heath. "Good. And no, it was suspiciously short. They very likely cut it down to fit their own agenda. But I can't prove that. Who else was there when it happened?"

"The other cop. A rookie."

Liam groaned. "Your word against two cops? I think we all know how that will end. But we'll add it to the list anyway. If this guy was in love with her, maybe he was stalking her, too. What else?"

"Her job," I said slowly. "The night she died she was going back to work because she wasn't happy with how a case was going. She'd been fighting with Boston—"

"Wait, you keep saying Boston. Do you mean Joshua Boston? He worked with your sister?"

"They were partners."

Liam swore low under his breath. "I like the guy, even though he busts Eve's balls constantly. But if he and Jayela were fighting, then that makes him a suspect, too."

Heath glanced over at the two names written on the legal pad. "Great. So all our potential suspects and witnesses are cops."

None of us needed to spell out how that was really no better than no other suspects at all.

I reached out across the table and squeezed Heath's hand, quickly withdrawing before Rowe could notice. "It's going to be okay."

"The police will never consider that one of their own could have been responsible for this. Come on, Mae. You know how they work. They have their guy. They aren't going to suddenly start investigating someone who's been on the force twenty years."

"Hate to admit it," Liam closed his files, "but I agree. They've wrapped this case up with a bow, patted themselves on the back, and called it done. Getting them to investigate *any* other suspect is going to be a battle."

My heart sank a little, but I couldn't just sit there and do nothing. I'd had my moment to mope, and I wasn't going to dwell on it. I'd started this, and I was going to see it through. "Fine. If they won't investigate, then we will."

24

MAE

The midday sun was blinding when Liam and I made it back out to the parking lot. I was grateful to sink into the cooler depths of Liam's car, air-conditioning cooling my heated skin.

He got in behind the steering wheel. "Well. That didn't exactly go the way I'd hoped it would."

"I know."

"We need more suspects than two cops, Mae."

"I know."

We both sighed in unison.

"I am going to call the police chief, though. I'll report everything Heath said about this DeWitt guy and a hit on Jayela. That'll include the possibility of Boston working with this gang... You good with that? You and he seemed kind of tight at Eve's place last night."

I nodded. "He's always been like an older brother to me. I honestly can't believe he would do something like that. He and Jayela were both so morally straight. Their compasses never even twitched."

"I'm sure you're right. This DeWitt guy is probably just

running his mouth. It happens a lot on the inside. Criminals aren't exactly known for being truthful. But I should report it anyway."

I agreed. "You have to. Jayela would have."

Liam started the engine and steered us out of the prison gates. I'd be back here to teach my class in a few hours, but until then, the day was my own. I had nothing to do except go home and try not to think. I didn't like my chances. I needed to go through Jayela's things and see if there was anything in there that might give us a clue as to who really killed her. There had to be someone else. A better option than cops and random gangbangers. But every time I thought about opening the door, I flashed back to that morning and her unseeing eyes as she lay murdered on her bed.

My fingers trembled, and I shoved them beneath my thighs so Liam wouldn't notice. I knew it had to be done, but I wasn't ready. Not yet. And I didn't want to be alone, thinking about it for the rest of the day.

"Do you want to come back to my place?" Liam asked, like he could read my mind. "I've told the office I'm not coming in. I'd really like to talk to you some more. I want a whole list of people your sister knew, or hell, even a list of people she might have once met. I want to be able to point the finger at least half a dozen people by the time this goes to court."

I agreed quickly, and it was only a few minutes before Liam hit a button on a key fob. Automatic garage doors on a very fancy-looking building in the middle of Providence rolled up, smooth as silk.

"Your apartment building is about as swanky as your office." I gazed up at the tall structure, taking in the sleek, modern lines and we drove beneath into the basement parking area. Liam parked in a space marked reserved, right by the elevators.

"Do you like it?" Liam got out of the car and headed in my direction.

I opened my door and went to climb out, but that stopped Liam in his tracks. He pouted at me.

I froze. "What?"

"Get back in the car."

"Why? You can't kick me out before you've even let me in."

"I'm going to let you in, you dork. I just like to open the door for you. You wreck my fun when you open it for yourself."

I stifled a smile. "Seriously?"

"Seriously. So shut your door and let me open it for you."

I fought back a laugh, kind of giddy. Yeah, okay. It was a 1950's thing to do. But I liked it and I was happy to play along. It was a nice moment of lightness after what had essentially been a pretty bleak morning. I pulled the door closed and waited with a smile for Liam to open it again.

"After you, madam." He chuckled, offering me his hand.

I took it and let him lead me across the parking lot to the elevator. Inside, he hit the button for the penthouse.

Of course. Knowing Liam's love of all things fancy, I would have been more shocked if he'd lived on the ground floor.

The interest in seeing Liam's penthouse was swamped by the realization he was still holding my hand. He was warm and sweet and here with me. Fighting for something I knew he really didn't believe in but fighting for it anyway. Because I'd asked him to. He didn't owe me anything. I wasn't even paying him.

"Why are you doing this?"

We exited the elevator onto the top floor, and he glanced over his shoulder at me, key poised in midair above the lock to his place. "Opening the door?"

He ushered me inside, and I blinked around at the huge open-plan space. My place wasn't exactly small. It was no top-floor luxury penthouse or anything, but it was a standard-sized two-bedroom condo. But Liam's place was bigger than even my father's. And my condo would have fit in his living room alone. "No. I mean, why are you helping me help Heath? You said yourself, this is a losing case. You could have just said no."

"I wanted that date with you." He led me into the industrial-style kitchen and dropped his keys on the countertop. He spun around, caging me in against the island bench, his hands sliding over my hips. To my surprise, he gripped them tight and hoisted me onto the countertop.

I let out a squeal of surprise and gripped his shoulders for balance. I'd worn one of my long floral skirts, my favorite one with the tiny daisies on a deep-navy background. The material brushed my ankles, so even when Liam pushed his way between my knees, I was still completely covered.

I kind of wished I wasn't.

He planted his hands either side of my ass, fingers wrapped around the edge of the granite countertop. We were similar heights, with me sitting on the higher surface and him leaning in. And when he brushed his lips over mine, my core did a happy little flip, yearning for him to fit his body completely against mine.

But Liam kept it PG. He moved back before I could deepen the kiss or pull him closer. And it gave me enough time for my head to clear, and to remember that I'd been asking him something. "I don't think so. You could have just asked me out, like any other guy."

"You would have said no."

"Probably. But we both know you're persistent. I hate to admit it, but you're kind of charming. You would have worn me down eventually. So I don't really buy that the reason you took this case has anything to do with me."

Liam backed away, not answering the question. "You hungry? I'm a good cook. I'll make something to eat." He turned around to open the pantry door. Or to hide in it.

To my surprise, the pantry was at complete odds with the rest of his house. It was of the huge walk-in variety, with floor-to-ceiling shelving and deep enough for a grown man to stand inside. But unlike the rest of his very minimalist apartment, the pantry overflowed with food. It was almost like he'd opened the door to his own personal supermarket. There were multiple boxes of cereal, at least a dozen packages of dry pasta, and enough canned goods to feed a small army for a month. They were stacked ten or more deep, disappearing into the darkness at the back of the shelves.

"What do you feel like? Stir-fry? Salad? Toasted sandwiches? Name it."

"Are you preparing for the apocalypse? You have so much food. Do you have a secret family I don't know about? A horde of teenagers as your roommates?"

Liam's shoulders stiffened.

I pondered over what I'd said and why it would have bothered him. But couldn't think of anything.

He grabbed a pack of burger buns, an onion, and a handful of seasonings from a rack, before dumping them on the countertop. "I just like to be prepared."

"You're a prepper?"

He glanced over at his stash of food, like he was only just

realizing how much of it he actually had. “Not exactly. Like, I don’t think zombies are coming. I don’t have a bug-out bag, if that’s what you’re asking. But yeah. I guess I like knowing I can feed myself for an extended period of time if something was to happen.”

I mulled that over. It seemed an odd habit to get into for someone as wealthy as he was. The man could buy anything he wanted, at any time. He hardly had a need to horde all this food. “What would stop you from just going to the supermarket, though? If not zombies.”

“Could be anything. Illness. Supplier shortage. Plus, money doesn’t grow on trees. If I lose my job, this all goes away tomorrow.”

I scoffed at that. “You’re one of the best lawyers around. You work for the top firm in the city. I don’t think this is all going away tomorrow.”

He took a package of ground meat from his refrigerator and dumped it into a bowl. “Doesn’t hurt to save for a rainy day, though, right?”

He avoided looking at me, and so I suspected there was more to the story than he was letting on. But I decided to let it go. The pungent smell of onions filled the kitchen as Liam sliced through them with a fancy knife, so I slid down from the countertop and wandered around his place. “Did you just move in?” I asked after a while.

He paused in his chopping. “No? I’ve been here two years.”

“Oh.” I found that hard to believe. There was nothing personal in sight. Not even so much as a jacket on a stand, an award on a wall, or a photograph on the side table. The furniture was so minimal it was about as homely as a store display. It was almost surprising that there wasn’t plastic on the couches. They certainly didn't seem as if anyone had ever sat on them.

The sizzle of meat on a hot frying pan caught my attention, and I wandered back to Liam's side, touching a hand to his lower back, leaning over to see what he'd created. The meat patties were perfectly round and full of colored spices. "That already smells amazing. Can I help?"

"Nope. Go sit your pretty little ass on a seat. I've got this. It's my turn to ask questions."

I dragged out a stool from beneath the other side of the island counter. It was so long, there was enough stools for eight people. I took the one right in the middle. "Okay. Fair enough. I was being kind of nosy. Ask away."

"Start talking to me about the people in your life. And the people in Jayela's life. Let's forget her work for a moment. Go personal. She didn't date, right? Not since Heath?"

"Right."

"Friends?"

"Besides me?"

"Unless you're putting yourself on the suspect list, then yes. Besides you. Were you two close?"

"Sort of? I mean, we lived together. So yes. We probably spent more time together than most sisters do. But we have other friends."

"Who? Tori?"

"Yes, Tori. And Will, her husband."

Liam rolled his eyes. "Okay. Any friends who haven't been in your life since you were five years old?"

I thought about it for a moment and came up pretty blank.

Liam glanced over his shoulder at me and raised an

eyebrow. "Have you seriously made no friends since high school?"

"How many have you made, Mr. Popularity? I saw you at Jayela's funeral. You were with the same guys you hung out with in high school. So don't give me attitude." I gave an indignant huff, but it was good-natured.

He chuckled beneath his breath. "I have a very demanding job. I don't have time to make new friends. What's your excuse?"

"Same."

"Okay, so we're both workaholics. Noted. Jayela, too?"

"Worse than I am. Her whole life was work."

Liam sighed. "Okay. So we're back to the work thing again. Exactly what we're trying to avoid. Let's try a different route." He paused to grab some paper towel and lined a plate with it. Then he lifted each of the burger patties onto the paper and pulled the buns from the oven. He assembled our burgers as he spoke, layering the buns with cheese, and lettuce, and the meat. "What about family? You lived with your dad in high school, right?"

Despite the fact I tried to stop it, my molars ground together at the mere mention of my father. "Yes."

Liam glanced up from putting ketchup on his burger. "You want to elaborate a little? He still around?"

"No."

"Oh. Sorry to hear that. When did he pass away? I didn't hear anything about it."

I forced my jaw to work normally. "He's not dead. I just kind of wish he was."

Liam paused with his hand halfway to the spatula. "Wow. Okay. I was not expecting that. Sounds like there's a story there, though, so start talking. If you want him dead, is there any chance that he wants you dead, too? Or more specifically, Jayela?"

I balked at the idea. "I'm exaggerating, Liam. I don't really wish death on the man. But honestly, he may as well be, considering how little he's been in our lives since we finished school."

Liam put the finishing touches on his burgers and capped them with the top of the bun, before sliding one across the countertop to me. My stomach gave a rumble of appreciation, and I took a huge bite, flavor exploding across my taste buds.

"He always seemed like the doting parent whenever there was a school function. He was always in the front row, clapping and smiling."

"All for show. He went to Edgeley Academy, too. So he's well-known in those circles. He's much like you and me. Still friends with the same people he went to high school with. So he has to save face. I don't think he could have cared less whether Jayela and I even graduated from high school, if it wouldn't have looked bad in front of his friends. But we had to graduate, and we had to do well, because otherwise his life would look less than perfect."

"What about your mom?"

I swallowed hard, suddenly not so hungry. "She actually is dead. Died when I was a baby."

Liam chewed thoughtfully for a moment. "Shit. I'm really sorry to hear that. It's hard to grow up without a parent."

I glanced over at him. He was staring at his plate, lost in his thoughts. His sympathy wasn't that of someone who still had both his parents in his life.

"Who did you lose? Your mom or your dad?" I asked.

"It's hard to lose somebody when they were never in your life in the first place."

I racked my brain, trying to remember the joint graduation ceremony we'd had with Edgeley Academy. I'd had my photo taken with my father on the stage after I'd gotten my valedictorian certificate. They'd invited him up, and he'd stood beside me, his arm around my shoulder like a proud parent, and beamed at the crowd who all clapped politely. I remembered vividly, because it had made me so damn angry. I'd worked my ass off to be top of my class. It was no easy feat at a school where excellence was expected from every student. He'd done nothing to help me, except pay my school fees. He'd never been around when I had a question on my homework. He'd never helped me with my science fair projects. The most involved he'd been was reading my report cards at the end of the year, and making sure I had all A's. And yet he'd stood up on that stage, like my victory was somehow his. Even years later, it made my fingers clench into fists.

But when Liam had been announced as valedictorian for Edgeley Academy, there had been no photo with his parents. It had been his grandfather who had gotten up on stage with him, from memory. "Did you live with your grandparents?"

"Not exactly."

I frowned, taking the last few bites of my burger. "Who did you live with then? I don't think I ever saw either of your parents at school events. I can only remember your grandfather."

He pushed his plate away and swiveled on his stool to face me. "We're supposed to be talking about your family, remember?"

"My family story is boring and depressing. I'd much

rather talk about yours. I feel like I don't know anything about you."

"Better that you don't. You like me now. You might go back to hating me if you knew more."

I poked lightly at his chest. "I doubt it. You've kissed me. And there was a lot to like about that kiss. It would take a lot to undo it."

He reached forward and fingered the button at the top of my blouse. "It wouldn't take much to undo this..." He popped the top button free from the hole.

He was trying to distract me. And though my breath had stuttered in my lungs, I wasn't quite willing to let him off the hook so easily. "You're avoiding the question."

He bit his lip and undid another button. "I know. But honestly, Mae? I don't want to talk about my grandfather, or my parents. Not now. Not when you're letting me undress you."

I glanced down and watched him slip the last two buttons from my shirt. I swallowed hard as he brushed the material away, exposing the lacy white fabric of my bra and the bare skin of my stomach. I sat up a little straighter, fully aware we were in broad daylight. It had been a long time since I was even this naked with somebody during the day. Most of my sexual experience came from late-night hookups and one long-term boyfriend who wasn't exactly the 'afternoon delight' type of lover. More like the 'roll on top of me in the middle of the night, three quick pumps, and all over red rover.' I'd never really felt self-conscious with them because they'd never looked at me in the way Liam was staring at me now. Liam's gaze devoured me, raking over my cleavage, my bra, and the skin beneath. My belly wasn't the flat, toned abdominals my sister had. Though I was a bit overweight, I liked the shape of my body generally. But I did have belly rolls when I sat. And my ass jiggled when I walked. Even without seeing Liam shirtless, I knew he probably had the body fat percentage of a cucumber.

He pushed my shirt from my shoulders, and we both watched as it fell to the floor. He finally lifted his gaze to meet mine. "Is this okay?"

"It's okay." I found I meant it. "I like the way you look at me."

He stood and moved in closer, working his way between my legs again, and forcing me to stare up at him. "How am I looking at you?"

A blush spread across my chest. I could feel it heating my skin as it went. "Liam…"

He ran his thumb over my bottom lip. "Does that embarrass you?"

"Maybe a little bit."

"You want me to tell you?"

I let out a shuddering breath. Desire raced through my body, and though I had exactly zero experience with the way this man was talking to me, I wanted to see where he was going with it. "Yes."

"I can't stop staring at you. All I can think about right now is reaching around and undoing that clasp on your bra that's stopping me from seeing what shade of pink your nipples are." His fingertips brushed past my arm and he did exactly that. He didn't ask this time. His fingers made quick work of the clasp, and then he was dragging my bra down off my arms.

He groaned the cups falling away, exposing me to his greedy gaze. He drank me in with slow, extravagant sweeps of his eyes that started at my face and ended with my nipples tightening with his attention.

But just as I was beginning to feel self-conscious, he

speared one hand into the back of my hair, tilted my head back, and claimed my lips. My eyes fluttered closed and Liam's tongue delved inside my mouth, harder and faster than he'd kissed me last night. This was a kiss of need. A kiss that promised more than just butterflies in my stomach. It was the sort of kiss that promised a night of banging headboards, take-me-now sex, and screaming orgasms. I drowned in it, soaking it in, when his free hand cupped my breast to tease my nipple.

Blindly, I groped for the buttons on his business shirt, but he pulled away, out of my reach.

"Just let me touch you. I'm not going to be able to concentrate with your hands on me."

He didn't even give me a chance to answer. He just lowered his head, kissing his way down my neck, across my collarbone, and over the swell of my breasts. "Put your hands on the stool behind you. Lean back. Relax. I got you."

I did. I gripped the stool behind me, fingers digging into the padded surface. Liam continued his slow, sexy path across my chest, until he reached my nipple. With one hand he teased and pinched the tip into a hardened point. And with his other hand, he held my breast, covering me with his hot mouth.

"Oh," I moaned. The warm wet heat of him at my breast was delicious. I shamelessly grasped the back of his head, lightly holding him to me.

His tongue didn't let up for a moment. He licked and sucked until I was mewling like a kitten. Then his hands dug into the sides of my hips, sliding my ass forward until I almost fell right off the seat, stopped only by my core ramming into the hard thickness behind his suit pants.

I gasped at the sensation of having him between my legs like that. He thrust himself once against me, and the nerve endings in my clit went wild at the contact. They roared, sending messages of delight through my entire body, building the anticipation of what was to come.

All too quickly he moved away.

I mourned the loss of him. I needed him there, between my legs, pressed to my core. I needed him there in that spot the most. "Liam…"

"Shh. I told you. I got you."

His phone on the benchtop buzzed, an earsplitting alarm piercing through the room.

Liam's groan was full of sexual frustration. "Fuck. What's the time?" He let out a shuddering breath when he glanced at the clock on his oven. "Seriously, just fuck. Apparently, I don't have you after all." He gazed at me with an expression full of regret and longing.

"What's wrong?"

"I had no idea what time it was. I'm so sorry. I've got to go."

I sat up straight. "Oh. Okay." Except it was anything but okay. I didn't want him to leave. Not just because I'd been building up to the first non-solo orgasm I'd ever had. But because somewhere in the last few days, I found myself actually kind of liking Liam Banks. He was fun to be around. And when I was with him, I didn't feel quite so sad.

I grabbed my shirt from the floor and found my bra on the countertop, then dressed quickly, fully aware Liam paused and watched me do it.

I liked that.

"Before you go," I said. "Tell me one true thing about you. I feel like I spilled my guts today, and you gave me nothing."

Liam stopped and stared at me. His gaze calculating, like

he was debating whether to distract me off with one of his jokes.

But I must have passed the vibe check.

He nodded once. “Okay. You want to know something truly real? Get your stuff and come with me. I want to show you something.”

25

LIAM

I couldn't just ignore that alarm, I knew exactly what it was for, and it was important. But dammit. I'd never wanted to ignore something so bad in my life.

I'd barely had my fill of Mae's lips, her neck, her tits. I'd forced myself to go slow with her, wanting to savor every inch of her body. But now, with my dick hard as steel, and no chance of getting it anywhere near her for the next four hours at least, I was kicking myself for not tasting her.

I parked the car out the front of the homeless shelter in the middle of Saint View and scrubbed a hand through my hair, breathing deep and trying to think of anything except the feel of her nipple beneath my tongue and the heavy weight of her tits in my hands.

So fucking beautiful. Even more than she had been in high school. Teenage Mae had been smoking hot, but Mae now was all woman. A woman I wanted to bow down to, taking my rightful spot on my knees in front of her.

I'd spend all day on my knees, with my face between her thighs if Mae would let me.

"I thought you didn't do pro bono?"

"Hey?" I blinked out of my thoughts.

Mae pointed up at the sign above the shelter door. "Isn't that why we're here? Are you meeting a client?"

"No. I volunteer here. Four hours, once a week, every week."

Her head snapped around, and she blinked at me. "You? You volunteer here? Like, actually voluntarily? Or did you get caught for drunk driving and this is community service?"

I chuckled. "Thanks. I'm really glad you think so highly of me that you'd assume I'd do something like that. I barely even drink."

She held hands up in mock surrender. "Sorry, sorry. I just didn't expect this from you."

"Why? Because I'm such a douche canoe?"

"Something like that."

I couldn't really blame her. I had been pretty secretive about my role here. Nobody knew. Not the guys on my baseball team. Not the people I worked with. This place was special. And it was a part of me I didn't share lightly. "Guess I'm just full of surprises then, huh?"

She studied me carefully. "I'm beginning to wonder if I know you at all."

"That's probably a good thing. Because the me you thought you knew, you didn't like. Remember?" I couldn't help but inject a little humor into the situation. Because she was fun to tease. "Though you did seem to like me okay when I had your nipple in my mouth."

"Just for that smart-ass comment?" She opened the car door. "I'm going to let myself out of the car."

She got out and slammed the door behind her, grinning at me across the roof.

I prided myself on my manners. And more than that, it

wasn't just manners that had me wanting to open doors for Mae. I liked making her smile. I liked treating her like she was special. Because she was. She didn't even need to tell me she'd dated a bunch of dickheads in the past. Guys who didn't know how to treat her right. I'd seen her with Mathew Jorley in high school. The guy had treated her like his gym bag. Only useful when he needed something and dumped in the corner the rest of the time. Maybe I wasn't perfect for her either, but the very least I could do was make her smile by holding a door once in a while.

I walked around to her side and slung an arm around her shoulders. "You cut me deep, Mae."

I liked the way she fit herself to my side, her arm wrapping around my lower back, her fingers tucking into my belt.

We strolled inside the homeless shelter like we were a real couple. We weren't, of course. Mae had made it pretty clear there was something between her and Heath that she wasn't giving up on, even if he was behind bars for the foreseeable future. That should have been fine with me. I never got serious with women. Hell, I rarely even remembered their names. The women I'd been with were a blur of nothingness, an attempt to fill a void that wasn't fillable.

And then Mae had strolled back into my life and reminded me that once upon a time, I'd wanted more. More than just a warm body for a single night. I had a full life. I had my job, my friends, baseball, volunteering. I liked women. I liked sex. But there was a reason I'd never brought anyone here.

I'd never been interested in anyone enough to show them something real.

Mae was different.

She'd always been different.

I didn't deserve her then, and I didn't deserve her now.

She was right to keep some distance between us. It was good that Heath was in the picture. It would keep me from thinking this could be more than what it was.

I was a fill-in, while she waited for him. I could be that for her. I could kiss her, and touch her, and not need more. I just had to keep my fucking head in the game.

Easier said than done.

I punched in the security code on the shelter door and waved to Junie on reception. She raised her head from the form she was helping an elderly man fill out, but when she saw it was me, she waved me on through.

I led Mae down the corridor toward the kitchens, passing the shelter regulars.

"Hoo boy, Mr. Liam looking fine today! All dressed up in fancy pants."

I grinned at Linda, a fifty-something woman who had been in and out of the shelter so many times I could barely keep count. I was sad to see her return two weeks ago, sporting a black eye from who knows where. It could have been a partner. It could have been a dealer. She might have just been in a fight. I hated that she was here, but here we could help keep her safe. And that was better than being on the streets. She was a favorite of mine, and I wished there were more I could do to help her. But making sure she had full belly and warm clothes on the nights she came to us for help was something. "Thought I'd make an effort, since my best girl is here, right?"

Linda fake preened at the compliments. But then she eyed Mae who I tugged along by the hand. Linda smiled at her warmly. "Looks like I'm not your best girl anymore, huh?"

Mae stepped forward and took the older woman's hand. "I'm Mae. It's lovely to meet you. And I don't think I'm his anything just yet. So you can keep the best girl title for a little bit longer."

Her comment shot disappointment straight through my chest.

Linda linked an arm through Mae's and pulled her tight, whispering loudly, "Girl. Are you crazy? That man walked in here holding your hand. Have you seen his face?" She stepped forward and patted me on the cheek but then spoke like I wasn't even there. "He's very handsome. And he's a good one. Always here, helping out when he could be off working his important job."

"No job is more important than this one," I told Linda. I meant it. Money was important to me. But this job, and the people here, had a hold on my heart that grew stronger with every shift I worked. They eased the guilt of the sins on my conscience. If I did some good here, maybe it helped make up for some of the bad I'd done in the past.

I rescued Mae from Linda's clutches and steered her into the kitchen. A chorus of hellos were shouted as we entered. I went straight for a rack full of aprons, taking two out, handing one to Mae.

She slipped it over her head, tying it at the back. It somehow looked good on her, stretching tight across her breasts and accentuating her narrow waist and the flare of her hips. While the others were all busy preparing food, I took the opportunity to pull her close and brush my lips over hers. "I might have to bring one of these aprons home. You could wear that and nothing else."

She grinned against my lips. "Funny. I was just thinking the same thing about you."

I chuckled and linked my fingers between hers, leading her through the kitchen, and out to the serving area where I normally worked. The eating area doors were already open, and the residents were streaming in, impatiently waiting in the cafeteria-like space with their brown trays, ready to receive their meals for the evening.

"You ready to do this?" I asked her. "It's pretty basic. The kitchen staff makes the food, we serve it up. It will get pretty busy in here for a while. This is the only shelter in Saint View, and it's generally at max capacity."

She nodded eagerly. "I'm glad you brought me. I've never done this before, but I'm glad to help. That lady back there, she seems lovely. They all seem to really like you."

"Do you?" The question slipped from my mouth before I could get a hold on it.

She grabbed a soup ladle, stirring a pot of chicken broth in a pot. "You fishing for compliments, Liam?"

I breathed out a sigh of relief. She'd taken it as a joke. That was better. I could work with that. "Maybe I just like knowing I'm adored."

She shook her head. "I liked how you made me feel last night. And earlier today. So I'll give you that. As for if I like you as a person? Jury is still out."

I sniggered. "Fair enough. Quit dripping soup all over the tray."

She elbowed me, which made my ladle of soup slosh, too. We went on like that for a while, serving up food, Mae chatting enthusiastically with each and every person she served. In between, the two of us teased each other. Nudging, elbowing, taking any opportunity to touch the other. It was the sort of fun I hadn't had in a very long time, if ever. She was cute, and flirty, and she didn't seem at all put out by the fact that we were in a shelter full of people who didn't smell particularly good, often had no manners, and some who were just downright rude. She took the good with the bad, and she took it all in stride. Two hours into my shift, I was more impressed with her than I had been as kids when she almost beat my grade point average.

Put short, Mae Donovan was still the most impressive woman I'd ever met.

As the line died down to a trickle, the rush over, Mae rested her hands on the countertop and glanced over at me. Her teasing smile from the last few hours morphed into something more serious. "Thank you for bringing me here, and for showing me this side of you."

Heat crept up the back of my neck. "No big deal," I lied.

Mae covered her hand with mine. "No. It is a big deal. This place is special to you. I can see that. How many other people have you ever brought here?"

"None."

"See? Special."

"I don't like to make a big deal of it. My reasons for coming here aren't purely selfless."

Mae cocked her head to one side, considering my words. "Does anyone ever do anything for purely selfless reasons? I mean, I love teaching seven-year-olds, and I believe wholeheartedly in education for everyone. But I also really like to get paid. So that's not entirely selfless. I took a job at the prison partially to help inmates, but mostly to ease the guilt over my part in Heath being in that place. That's what people do. We help other people, sure. But none of it is completely selfless. No one says it has to be."

She tapped a finger on the table when I didn't answer. "What makes this selfish for you?"

I blew out a long breath. "It eases my guilt," I admitted. "I've done some bad things in the past. I don't feel good about them, but this place makes me feel a little better."

She leaned her hip on the countertop. "You're a lawyer. You get justice for people. Doesn't that make you feel good?"

"Sometimes. Sometimes it makes it worse. Depends on the case. But the things I've done as a lawyer aren't the things I'm trying to make up for."

"What then? What could you have possibly done, pre-lawyer, that has you feeling this bad about yourself?"

She seemed bothered by that, like my pain was tangible. And maybe to her it was. She cared about people in a way that most didn't. That was clear in what she was doing for Heath. And in the way she'd addressed each person in this shelter, treating each of them with respect.

Something squeezed around my heart. A sudden urge to tell her everything. To spill all the lies. All the secrets. Everything I'd kept inside since I was just a child. Mae was actually interested in getting to know the real me. The one I locked behind the cocky, arrogant exterior. It had always been a farce. A wall. A way of keeping people out because I didn't want them to know the truth.

It was the whole reason that even though I'd been desperately attracted to Mae throughout my entire high school experience, I'd never asked her out. Because even back then, I knew she'd be my undoing. She watched in a way that the other kids hadn't. Maybe it was because we were always competing for the same things. We were so far ahead of all the other kids, nobody else could touch us. Nobody else studied me the same way she did. I was just another one of the popular crowd. I fit in. I made sure of that. Nobody paid attention to you when you were always surrounded by friends. I wasn't as brave as her. Her ability to stand alone, to be different, to not need to fit in the way that I did... I envied her. I always had.

"Do you remember before, when you asked me, why I'd taken Heath's case?"

"And you told me it was just because you wanted a date?"

I grinned at her ruefully. "Well, I did want the date. But you were right. There was more to it than that."

She waited patiently.

"I see me in Heath. If things had been even slightly different, it could have been me in Heath's shoes." I shrugged.

Mae frowned. "How? Your life and Heath's are not even remotely similar."

I bit my lip. I wanted to tell the truth. God. I wanted to tell the truth so bad. But a cold sweat broke out across my skin. I'd spent half my life keeping these secrets, the secrets of who I really was. And suddenly opening them up to someone was terrifying. I couldn't force the words out of my mouth.

So I chickened out. Instead, I came up with a stupid lie. "If I hadn't studied, you know? If I wasn't naturally smart and driven, it could have been me taking a dead-end job, getting in with the wrong crowd." I cringed internally even as I said the words, because I knew exactly how they'd sound, and I wasn't proud of them. I sounded like an elitist jerk, the role I'd spent half my life playing.

When the truth was, I was just a coward, too scared to be honest and locked in a lifetime of lies.

Mae nodded slowly and went back to serving food without a word.

"Fuck," I muttered. She didn't even need to tell me that I'd disappointed her. And she'd seen right through my lame story. It was written all over her face. "Mae..."

She shrugged. "It's fine, Liam. We barely know each other. You don't have to tell me anything. But don't lie to me." She turned back and smiled at the next woman in line. "What can I get for you?"

I grabbed her hand. "Mae, wait. I—" I turned to the woman at the head of the line. "Sorry, ma'am. I just need to..."

The words died on my lips as I took in the woman's long blonde hair, her ageing face, and the cheap clothes, ratty with overuse.

"Liam?" The woman's eyes widened in shock.

Her expression had to mirror mine.

Right down to the identical blue eyes.

Eyes that belonged to my mother.

26

ROWE

Reception shifts weren't my favorite. I'd much rather deal with prisoners and their petty dramas than deal with their families and friends wanting to visit them. The number of stupid questions I was typically asked made me contemplate grievous bodily harm myself.

After not so patiently explaining to one woman why she couldn't take in a folder full of dirty magazines for her darling little bank-robbing son, I could feel the aneurysm growing in my brain.

Colt spun around on one of the office chairs and raised an eyebrow at me. "You need a day off. You're being a grumpy prick, even for you. And that's saying something coming from me, because I'm not exactly sunshine and rainbows either."

He wasn't wrong. I'd been working my ass off for months. Double shifts, triple shifts. Sleeping in the guard's room where there was a couple of bunks instead of going home. Anything to avoid going back to my empty house.

The alternative was worse. Being alone was better. Safer. No ties to anyone.

But fuck it hurt. Instead of getting easier, it killed me a little more inside every day.

At least here, the only hurt I had to deal with belonged to other people.

The alert system pinged, letting us know there was another visitor on the outside who needed to be buzzed in. Colt checked the monitor and hit the 'door open' button. "It's Boston. Were we expecting him today? Didn't see him on the schedule."

I shook my head. "Not that I know of." We often had cops in here, though. We knew all their names and had an amicable working relationship with most of them. Boston was one of the good guys. Some of the older ones looked down on the guards as wannabe cops who'd never made the cut. But Boston and Jayela hadn't been like that. They knew this job wasn't for the faint of heart. It was rough, hard, and you had to be constantly aware of your surroundings. It wasn't unlike being a cop in that respect. They got that.

I frowned as Boston rushed in, disheveled like he'd been out on a two-day bender. His hair was a mess, the top button on his normally pristine uniform was undone, his shirttails partially sticking out from his pants. His eyes were slightly wild and unfocused when he approached the bench.

I peered at him through the plastic shield. "Hey, bro. You okay?"

Boston forced a smile that didn't reach his eyes. "Yeah. Fine. I need to talk to a prisoner, though."

I cocked my head to one side, hearing something in his voice that wasn't normally there. "In an official capacity? Or as a visitor?"

Boston narrowed his eyes. "Official, of course. Why the fuck would I be visiting any of these morons? They don't exactly run in my social circles."

I held up my hands, surprised by his snappy tone. "Fair enough. Just asking. Don't shoot the messenger. You're here at visiting hours, and you don't have a partner with you."

I immediately realized what I'd said. And it was written all over Boston's face, too. The mention of him not having a partner here just reminded everyone that the reason he didn't have one was because Jayela was gone.

"Shit. I'm sorry, man. I wasn't thinking."

Boston blew out a slow breath. "No. It's fine. Sorry. Just a lot going on at the moment."

"Yeah. Of course. I get it. We're good. Which prisoner do you need?"

"DeWitt."

"You got it. You take interview room two, and I'll go get him. Colt, you got reception for a bit?"

He mock saluted me, like the smart-ass he was, and so I stuck my finger up at him in return. But we were both grinning at each other. We really were similar. We got each other in a way that had made us instant friends.

I let myself through another security door and headed back to General Population, punching in the code to open that door as well. "DeWitt! You got a visitor." I had to yell over the low din of fifty prisoners milling around and talking shit with each other.

DeWitt looked up from his kingpin position at the head of the table. On autopilot, I quickly took in the other men sitting with him, silently noting each one, and how they interacted. No Michaelson. Interesting. I'd already noticed the growing power DeWitt seemed to have in here. He hadn't been here long enough to warrant it. I wasn't concerned just yet. But I was definitely keeping an eye on them. When prisoners got too comfortable, they started thinking they ruled the roost. They didn't. I ruled the fucking roost. And I'd make sure they remembered it if I had to.

The big man stood, throwing down his cards. "I wonder which of my ladies it is today? Maybe the hot blonde with the big tits? Or the skinny brunette who likes to talk dirty in my ear."

He sauntered toward me while the others hooted and hollered.

I didn't even bother dignifying his bravado with a response. It was the same shit I heard all day every day, and it was boring. So much about this job was just boring. I didn't hate it. But if I could have been doing something else, I would've. In a heartbeat. But this was what I knew. This was what I'd always done. And there was something about it that called me. Better the devil you know, perhaps.

In the corridor I told DeWitt to stand against the wall while I cuffed him. It was a procedure all the prisoners were used to. We didn't let them meet with cops or lawyers uncuffed. That had ended in disaster before. Nobody wanted that again.

DeWitt ran his mouth the entire time, but I didn't bother listening. Once he was ready to go, I led him to the interview room, where Boston waited for him.

"Well, this is a surprise," DeWitt said as we entered the room. "To what do I owe such a pleasure, Officer Boston?"

I cuffed DeWitt to the table and backed off to the corner of the room. "You good?" I asked Boston, meaning was he okay if I left the room. He was a cop, not a lawyer. So this interview wasn't privileged. I didn't have to leave. But Boston was more than capable of holding his own. I'd never bothered babysitting him before, though his agitated behavior had me questioning if he was actually nervous. Some of the newer cops were when they first started coming here. You could tell by the way they fidgeted, their gazes dancing around the room. Having a guard in here with a dangerous prisoner helped put them at ease. But Boston was a seasoned pro. The fact he was acting weird today was completely out of character.

"Yeah. I'm fine."

I nodded and walked out, closing the door behind me. But something prickled at me. That sense of awareness that made me an excellent guard. It kicked to life, demanding attention, shouting at me that something wasn't right here. I turned around and stared back at the door. Boston had told me he didn't need me in there. I didn't want to undermine him with the prisoner. But there was something about the whole situation that felt off. And I couldn't just let it go.

So instead of heading back to reception to help Colt, I detoured to another room, filled with screens recording the entire prison. There was a single guard inside, monitoring each screen, ready to call for backup if there was a disturbance on any of them. He glanced up when I entered, relief flushing his expression. "Hey. You here to take over? I called someone up ages ago. I'm about to piss my pants."

I frowned and waved a hand at him. "Just go."

Suited me to be in here by myself anyway. I slid into the man's chair and gazed around at the plethora of monitors. Grainy black-and-white images filled each screen, the prisoners moving about on them, all doing nothing of real interest. This was the most boring job in the world, unless it was a day were a fight broke out. But I wasn't looking for a fight right now. I located the camera recording in interview room two, where I'd put Boston and DeWitt. Kicking the door closed behind me, I hit the sound button for that room and leaned forward, peering at the screen and the two men sitting across the table from each other.

My instincts weren't wrong. While I didn't expect for DeWitt and Boston to be best friends, chatting gaily with a cup of tea and scones, one look at them on the screen told me that this wasn't just any old interview. I instantly tensed at the expression on Boston's face. While it would be no loss to me if he reached across the table and throttled DeWitt, it'd be a shitload of paperwork that I didn't really want to deal with. "Shit."

Boston's expression was murderous. His fingers curled around the tabletop, nails pressing hard into the solid wood, as if he was trying to hold himself back. And when his voice came through the speakers, it was with barely concealed rage. "Who did you tell that I was on the take?"

DeWitt sat back, crossing his arms across his broad chest. "I've no idea what you're talking about."

"Don't bullshit a bullshitter. I've just had my chief up my ass about it."

DeWitt grinned slyly. "You ever tried that? You'd probably like it."

I could practically hear Boston's molars grinding. "Who did you tell?"

My mind spun. There was no way Boston was on the take. I couldn't believe that for even half a second. The man was as straight as they came. Even the notion of him being dirty was completely inconceivable to me.

DeWitt leaned forward, the smile dropping from his face. "Don't worry about it. I'll deal with it."

"I've been letting you deal with it for months. How about you start talking, and I deal with it."

What the fuck?

DeWitt drummed his fat fingers on the tabletop. "The new guy. Michaelson. You know, the one you put in here for your bitch partner's murder? You guys fucked up there.

There is no way he did it. You and I both know that, though, don't we?"

Boston shoved to his feet and launched across the table, grabbing DeWitt by his shirt.

I didn't stick around to see what Boston's reply was. I slammed out of the tiny security room, racing back around the corner and down the hallway to the interview room. By the time I got there, Boston had DeWitt up against the wall, his fingers around his throat.

DeWitt appeared to be enjoying it. Sick bastard.

I yanked Boston away, pushing him to the other side of the room. "What the hell are you doing?" I got right up in his face, going nose to nose with him. "Have you lost your goddamn mind?"

It took a moment for Boston's gaze to refocus. He blinked hard when he finally looked at me properly, and then I felt the fight go out of him, his body relaxing enough that I knew he wasn't going to try again.

I loosened my grip on him. "You good?"

"Yeah. I'm fine."

"You know that was all on tape, don't you?"

Boston narrowed his gaze at me. "It's not what you're thinking."

I backed off. "It doesn't matter what I'm thinking. That's between you and your chief. Ain't got nothing to do with me."

DeWitt piped up gleefully. "Pritchard probably likes you better now he knows you're dirty. I get the impression our guard friend here likes a lot of things kinda dirty, right, Pritchard?"

I glared at him over my shoulder. "You want to shut up? Or will I let Boston try to kill you again? Seriously, man. Learn to close your mouth."

Boston shrugged out of my grip and made for the door. But he paused, fixing me with an eagle-eyed glare. "Don't believe his talk."

I nodded. Boston seemed satisfied with that, spun on his heel, and left the room.

DeWitt chuckled. "You're as big a liar as he is."

I didn't dispute that fact. I just shoved DeWitt out of the room and back to the cells.

27

MAE

"Mom?"

My gaze darted between Liam and the woman. Her fingers trembled, the thin soup I'd just placed on her tray spilling over the edges of the plastic bowl. She shook her head viciously and put the tray down on the countertop.

Her eyes widened, darting between Liam, me, and the door. "I'm sorry. I need to go."

That spurred Liam into action. "No, Mom. Wait. What are you doing here? Do you need help? Food? Why haven't you been cashing the checks I send you?" He dropped his ladle back into the soup pot and hurried to the door that would let him out into the dining area. "Just wait a moment. I'm coming out."

But the woman shook her head again. "No. Please. I don't want to be a bother. I shouldn't have come here. I wouldn't have if I'd known..."

Liam's hands faltered over the doorknob, and hurt flashed across his face. I knew what he was hearing.

His mother wouldn't have come if she'd known he was here.

I cringed.

But Liam's hurt was quickly replaced by determination. He turned the handle, but it barely moved. Liam cursed under his breath and fumbled for the keys in his pocket to unlock the door.

Meanwhile, his mother was already at the main exit that led to the alley outside. The late-afternoon sunlight flashed, marking her escape, and then it slammed closed behind her.

The other men and women in the room all turned to stare at the scene they were making, curious conversation rippling around the space.

"Mom! Wait!" Liam finally jabbed the right key into the lock and twisted it so viciously it was probably at risk of breaking. "Please."

His voice broke on the word, and before I really could analyze what I was doing, I was rushing to his side. I followed him through the exit.

There was no sign of his mother in either direction. Just an empty alley, the dirty concrete ground glittering with broken glass, the walls of both the homeless shelter and the building next door covered in multicolored graffiti.

Liam slumped against the wall and drove his fist back against it. "Dammit."

He rested his head on the bricks, his face turned up to the skies splashed with the pinks and oranges of the setting sun. They danced over his features, strangled with pain.

I took up the spot beside him, standing shoulder to shoulder. Without saying anything, I found his still clenched fist and slowly worked his hand open, massaging each finger as I went, before fitting my palm to his.

When he finally glanced over at me, the hurt in his eyes buckled my knees.

He peeled himself off the wall and wrapped himself around me, his face burying into the side of my neck and inhaling my scent deeply. His big body pressed me into the wall, and I put my arms around his back, pulling him even closer, engulfing him in a hug that tried to absorb some of his hurt. "Shh," I soothed. "It's okay."

But I could tell it wasn't. Seeing his mother had triggered something in Liam. I wanted to talk to him about it. I wanted to understand what had happened and why she'd run from him. Why her disappearance hurt him the way it obviously was.

But I also knew what it was to not have a mother in your life. And to be so completely and utterly broken by it, that at times, all you could do was just stand there and let somebody hold you.

I found myself wanting to be that person for Liam.

I drew his face away from my neck and stared up into his eyes. For once, all his walls were down. The cockiness was gone. The arrogance disappeared. All that was left was the real him. The him he tried to hide from everybody else.

I lifted up onto my toes, took both sides of his face in my hands, closed my eyes, and let my lips meet his.

There was no surprise, no hesitation in his kiss. He kissed me soft and slow, and it was just like that first night, where he'd stolen my breath and maybe even a little piece of my heart all in one moment without even trying. I held him to me, let our tongues mingle, drawing him deeper and closer, until the kisses changed.

The kisses woke something in him that in turn called out to me. His lips became harder and more demanding as he took control, pressing me into the wall.

"I want you," he mumbled over my mouth.

"Here?" I breathed.

"Everywhere. I wanted you back at my place. I wanted you in the car. I wanted you at your sister's funeral. I wanted you every fucking day I saw you in high school. So yeah. I want you here, Mae."

A tiny moan escaped my throat. I tugged his head down again, taking his kiss, surrendering to it, blocking out any concern that we were in a public place, and anybody could walk down this alley at any time. I didn't want him to feel the way I had for my entire life. If I could take even a tiny part of that away from him right now, then I would. Because I hurt, too. And surrendering to him meant him taking some of my pain as well. Somewhere in the back of my mind, I could hear my therapist saying that this was not a healthy exchange. But I didn't care. Because Liam's kiss was easy to drown in. And I wanted to sink right to the very bottom, where only he and I existed.

He kissed me deep, his tongue plunging, taking what he needed and yet giving me what I craved at the same time. It felt like hours before he'd had his fill, moving off my mouth and on to my neck. He sucked and bit and licked at the soft skin there, while my nails raked down his back, searching for a way to get beneath his clothes to touch him. His hips pressed to mine, his cock hard and long beneath his pants. He ground against me, trailing his lips across my neck and my throat.

Kiss by kiss, touch by touch, all my reservations fell away. Until it was just him and me. We weren't two broken souls, desperately clutching to each other in a ghetto alley. We could have been anywhere in the world. We could have been in a multimillion-dollar mansion, and it wouldn't have made an ounce of difference. Because the setting didn't matter. All that mattered was him and me and the connection sparking to life between us.

I got my hands up beneath his shirt, fingertips chasing over his warm skin. Every ridge of muscle delighted me, but better was the way his skin turned to goosebumps everywhere I touched him. Once again, I reached for his belt, only to be stopped by thick fingers wrapping around my slender wrists. He dragged them up above my head, holding them with one hand.

"Stay there." It was more of a promise than a demand. But he held me tight enough that I didn't want to argue.

The backs of my hands and arms rubbed on the brick wall, the rough surface scratching my skin. I barely noticed, because Liam's other hand skated down the side of my body, dipping in at my waist and out at my hips, before moving across my belly. He thrust his hips toward mine, his erection not quite hitting me in the right spot, but the intent was there. Need lit up inside me, starting low and spiraling down and out. Every second of it was blinding, fireworks arcing through a dark night sky.

His fingers traced along the elastic band cinched around my waist, holding my skirt up. It was nothing for his fingers to slip below it, palm flattening on my belly and inching lower until his fingers brushed over my mound. He snatched my breath when he reached lower to cup me, fingers navigating between my thighs, and widening my stance.

"I'm supposed to be making you feel better," I murmured.

"This does make me feel better. So much better." His lips skated along my jaw until they tickled my ear, his words barely more than a husky whisper. "Nothing is better than feeling how wet you are right now."

A blush heated my cheeks.

Liam chuckled in my ear. "Does that embarrass you?"

"No."

"I'm a lawyer, Mae. I know when people are lying."

"Damn you and your Secret Squirrel lawyer powers."

The rumble of his laughter vibrated through my chest, my nipples hardening at the sensation. He slipped one finger farther between my legs, nudging apart my folds and sliding through the silky wetness there. There was nothing I could do but surrender to his touch. My eyes fluttered closed, letting the sensation he created take control of my body.

He circled my clit, exploring the most intimate part of me with gentle fingers. But when he found the sensitive bud of nerves, his touch changed. He went from slow, barely-there glides, to a more insistent rub. It built in intensity until he had a rhythm going that made my head spin. I was completely at his mercy, his hand still locked around my wrists, and I wanted nothing more than to surrender to him fully.

"Liam," I murmured.

His lips and tongue trailed a path down my neck. "I know what you need."

"I want to touch you."

"Not yet. Don't move your arms, Mae. Got it?" He gave my clit a pinch that would have had me agreeing to any condition he put forward. As long as he didn't stop.

"Say it."

"I won't move."

"Good girl."

Fuck. Why was that so hot? I should have expected Liam would like to be the dominant one. He was well used to being the center of attention. The one running the show.

It made sense that he'd like that control in all areas of his life.

I was more than willing to reap the benefits.

With an extra hand to work my body into a tailspin, he slid his hand up my shirt to cup my breast through my bra. His thumb flicked over the stiff peak of my nipple, adding a new magical spot to my body already lit up like fairy lights.

But it didn't distract from finally pushing one finger up inside me. I let out a cry that he muffled with his lips. He kissed me hard, his tongue spearing into my mouth in the same tempo that his finger drove into my heat. His second finger hit that spot inside me so deliciously I couldn't leave my hands on the wall any longer. I wrapped them around Liam's neck, thrusting my fingers into his thick hair, and mirrored the action with one leg, hooking it around him and letting my hips roll in time.

I groaned, moving faster, meeting the jerk of his hand, my orgasm building deliciously within.

"I want you inside me," I whispered. I wanted him to yank my skirt up and free his cock, only to slam it inside me in the next instant.

"Good things come to those who wait." His voice was barely more than a whisper, but the inherent promise in his tone had me panting with need. With want. And yet somehow, I knew that if I followed him and let him lead, he'd make it so very worth my while.

Like he'd read my mind, his thumb expertly found my clit and nudged it in time to the movements of his fingers. It was all it took—the combination of his fingers filling and stretching me, with the added friction on my clit—and I fell over the edge, hard. My fingers curled around the strands of his hair, tugging and pulling as feeling exploded through me, a powerful gust of sensation that had me making noises

I never had before. My hips rolled wantonly, taking what I needed with no direction from my brain, my body just hell-bent on milking out the best orgasm I'd ever had in my life.

The only orgasm I'd ever had at the hands of someone else.

Liam knew exactly what I needed without me having to say anything. He picked up the cues my body gave him and worked me until I couldn't bear for him to touch my sensitive flesh for even a moment longer.

It was only then that he withdrew his fingers, bringing them to his mouth to lick them clean.

He leaned in close, the stubble across his jawline brushing my chin. "You're embarrassed again. You shouldn't be. You taste like fucking sin and Heaven all rolled into one. But next time I taste you, it's going to be with my head between your thighs."

I moaned and let him kiss me once more before we both reluctantly pulled away. He straightened my clothes for me, and I swiped a finger over the lipstick that had transferred from my lips to his. We both grinned like two naughty kids who'd been caught kissing on the porch past curfew.

Liam glanced over at the door reluctantly. The relaxed pleasure on his expression slowly disappearing as the real world sank slowly back in.

"Do you want to talk about your mom?" I asked gently.

He raked a hand through his hair and turned his gaze back on me. "Can I just make you come again instead?"

I grinned. "Rain check?"

He fake groaned. "Fine. But just so you know, I'm not going to be able to wait long."

I wasn't about to argue.

28

MAE

By the end of my first week at the men's prison, my class had more students than I had room for. Every evening, there had been a steady stream of men filing in the door. At first, I'd been pleased by the turnout, truly believing that word must have got around about my class, and that I could help them make something of their time in here. But it quickly became obvious that for the most part, that was a pipe dream. Out of a class of twenty, I was lucky if two listened to a word I had to say.

DeWitt was one of the first to sign up, along with some of his sidekicks. I handed out worksheets, and when I passed one to the big prisoner, he gave me a sly grin.

"Well, thank you, little mouse. I see why Michaelson has a hard-on over you. You are a sweet treat, aren't you? I'd like to eat you right up."

I blanched in disgust.

Rowe grabbed him by the back of the shirt and hauled him out into the hallway before I could even open my mouth to respond. He kicked out DeWitt's friends just for sniggering, and then helped cull the rest of the class by removing anyone who so much as dared to blink out of turn.

But then the next night there'd be another dozen new guys who were just as rowdy and disruptive.

I gave up trying to engage them all, letting Rowe deal with most of them, and instead focused on the two or three who showed promise and a real commitment to wanting to learn.

"Right." I clapped my hands together, trying to get the attention of the room. "Let's work on this math problem. If X equals twelve, and Y equals six, X divided by Y gives you what?"

I waited for any of the guys to raise their hands or call out the answer. It wasn't even close to the work I should have been teaching these guys for their GED, but I'd found their average level of education was barely sixth grade at best, so I'd had to start from the very beginning. When nobody put up their hands to offer an answer, I let out a sigh. I focused in on one of my more promising students. Vincent seemed out of place amongst the other men, with his quiet, intelligent way of working. "Vincent? X divided by Y gives you…?"

"Gives Vincent a hard-on because a woman is speaking to him."

The room burst out into hysterical laughter, and I rolled my eyes as Rowe kicked yet another man out into the corridor.

Vincent looked down at his sheet of paper, the tips of his ears turning bright pink. I cringed internally. It was obvious the man was trying to fly under the radar and I'd just dumped him in it. I walked by his desk, and though it was against the rules, I placed a sympathetic hand on his shoulder.

He stiffened beneath my brief touch, but he didn't say a word. He just slid his paper in my direction. In neat handwriting, he'd written the math problem, along with the right answer. I grinned to myself but didn't put Vincent in the spotlight any further by commenting on it.

The class carried on, and I did the best I could, but there was one noticeable absence. Heath hadn't been in my class all week. Rowe had refused to give me any information on where he was, so I'd had Liam inquire instead. He was told that Heath was fine, and in good health, which led me to believe that he wasn't in my class right now because Rowe was trying to keep the two of us apart.

I hadn't bothered confronting Rowe about it, knowing he'd just give me the runaround. My life at this prison was easier if I wasn't constantly arguing with the man.

Rowe called time on the class, and the men gathered up their single sheets of paper and filed toward the door. Rowe confiscated their pencils before letting them out, and I slowly picked up my own things, packing a file of teaching materials away into my oversized bag.

Rowe was watching me when I looked up. He seemed tired tonight, a slight trace of circles beneath his deep-brown eyes. But nothing could dull how sinfully beautiful he was. Nothing could make me forget the way his biceps strained against his uniform as he'd manhandled prisoners out of my room all evening. Or the way his dark gaze followed me around, always making sure I was safe, even if he did hate me being there in the first place.

"What?" I asked.

He shook his head wearily. "How long are you going to do this for?"

"Teach seventh grade math?"

"Teach seventh grade math here."

I shrugged. "Until I get what I came for."

Rowe leaned against the doorway like he needed it to hold him up. "Michaelson added you to his visit list. Can't you just be a normal woman and see him during visiting hours? Why make this so difficult for me?"

I patted him on his solid, hard biceps, and fought the urge to leave my hand resting there. "Some things aren't all about you, Rowe."

"Mae."

Rowe and I both snapped our heads around to face the corridor. Heath stood on the opposite side, too handsome to be real. Even in his ugly prison-issued clothes, the man made my heart thump and my stomach flip. His hair had grown out slightly, and the stubble on his cheeks verged on a full beard. He seemed just as tired and worn out as Rowe did. But I drank in the sight of him like a woman who'd spent too long in a desert.

"What are you doing here, Michaelson?" But Rowe's question had no real energy behind it.

"I just need a minute of Miss Donovan's time."

"You just need to go back to your bunk. You know you're not supposed to be here."

I stiffened, waiting for Heath to fire up or run his mouth. But he didn't. He just stared at me with pure desperation in his eyes, and then turned that same face on Rowe. For the tiniest of seconds, their gazes collided, Heath's earnestly searching the guard's face. "Please."

To my surprise, Rowe didn't turn away. Instead, he studied him carefully and then blew out a long sigh. "Fine. Get in here. You've got one minute. You touch her, you're dead. Got me?"

The fierce protectiveness in Rowe's voice took me by surprise. As did his willingness to let Heath speak to me. But then Heath was in the room, and Rowe closed the door, locking the three of us inside.

I wasn't about to look a gift horse in the mouth. I had no idea why Rowe was suddenly being so generous, but I wasn't about to question it. I forced myself to stop a few inches away from Heath, though, and pressed my palms to my sides to keep from reaching out for him.

God, it was hard.

Heath appeared to be fighting a similar battle himself. "What's happening with you and Liam?"

Shock punched through me, thinking about what Liam and I had done just hours ago in the alleyway outside the homeless shelter. But there was no way Heath could have known about that. And after the shock wore off, I realized he was talking about the information he'd given us about Boston. "Liam spoke to Chief James."

Heath's eyes widened. "You went to the cops? About a dirty cop?"

"Where else were we supposed to go? Liam had to say something."

Heath ran a hand through his hair. "That isn't gonna get us anywhere. The police are literally useless to us right now. And if it gets back to DeWitt that I've been talking..."

I swallowed hard. "Are you in danger?"

He shook his head. "Don't worry about it. I can handle it. What did the cops say?"

"They're looking into it."

Heath sighed. "In other words, they don't believe me."

I shook my head hard. "I know the chief. I've met him many a time. And I know my sister believed in him and in her department. They'll take the accusation seriously."

"Yeah. But until DeWitt told me that Boston was on the take, we all thought he was a good guy, too. Who's to say that the chief isn't in on it as well? I'm telling you, Mae. The cops can't help us. We've gotta go past them. Around them. Whatever it takes."

I kept shaking my head. I'd spent so much time with my sister in the past ten years, watching as she trained and then dedicated her life to her job. She had such high ideals. She was so by the book, right down to the very letter, and she believed in law enforcement and following the rules. It was impossible for me to believe that she'd worked day in and day out with people who didn't have the same high morals as she did. "I still don't think Boston has anything to do with this."

Rowe cleared his throat. "DeWitt knows you ratted him out to the cops. Boston was down here yesterday chewing him out about it." His lips pressed together for a moment. "I know Boston, and even though I admit that what I saw yesterday sounds bad, I believed him when he said it wasn't what it looked like. Forget Boston. DeWitt is your bigger problem now. I doubt he's impressed that you've been blabbing your mouth to save your own skin."

Heath and I both stared at Rowe with open mouths. It was a moment before either of us could say anything.

Heath recovered first. "What was I supposed to do? The man admitted I went down for a murder his gang committed. A murder he put the hit out for."

Rowe's eyes widened. "You fucking serious?"

Heath's gaze met his. "Deadly."

Rowe swore low under his breath.

Heath cocked his head to one side, studying the guard. "You believe me?"

I held my breath. This was huge. If there was even a smidgen of doubt in Rowe's mind, then maybe we could place that same disbelief into the minds of others. The minds of people who could get Heath the hell out of here.

"I don't know what to believe. But I'll admit there are things that don't add up here. I've been chewing that over since I overheard Boston and DeWitt's conversation."

I let out the breath I was holding. It was something. A seed of doubt that we could work on.

"Thank you." Heath nodded at Rowe.

"Don't bother thanking me. It's not like I can do nothing. I've got about as much pull with the cops as you do. And now not only do you have the cops side-eyeing you, but you've put yourself on DeWitt's shit list. And I don't know who that guy is on the outside. But in here, if I were you, I'd watch my back."

For once, Rowe didn't have anything to say as he walked me to the prison exit. He was stoically quiet, punching in the code to the security door and waiting for me to walk through it into the quiet reception area. Visiting hours were long over, so there was no one behind the reception window. I opened my mouth to say goodbye to Rowe, but he followed me right to the main exit door, holding it open for me like we were on a date. Or like a bouncer, kicking me out.

Knowing Rowe, it was more likely the latter.

But the night outside was nearing on balmy, and the scent of summer was truly in the air. So when Rowe walked side by side with me across the dark parking lot, I didn't comment. I didn't want to ruin the nice moment. It felt suspiciously like a truce.

"Thank you," I said quietly.

Rowe shoved his hands deep in the pockets of his uniform. "Yeah, well, you kind of forced my hand when you showed you had no real regard for your own personal safety. Don't you know how many women are attacked in dark parking lots every day? Just because there are big-ass security gates, doesn't mean you're safe, you know? An attack can come from anywhere at any time, and especially when you're paying more attention to your phone than what's going on around you."

Truce over, apparently. "I pay attention," I huffed.

He scoffed.

"I do!"

"Where are your keys then? Do you already have them out, ready to enter your vehicle? And are you aware that there's a man in his car, just three space down from you?"

My fingers tingled, empty and irritated by the fact he was right. My keys were still buried somewhere in my bag. But when I glanced to my left, squinting to try to make out anyone sitting in a vehicle, I couldn't see a thing.

"Oh, for Christ's sakes." He reached out and grasped my chin between two fingers.

Our gazes crashed, and for the tiniest of moments, he held it.

The annoyance in his expression flickered into something different. Something more. Something that made parts of me come alive with realization of what that look could do to my body if only he allowed it out.

But he didn't. He locked it down tight and twisted my face in the opposite direction. Away from him, and the possibility that if he let it, standing like this could have led down a completely different path.

"There," Rowe said, pointing to a car to my right. "Black

Nissan Skyline. Unidentified male sitting in the driver's seat, and you had no idea."

I hated that as his fingers fell away; I instantly missed them. I swallowed down the urge to find a new way to get him to touch me and focused instead on the fact that he was actually right.

There was someone else in the quiet parking lot with us, and I hadn't had a clue.

Dammit. I hated when Rowe got one up on me.

The car door opened, and the male in question got out, pausing to grab a lunch bag from the back seat. When he straightened, the light from the interior of the car lit up his guard's uniform.

I elbowed Rowe. "He's a guard, you jackass! He's hardly about to attack me!"

Rowe turned a withering gaze in my direction. "It's always the ones you least suspect."

I raised an eyebrow in challenge. "So I need to be worried about the guards now, too? By that logic, I should be wary of you."

"You probably should be."

"Oh, please. You talk the talk but you're about as scary as a lamb with a bow tie."

Rowe wrinkled his face in what was probably supposed to be disgust but on him still managed to be hot.

The other guard wandered over and slapped hands with Rowe before turning to me. "Hey, you're Miss Donovan, right? The teacher? We haven't met yet. I'm Colt."

The name set off a bell in my head. "Oh! Colt!" I rushed forward and engulfed him in a hug, wrapping my arms around him and squeezing him.

Over Colt's shoulder, Rowe folded his arms across his chest and glared at me.

He could pretend he was annoyed all he wanted. But I had the sneaking suspicion that there was a hint of jealousy behind his actions. That was interesting. Partially because I liked having ammunition to use in our verbal sparring matches. And partially because Rowe intrigued me. The man was beautiful and smart and the fact he was guarded and closed off only made me want to dig deeper, push beneath the layers, and find out who he really was.

Because no one was as permanently grumpy and scowly as he was. Not without a good reason.

Locked in a stare off with Rowe, I'd almost forgotten I was still hugging Colt. And that it had now been going on for an uncomfortably long time. Colt was stiff in my embrace and awkwardly patting me on the back, like he was considering pulling out his cuffs and taking me off to the psych department on the third floor.

I stepped back quickly. "Sorry! I'm not normally so over-enthusiastic with my greetings, I swear. That was from Selina. She said to tell you happy birthday."

His body relaxed as he stepped back and grinned. "You saw her?"

I smiled at his enthusiasm for his mother-in-law. "She joined my class at the women's prison."

He chuckled at that. "You know she went to a fancy private school and has a college degree, right?"

I gaped at him. "She does? What on earth is she doing in a prison GED class then?"

He shrugged. "She got five years for taking her husband out. Probably just filling her time."

"What?" I struggled to comprehend how the tiny, quiet woman I'd met could have killed someone.

Colt patted me on the shoulder. "Don't worry. She had a

good reason. She's harmless, and she'll likely be your best student."

I hoped so. Because I liked the woman. But it was a reminder that Rowe was probably right. There were dangers lurking here, not just in the darkened parking lot, that I needed to take more seriously.

An odd shiver rolled down my spine, and I told myself to stop being stupid. This job was perfectly safe when I had Rowe by my side. I wasn't even in the prison anymore and wasn't due back until next week. My first week was officially over.

"So, what are you doing for your birthday?" I asked Colt.

He shifted his backpack higher on his shoulder and cringed. "My girl is throwing me a party. It's a surprise."

I chuckled. "Not much of a surprise if you know about it."

He grinned. "Yeah. Lacey and Banjo are pretty much the worst secret keepers in the history of forever. I worked them out about five minutes after they decided they were doing it."

"And they don't know you know? You didn't tell them?"

Colt lifted one shoulder, a small, fond smile playing around his lips. "Nah. Why ruin their fun? That sort of shit makes them happy. And I'm happy when they're happy."

His partner was a lucky woman. I glanced over at Rowe and his annoyed scowl. I threw my hands up in annoyance. "What now?"

"Are you ever gonna quit blabbering about Colt's partners and get going? Some of us haven't finished our shifts, you know?"

I ignored his complaining and focused instead on something else he'd said. "Partners?" I asked Colt. Then I rushed on, realizing what a busybody I was being. "Sorry. None of my business."

But Colt was quick to smile. "Nah, it's cool. Everyone is always curious. Come to my party on Saturday night. You can meet everyone. Lacey would love to talk to you about Selina, I'm sure."

"Pretty sure she's busy," Rowe interjected.

Colt and I both looked at him.

"Despite what Rowe seems to think, I am actually capable of speaking for myself." I glared at him to prove my point. I got it. He didn't want me encroaching on his social space. But I'd hardly just invited myself or rocked up without an invite at all. So Rowe could just pull the stick out of his ass. I needed friends in this place. Plus, it was fun to piss off Rowe. I turned back to Colt. "A party sounds great. I'd love to come."

Rowe groaned and mumbled something about having to wash his hair that night.

We both knew he wouldn't. He'd be there.

29

MAE

Colt had given me a Providence address for the party, which I hadn't really thought twice about until I was actually driving through the familiar streets I'd grown up on. The elementary school I worked at was on the other side of the main road that cut through the center of the suburb, as was Tori and Will's place, so for years now, even though I worked mere minutes away, I'd managed to avoid coming to this side at all.

Driving past my childhood home wasn't exactly something I did for fun. Fun and that house just didn't go together in the same sentence.

I checked the GPS and parked a few doors down as instructed, since this was supposed to be a surprise party after all. I walked the rest of the way, past sprawling mansion after even bigger sprawling mansion. Despite the fancy neighborhood, Rowe's warnings about safety echoed in the back of my mind, and I sighed grudgingly and gripped my keys a little tighter, instead of putting them away in my bag. I should probably buy myself some Mace. Jayela had always harped on about that, too.

A dark chuckle behind me had me spinning around so fast I actually dropped the keys. "Shit!" I scooped to grab them, but Rowe beat me to it.

He plucked them from the ground. "Well, I was about to commend you on the fact you at least thought to have your keys out, ready to use as a weapon, but then you went and screwed it up by dropping them."

"You scared me!"

"And what would an attacker do? Walk up politely and offer you a bunch of flowers before he jumps you?"

He had a point, but I was annoyed. Both at the fact he'd caught me unawares again, and at the fact I'd dropped the freaking keys. I wasn't some helpless damsel. I was a perfectly capable, full-grown woman, but something about Rowe seemed to short-circuit all of that and leave me fumbling.

Rowe out of uniform was even more mind-melting than Rowe in uniform.

I drank in the jeans that looked as if they'd been made especially for him, and the button-down short-sleeved shirt worn open over a tighter-fitting T-shirt that hugged his abs.

Lucky freaking T-shirt.

We fell into step and turned down the drive simultaneously.

"Jesus, this place is insane," Rowe muttered.

"You haven't been here before?" I asked, making idle chitchat to cover the fact I was also busily inhaling the delicious, clean, fresh scent of him. Whatever cologne he wore had me wanting to suck in deep, greedy lungfuls.

"I have. Just to pick Colt up or drop him off. But it still kind of takes my breath away every time."

It really was a beautiful house. One that reeked of money. "Why is Colt working the graveyard shift at the prison if he lives here? He can't be short of cash if he can afford the rent on this place."

We reached the front door, but Rowe touched one hand to my lower back and guided me around to the side of the house, and along a pebbled path that led to the backyard. The gate was open, and the quiet hum of chatter met my ears as we moved farther in.

I gasped at the huge swimming pool and the crazy number of fairy lights strung up across the rafters and through the trees that edged the property. A crowd of people gathered in an entertaining area, and a small bonfire flickered in the center of a stone pit.

"Yeah, he definitely doesn't need the money. But this is his girl's place. She inherited when her aunt went to jail. She and the aunt were real close. The woman raised her like she was her daughter, so when she went away, it all went to Lacey."

"Selina's her aunt?"

He nodded. "Colt's from Saint View. He's used to having to work for every cent. It doesn't sit well with him to just let Lacey pay for everything. And working at the prison pays a whole lot better than working at McDonald's."

"Yeah. But at least nobody tries to kill you at McDonald's."

Rowe raised an eyebrow. "You've obviously never eaten at the McDonald's in Saint View then."

I widened my eyes. "Is that true?"

He laughed at me. "So sweet and innocent."

That irked me. It was the automatic assumption that everybody made about me. Blonde hair. Soft, curvy body. Teaches elementary school. All seemed to add up to: must be completely naïve.

"Did I tell you I was in a drive-by shooting the other

day?" I dropped it so casually, like I was talking about getting milk from the supermarket.

Rowe snorted. "Yeah, okay. I'm sure they shot up your uptown apartment real good."

I didn't say anything.

Rowe stopped walking and spun on me. "You fucking serious?"

"As a heart attack. Which is what I nearly had when bullets started coming through the walls." I laughed, though it was strained. The memory was still a little too fresh in my head to be making jokes about it.

"Why didn't you tell me?"

I frowned. He seriously seemed annoyed. That was a bit rich. "I'm sorry. Did you turn into my father when I wasn't paying attention? Why would I have told you?"

"Oh, I don't know. Water cooler conversation, perhaps? Generally people share that sort of information with their friends."

I glanced at him in surprise. "Is that what we are?"

He shrugged. "Co-workers. Same difference."

But I turned away and smiled to myself. Co-workers and friends were two completely different things. They were not the same at all. "You like me."

Rowe rolled his eyes.

I was just about to tease him some more, but a tall, cute, blond guy who looked like he'd just stepped off the beach, started waving his hands in the air and shushing everyone. "Hey. Shut up, you guys. He's coming."

"Prematurely. As always," a dark-haired guy called out, and there was a titter of laughter around the group.

"Stop it, Rafe," scolded a young dark-haired woman with a baby on her hip. But she wrapped her free arm around him, tucking herself into his side.

The blond man joined the couple, kissing the woman on the top of her head. "Yeah, behave. You know Colt can't take a joke."

I took in the three of them standing together, natural and easy in each other's company. "Is one of them her brother?" I asked Rowe quietly.

He grinned devilishly. "Oh, you ain't seen nothing yet. Just wait."

I wasn't sure what he meant by that, but then Colt strode into the backyard.

"Surprise!"

"Wow. What's everybody doing here?" Colt called in the most wooden, stilted voice I'd ever heard. His acting was awful. Like, seriously bad. If there had been a critic here, he would have handed Colt whatever the opposite of an Oscar was.

People rushed forward toward the guest of honor, but Colt sidestepped them deftly. He made a beeline for the two men and the woman with the baby on her hip. He stopped a mere inch in front of her and grinned.

She pouted up at him. "You knew?"

"Yeah. I knew. You and Banjo are the worst secret keepers ever. But I still love you."

He bent down, taking her face between his hands and kissing her. He didn't seem to care that she had her arm wrapped around another man, or that a third was hovering nearby. He claimed her lips like he owned them, and she kissed him back deeply, sinking into his touch.

The baby patted them both on the face with delight, her chubby hands flapping.

They broke apart laughing, and Colt plucked the baby from the woman's arms. "You want a kiss, too, Luna? I got all the kisses in the world for you, baby girl."

I turned wide eyes on Rowe. "Spill the tea, sis."

He chuckled. "Love is love. Why choose when you can have them all?"

"But how...? Did they...? I don't even know how that would work."

"You need me to draw you a diagram?" He was battling back laughter.

I gave him a withering look. "You probably perfected those in high school, right? Pornographic stick figures?"

We shuffled toward Colt, who had let go of his partner long enough to allow his guests wish him a happy birthday.

"Like you can talk. I heard all about what you drew on the chalkboard in the women's prison." Rowe's amusement danced in his eyes.

"You did?" Well, that was kind of embarrassing.

"The massive dick?" Colt interrupted. "The whole prison heard about that. Pretty sure someone took a photo and posted it in the staff group chat. Thanks for coming by the way. Mae, this is my daughter, Luna. And this is the rest of the family." He pointed to the smiling young woman at his side, then the dark-haired man, then the blond. "This is Lacey. Rafe, and Banjo."

The woman stepped up and hugged me. "I've already heard all about you from my aunt. She really likes you. It's great they've got a teacher in there now. That must be so hard but rewarding for you, I guess? Are you enjoying it?"

"I am." A tiny stab of guilt curdled in my stomach, knowing I wasn't there just for the sake of educating prisoners.

"Well, thank you. I know it means a lot to my aunt, to have something to help fill her time."

Her eyes turned a little glassy, and Colt put his arm

around her, squeezing her shoulders. "She'll be out soon, Princess."

But we all knew it would be years before Selina was released. I could only imagine how difficult it was. I couldn't even let myself think about the possibility of Heath being in jail for years, with a sentence set in stone, and no chance of leaving. At least Heath's case hadn't gone to trial yet. No sentence had been passed down, so there was still hope.

Colt's little daughter made a happy, gurgling sound and smiled a gummy smile in my direction. I smiled back at her, touching her soft cheek. "Colt, she's gorgeous. She looks just like you."

Banjo groaned. "Erg. Don't get him started about having the strongest swimmers. He's been bragging about that ever since Luna was born."

"I can't help it if the truth hurts you, Banjo."

Luna laughed like she'd understood the joke and reached chubby hands toward me.

I blinked in surprise.

"Do you want to hold her?" Lacey asked.

My ovaries gave a little leap of delight. I did very much want to hold her. She was adorable, with a navy blue bow in her wispy dark hair, and a tiny navy blue with white polka-dot dress. "Yes please."

I reached for the baby, taking her carefully from her father and nestling her on my hip. I couldn't resist the urge to smell the top of her baby head. My maternal urge was strong. It always had been, and it was part of why I'd gone into teaching.

Lacey grabbed Colt's hand. "Excellent. Because I want to dance with the birthday boy."

He groaned good-naturedly but willingly followed her onto the makeshift dance floor they'd created to one side of the pool. Lacey glanced back over her shoulder at me. "If she gets fussy, her grandparents are around here somewhere. Or just hand off to one of the other guys. Or anyone here really! They all know and love her to pieces. Anyone will take her off your hands when you've had your fill of baby smell."

But Banjo was dragging Rafe out onto the dance floor as well. The four of them were all smiles, looking happy and carefree, and I imagined that between having a baby and being in college and working, they might not get much time to just be young and in love.

"We'll be fine," I called. I shifted Luna on my hip and then searched around for Rowe.

But he'd disappeared into the crowd. "Okay, then," I said to Luna. "That was rude, huh?"

Luna just gave me another smile.

I wandered around the edges of the pool with the baby, showing her the lights and letting her touch my necklaces. The party was in full swing, the dance floor full of bodies, most of them a few years younger than me, making me feel kind of old. I suspected most of the guests were friends of Colt's from high school or college. Though there were a group of older adults sitting at a table, chatting among themselves, Rowe wasn't with them.

Luna grew fussy but then laid her head down on my shoulder, and I realized she was tired. I wandered further into the backyard, away from the dancing bodies and the loud music and rubbed the little girl's back soothingly. Her chubby fingers twisted in my hair as we wandered beneath the starlit sky and trees full of fairy lights with a warm summer breeze washing over us.

At the far end of the yard, a shadowy figure leaned against a tree, gazing up at the stars. I stopped abruptly, watching Rowe. He had his hands shoved deep in his pockets, one foot propped up on the tree behind him. I almost didn't want to speak. There was something reverent in the way he studied the sky, and pulling him out from wherever he'd gone in his head felt wrong. I turned quietly, intending to walk away, when Luna gave a tiny squawk.

Rowe glanced over.

"Sorry for interrupting. I didn't realize you were down here. I wasn't following you, I swear." I didn't know why I'd added that last bit. It was hardly necessary. But I did kind of feel a little bit like a Rowe stalker. I mean, I was here, at a party that I probably only agreed to attend because he told me not to. These were his friends, not mine.

"It's fine."

I rocked side to side, trying to settle Luna who was still squawking. "Know anything about babies?"

There was a long pause. Then, "No."

"Fair enough. Me neither." I bounced around awkwardly, trying to settle the fussing baby.

Rowe's dark gaze tracked me, sending tingles down my spine. There was something about the way he looked at me that was both dark and delicious and all-consuming all at once.

"Hold her higher."

I blinked out of my Rowe trance. "Sorry, what?"

"You're holding her too low. If you hold up a bit higher there will be more pressure on her belly. Colt said that she gets colic."

I wasn't even entirely sure what colic was. But Rowe spoke with the confidence of a pro. So I shifted Luna higher, and almost instantly, she quieted.

I peered at Rowe, expecting to see a self-satisfied or

smug grin on his face, taking glory in the fact he'd been right. But there was nothing but sorrow in his expression.

"I thought you didn't know anything about babies," I stated quietly.

Rowe pushed off the tree and walked past me. "I don't. Not anymore."

30

MAE

In the middle of a crowded party, Liam and Heath surrounded me. Liam pulled me tight to his side, and Heath dropped a kiss on my head. Warm feelings floated through my body... Security mixed with a healthy dose of attraction. Rowe appeared through the crowd of people, and with the glow of fairy lights dancing over his face, he crossed the room, his entire focus on me.

There was no respect for personal space as he stopped toe to toe with me, gazing down with an expression I'd never seen before. He briefly looked to the other two guys, and I felt, more than saw, their nods. Something crackled in the air between the four of us, an intense swirling of desire that was so thick it was almost tangible. Music twirled through the air, a thumping beat starting up that mirrored the one inside my chest.

Thump. Thump. Thump.

"What are you waiting for?" Liam asked.

He grasped my chin and twisted it toward him, lowering his head and kissing my mouth. When he pulled away, he turned back to Rowe. "Kiss her."

Tingles shot deep between my legs. "You're okay with that?" I whispered to him.

Liam didn't answer. I glanced at Heath and saw nothing but fire in his gaze. There was no hint of jealousy. And when he urged, "Go on, Mae," my breath faltered in my lungs.

"You want this, too?" I asked him.

He didn't answer either, but then Rowe was drawing me into his arms, his lips skating along my jawline and over my ear. "We all want you."

"I can't choose," I protested.

"You don't have to."

I didn't know who said it. The beat picked up, crashing in my ears. *Thump. Thump. Thump.* It drowned out their words, until all that was left was the three of them, the beat, and Rowe's lips hovering over mine.

Thump. Thump. Thump. "Mae!"

I jerked upright, sweat beaded across my skin, sheets tangled around my bare legs. The comforter was on the floor in a heap, and the delicious dream disintegrated, leaving behind only the tingle between my thighs.

And an incessant thumping on the front door.

"Mae!"

"Coming!" I yelled back.

Not coming in the way I wanted, though.

I scrambled off the bed, yanking my nightshirt down over my ass, and hurried out of my bedroom. I jerked the door open without checking the peephole because I was pretty sure I recognized the voice.

Yep. I was right. Liam stood on the other side, eyes wide, hair slightly mussed and wearing running shorts and a tank top. My gaze immediately zeroed in on the bulge of his tanned biceps.

He slumped against the doorframe, relief smoothing out

the fine lines across his brow. "Fuck. You scared the shit out of me. I thought you were dead in there. You do remember your sister's murderer is still out there somewhere, don't you? Assuming that is, we believe Heath when he says it wasn't him."

"Which we do."

Liam shrugged.

"Liam! We do!"

"Yeah, yeah. We do. But frigging answer your phone and your door in a timely manner, will you? I was seriously afraid I was going to have to kick this door down only to find your messed-up body on the other side."

I blinked. "Well, shit, Liam. Thanks for putting that idea in my head. I won't sleep tonight now."

His gaze ran over my body, lingering on my legs. "Is that what you were doing? Sleeping?"

Sleeping. Dreaming about having three men at once and them all just being fine and dandy about it. Same, same. "Yeah, I was sleeping."

He cocked his head to one side. "Liar."

Damn his stupid human lie detector abilities! "I was!"

"You protest too much. Why are you flushed as pink as cotton candy then?"

I could suddenly see why he was good at his job. He'd barely even asked me two questions, but just the look on his face had me feeling like I needed to tell the truth. Like we were in a courtroom and I was under oath. "Nothing. I was just hot."

A slow grin spread across his face. "Hot dream?"

I couldn't help mirroring his smile with one of my own. "Maybe."

He straightened a little. "Was I in it?"

I debated over lying again, but I was obviously no good at that when it came to him. "Yes."

He inched closer and lowered his voice like we were sharing secrets. "It was a sex dream, huh?"

"Maybe."

He fist-pumped the air silently as I giggled at him. "Stop! You'll wake the neighbors." If he hadn't already with his incessant thumping on the door.

He calmed down but then studied me again. "Tell me about it."

"Oh, hell no. You do not want to know." I turned around and walked back into my entryway, leaving the door open for him to follow.

He was all up in my personal space in seconds, his hand running up my bare thigh. "Oh, but I do. And don't lie because I can read you like a book. Tell me every little detail, and maybe I'll make it come true."

I snorted. "I don't think so."

He grinned. "That dirty, huh? Kinky? I can be kinky if you want me to be..."

Yeah, I didn't doubt that. I still remembered the way he'd pinned my hands above my head in the alley as he'd made me come. But I somehow didn't see Liam as the type to share. I'd watched Colt, Lacey, Banjo, and Rafe at the party last night. I'd seen their easy manner with each other, and the completely unashamed way they loved each other, and their daughter. Nobody at the party had even blinked an eye at them. And even I, a complete stranger, could instantly see how perfectly the four of them just fit together.

It was where my dream had stemmed from. That much was obvious. I'd been so vanilla all my life, I'd never even contemplated the idea of a threesome...let alone more. There was a reason I'd suddenly started visualizing myself surrounded by three eye-wateringly hot men. But if my dreams were anything to go by, there was a part of me that was curious about what it would be like to be wanted like that. To be someone's missing piece. To have a bond not with just one man, who made you feel safe and loved, but with three. To have an instant family.

Hell. It would make the feelings I had for Heath and Liam and the attraction I had to Rowe a whole lot easier to reconcile.

"I was dreaming about you, yes. But you weren't alone."

Liam's eyes widened. "Threesome?" he not so subtly groaned and adjusted himself in his shorts. "I can get on board with that."

I giggled. "It wasn't another girl. It was me, you...and two other guys."

Liam let out a surprised cough. "Okay then. I did not see that coming from you, Valedictorian. Whatever would Principal Jones say if he knew? Wait, Principal Jones wasn't in this dream as well, was he? He wasn't one of the other guys? I don't think I can get down with seventy-year-old wrinkled balls and flaccid dick."

"Oh my God." I burst out laughing. "Stop! You're awful. I'm sure Principal Jones can get it up just fine."

We both cringed and made faces at the very idea. Gag me with a spoon.

When we settled down, I pulled two bowls from the kitchen cupboard and a box of cereal from the pantry. I shook the box in Liam's direction, and he nodded, grabbing the milk from the refrigerator for me. I smiled at the easy and familiar gesture, silently happy that he was making himself at home in my apartment. I kind of liked it. It was nice to have someone here again, and for there to be laughter in this room. That hadn't happened since...

"Okay, are you ready to hear about who else was really in the dream?"

Liam did a little jog on the spot, shaking out his arms and legs like he was warming up for a marathon. "Okay. Give it to me quick. Rip the Band-Aid off. Who was getting jiggy in this dream with us?"

"Heath and Rowe."

To my surprise, Liam's mouth didn't drop open in surprise or disgust. He pondered the idea for a minute, then said, "Okay. I can handle that."

I paused in my cereal pouring. "Excuse me?"

He shrugged. "Honestly, if I was going to have group sex with you and I had to pick two other guys for it, they're exactly who I would have picked."

My mouth dropped open. "Seriously?"

"Seriously. Rowe is hot. I don't think there's a single human being on this planet who could truthfully say they didn't find that man attractive. What he's doing working in a shitty Saint View prison when he could be posing in front of a camera is beyond my comprehension."

"Totally agree. And Heath?"

Liam shrugged. "Not saying I'm into guys. But he's got that older mountain man, gruff and grumpy thing going on." He held one hand up. "Assuming that is, he actually didn't kill your sister, because I don't care how ruggedly handsome someone is. If they're into the stabby stabby, then it's a deal breaker."

I just stared at him. "The stabby stabby? Did you seriously just say that to me?"

He cringed. "Yeah, maybe that was a tad insensitive."

I snorted on my laughter. "No. It was actually pretty funny. Nobody else would dare make a joke like that with me, you know? Everybody walks on eggshells now."

"Lawyers aren't much good at that. I'm a bit like a bull in a china shop."

"I like it," I admitted.

"And I like you."

"Yeah?"

"Yeah. And while there isn't a whole lot I can do right now about getting Heath and Rowe in on the action, there are things I can do solo..."

His hand flattened on my thigh again and crept up toward my panties. Those tingles left over from my dream lit up again, urging his hand higher. But there was something my brain wouldn't let me move past without confirmation. "But if they were here, and willing..."

His fingers reached my hips and hooked around the fabric of my panties, slowly inching it down to bare my ass. "If they were here and willing, I'd be interested to see what happened. Now hold on to the countertop. Tight."

I sucked in a breath as he yanked my panties lower, until they pooled around my ankles. I did as I was told, holding on to the counter.

He stood behind me, drawing his fingertips up the backs of my legs, and then over my ass, until he found the hem of my nightshirt. He pushed it up, inch by agonizing inch, tugging it over my head. "Good girl," he whispered in my ear.

My core lit up in expectation, my nipples beading. I hadn't worn a bra to bed, so I was now completely naked, and he was still fully clothed.

But I already knew better than to try to touch him. He'd stop if I tried, and I really didn't want him to stop. Not after that dream. I needed the relief, either by my own hands or by his. And damn it, I wanted it to be his.

"Spread your legs. And lean forward a little. I want to see all of you, Mae."

I moaned, turned on by his dirty words and the wetness building at my core. He settled on his knees, and my own trembled at the knowledge of what he was going to do.

"Bend right over that countertop. I want to taste you."

Without any more warning than that, his hands parted my thighs and his face pushed up between them. His tongue was one long, tantalizing slow lick from my clit and right through my slick arousal.

He buried his face at the junction my legs like he'd been born for the job, no hesitation. His fingers dug into my thighs, almost to the point of punishing, but with the sole intent of not letting me move. His tongue was a wicked pleasure, one that I had little experience with, and none in the way he was doing it now. My ex had been halfhearted about going down on me at the best of times. But Liam ate me out as if determined to get a gold medal. When my legs trembled, he stood and spun me around, claiming my mouth instead, letting me taste myself on his tongue.

It should have been weird, or gross, but on Liam, it was just sinfully hot, and I wanted more.

Like he could read my mind, he hoisted me up onto the counter, the breakfast pushed aside and forgotten. And then he was laying me out, as if I was the meal. The stone countertop was cold at my back, but Liam's mouth was hot against my clit, and that warmth radiated through my entire body. On autopilot, one hand drifted to the back of Liam's head, the other to my breast. I rolled my nipple between two fingers, pinching it into a stiff peak that begged for more attention. I stroked my other hand through the lengths of his hair to stop myself from pushing down on the back of his head and holding him to me like I really wanted to.

Apparently, I wasn't the only one who wanted that. Liam's hand covered mine and planted it firmly on his head, encouraging me to hold him in place.

"Wanna fucking drown in you, Mae," he mumbled against my core.

When he was sure I'd received the memo, he removed his hand and instead used it to drive me higher. His fingers slipped up inside me, two from the very get-go, because I was so wet and ready for him. I writhed on the counter, my hips moving with a mind of their own, bucking and lifting off the surface, while my hand pressed down on his head, providing resistance to the ache growing inside me. His fingers started a slow pump, in and out, soft at first but then with a growing intensity that matched the need rolling through my body, demanding relief.

I drew my legs up so my heels dug into the countertop, my knees alternating between flopping wide to give him access to every inch of me, and clenching tight around his head as my orgasm tried to drag me under.

"Faster," I urged. "God, Liam. Harder."

He groaned, the noise muffled by his lips and tongue flush with my pussy. But his fingers picked up the tempo, fucking me with abandon until I was screaming his name. A bowl was knocked onto the floor. It shattered, but I barely noticed and I certainly didn't care. The need to come was overpowering, and I teetered on the edge.

"I need more," I moaned desperately. "I need your cock."

A third finger did the trick instead. I hurtled over the precipice and free fell into nothingness. The room swirled in a mass of colors behind my eyes, and sensation blocked out everything else. The orgasm roared like a lion released from its cage, and I bellowed Liam's name right along with it. He stroked my G-spot and clit simultaneously, while my toes curled and muscles clenched and relaxed around him, over and over until I was completely exhausted.

Eventually, I caught my breath, and my knees fell wide, releasing Liam from between my thighs. He stood slowly, reluctantly, and stared down at the junction of my thighs, still swollen and pulsing from being so thoroughly and utterly devoured. His lips shined with my arousal.

His erection strained long, hard, and thick behind his running shorts, absolutely nothing left to the imagination.

I sat up, scooting my ass to the edge of the countertop, so my legs dangled down, and drew him into me. I wrapped my arms around his neck and touched my breasts to his chest. Another kiss, just like the others we'd shared, spun my head.

He let me take control, let me thank him for the best orgasm ever with slow strokes of my tongue and presses of my lips. I liked the way he tasted of slick heat, and it only made me want to taste him more. The fabric of his shorts rubbed on my still sensitive flesh, and I wanted to take it away, to feel him skin to skin, and to make him feel as good as I felt right now.

I reached for the waistband of his shorts hesitantly, testing to see what he'd do. He groaned as my fingers slipped beneath the hem of his shirt and skated along the ridges of his lower abs. But he caught my wrist before I could get any farther. "We can't. We just lost an hour I wasn't counting on."

I glanced wildly at the clock on the oven and realized he was right. The man had been going down on me for an hour without a break, and I hadn't even offered him a coffee. There was also the mess the shattered bowl had made, that both of us had ignored. "Who cares about the time? I've got nowhere to be."

I kissed him again, the promise of more in the way I slid my tongue suggestively with his. But he pulled away, breathing hard. "Maybe not, but I do. I spoke to the police last night, and they've found no basis to Heath's claims that there was a gang involved in Jayela's murder."

My mouth dropped open, sexy times forgotten. "What? How can they say that? Heath's cellmate admitted it!"

"Prisoners talk shit. And talk is cheap."

My mind whirled. I watched our only real lead swirl around the drain, ready to disappear. I wanted to shove the plug in and capture it before it could. "What can we do?"

Liam bit his lip. "Remember what Heath said about going around the police? Doing whatever we had to? Well, I know a guy..."

I raised one eyebrow. "That sounds ominous."

Liam grimaced. "He's in the gang Heath mentioned. He might know something."

I slid down off the countertop and grabbed my nightshirt, tugging it over my head quickly, because I couldn't have this sort of conversation while I was stark naked. "Okay, so let's go."

"Not a chance. I'm keeping you in the loop, but I'm doing this alone."

I glared at him. "I'm going."

"Do you not remember what happened last time I took you to Saint View?"

"Yeah, I had a mind-blowing orgasm in an alley!"

He blinked and then let out a laugh. "Okay, I meant the drive-by shooting, but I suppose I should have been more specific."

The light moment broke the tension between us. And I threaded my fingers between his. "I'll be fine," I said softly.

"Don't shut me out. Nothing will piss me off more than you babying me."

"I'm just trying to look out for you... If anything happened to you..."

My heart flickered. Because that sounded like feelings talking, not just attraction. A little cloud of happiness started to form around me, but I had to ignore it because we had other things to do. I could unpack Liam's not-so-hidden intentions later. "I'm coming."

He sighed. "Then get dressed, because we won't be getting any information from these guys if you rock up with your gorgeous ass peeking out from beneath that shirt."

"It might help?" I grinned.

But Liam just glared at me. "I might have considered sharing you with Heath and Rowe, but don't even joke about a gang of thugs seeing you like this. No fucking way, Mae. I already have one murder trial to deal with, I don't need to be preparing to defend myself as well."

31

MAE

Even in the middle of the day, with a bright sun overhead and a flawless blue sky, Saint View was still a hard place to be. The light only showed the state of disrepair and poverty in this area more clearly. At night, shadows helped hide the graffiti on the abandoned houses. And the darkness covered the thugs that roamed the downtown strip, their gang tattoos worn proudly on their bare arms now that the weather was nice enough for it.

In the middle of the day, there was no hiding anything.

Except for the guy we'd come to look for, apparently.

"We're going to have to get out and ask around," Liam muttered, after we'd cruised the neighborhood for an hour, then abandoned that idea in favor of checking the strip.

I eyed three men standing on the corner, their motorcycle cuts declaring them members of a biker club. Their perfectly shined motorbikes gleamed in the midday sun, the light glinting off the polished chrome. All three turned in our direction as Liam parked his car at the top of the strip.

I unclicked my seat belt and waited for Liam to come around and open the door for me. By the time I got out, the three men had gone back to their conversation, seemingly uninterested in us. I breathed a sigh of relief. Liam and I had both dressed casually in jean shorts and T-shirts, and yet somehow, I was sure we stuck out like a couple of sore thumbs.

We moved slowly down the street, Liam reaching for my hand and threading his fingers between mine. He peered into the window of the tattoo shop but pulled away, shaking his head. At the barber shop, he opened the door and called out to the guy cutting hair. "You seen Hayden Whitling around lately?"

The man shook his head, and Liam sighed before moving on. We passed supermarkets and a gas station then stopped outside a building with a faded neon-pink sign that read Saint View Strip. It buzzed loudly, like it needed a good service. Liam tugged me toward the door.

I paused and grinned at him. "Bit early for a lap dance, don't you think?"

He chuckled. "You don't recognize the place?"

I peered past him to the painted black walls and the single door. There were no windows to give away what was going on inside, and it was the same as any other building on the strip to me. "No, should I?"

Liam led me over to door and stuck his finger in a small round hole in the wall beside it. "Eve missed one."

I did a double take, realization sinking in. He had his finger in a bullet hole. "Oh shit. This is Eve's place?" I hadn't even recognized it. We'd only gone in and out the back doors when we'd been here last.

He opened the door and led me through, into a darkened hallway. A guy about our age, his shoulders broad and strong with muscle beneath a tight black T-shirt, glanced up from his phone.

"Hey, Augie," Liam greeted.

"Eve ain't here," he replied, taking in Liam's outfit. "You look weird. Where's your suit?"

"Not here on official business for once."

Augie eyed Liam cautiously. "That's new. What do you want then?" His grin turned into something more suggestive. "I'm not working 'til later, but I could be persuaded to start early for the right price."

Liam chuckled. "Told you last time, bro. You ain't my type."

Augie's gaze ran along Liam's arm, taking in our joined hands, and then traveled up mine, finally settling on my face. "Yeah, but we all know you ain't fooling anyone. I like women, too, but ain't nobody saying you gotta pick a team. Or maybe your missus would like a show..."

Liam shook his head. "Not going to happen. But seriously, I came for a reason. Have you seen Hayden around lately? In the last week even? Anything?"

"Hayden?" He rolled the word around on his tongue like it was hard to pronounce. "Shit, that name's a blast from the past. Yeah, I seen him. But it'll cost ya."

Liam shook his head and pulled a fifty from his wallet, handing it over to the man. "You're a hustler. I'm adding that to your next legal bill. Start talking."

"His crew have been hanging out on Simpson Street. Holing up in the big house on the corner. You know it? Or you conveniently forgotten where that is? A private tour will cost you more."

Liam sighed. "Yeah, I know it. Thanks. Tell Eve I said hi, yeah?"

"She'll be pissed you didn't hang around and wait for her."

"Not today."

Augie shrugged. “Your funeral.”

“I’ll take my chances. See you around.”

Augie had already gone back to his phone, his interest in the two of us evaporated now that there was no chance of him getting any extra money.

Liam and I emerged back onto the strip, blinking rapidly in the bright light while our eyes adjusted from the dim of the strip club. He held my hand a little tighter as a wolf whistle pierced the air from somewhere down the street. “Just ignore it.”

I nodded and followed him further down the strip. We passed more tiny shops, each one dingier than the last. But the people inside didn’t seem to mind. There was laughter in the air as we passed a carryout place, and two women leaning against the wall of a healthcare clinic called out to Liam, saying it was good to see him. The shops gave way to government housing, and I gazed up at Liam, questions in my eyes. “I thought you didn’t do pro bono.”

The set of his jaw was tight, and he stared straight ahead, his gaze fixed on a house at the end of the street. “I don’t.”

“And yet everyone here seems to know you.”

“That’s different.”

“How?”

But Liam’s distracted gaze flickered all around us, instead of focusing on me. He darted a glance over his shoulder, back toward the strip we were leaving behind. “Walk faster.”

He picked up the pace, lengthening his stride and urging me to do the same.

“What? Why?” I glanced over my shoulder as well, following his line of sight.

A group of men strolled down the street behind us. There was nothing immediately threatening about them. No obvious weapons, or even any noticeable interest in us. They talked and laughed as they wandered like this was a Sunday afternoon and they didn't have any place else in the world they needed to be.

Liam didn't answer. Just hauled me along, and I doubled my pace to keep up with him, my heart picking up a more rapid beat, both from the increased physical effort of a faster gait, and from the vaguely threatened tone of Liam's voice. "Liam, talk to me."

"Those guys behind us are Saints."

"Not the nice kind who do good deeds and live a life of poverty and servitude, I'm guessing?"

"The poverty bit sounds about right, but not so much about the rest. They're part of the gang that run these streets. That DeWitt guy Heath told us about? He's in this crew, too."

I glanced over my shoulder again. There were five of them. Two of us. Maybe it was the rising sense of dread clouding my eyesight and turning a perfectly ordinary situation into something more, but it seemed as if they were a little closer than they had been a minute ago.

I suddenly had a vision of sheep being herded into a pen by a sheepdog. The dog didn't need to touch the sheep to get them to move. And yet he still managed to get them exactly where they wanted them.

"Should we go back to the car?" I clutched his fingers tighter, the faster pace no longer seeming like an inconvenience. Adrenaline started to fill my body, fueling my muscles.

"No. I think we're past that point. If we turn around, I'm one-hundred-percent sure they'll confront us. So unless you have hidden ninja skills I'm not aware of..." He threw me a wry grin.

But that nervous energy was taking a hold on me, and I couldn't return his smile.

He sobered quickly. "Hey. I got this. I got you. You don't need to worry, okay? We'll be fine. Just follow my lead."

Maybe he was using his secret sauce lawyer superpowers on me, but in that moment, I was willing to believe it. I sucked up Liam's assurances and the strength in the tight grip of his hand on mine. I let his confident posture and determined stride wrap around me like a safety blanket. And then I lifted my chin and strutted right alongside him.

"That's my girl."

"I like the sound of that," I whispered.

"Me, too."

A warm glowy buzz of happiness settled over me.

Only for it to disappear instantly as Liam led me up the path of the house on the corner.

It looked like we'd arrived.

32

LIAM

I banged on the wooden front door, cursing softly when a jagged splinter peeled off and stuck in my skin. I pulled it out quickly, leaving behind a drop of blood.

"You okay?" Mae asked.

"Yeah, fine."

We both knew we had bigger problems than a splinter.

I banged on the door again, ignoring the tiny spot of red that marred my hand. "Hayden! It's Liam."

The door opened, and a weedy-looking white guy with a plethora of tattoos covering every inch of exposed skin filled the doorway. "Quit fucking banging." He eyed me with a distinct lack of interest, and then his gaze slid to Mae. The man was missing a handful of teeth, and even from across the threshold, he reeked of weed. I somehow doubted that was the only drug he took. The missing teeth were a telltale sign of a meth habit.

Instinctively, I stepped an inch in front of Mae, partially shielding her.

She plastered herself to my back.

The gang member's perverted gaze had me wanting to

take a hot shower, I could only imagine how it made her feel. Even with me blocking his view, the man craned around, his gaze locked on Mae like he hadn't seen a woman in months. Anger and protectiveness rose in me all at once, but I needed to keep a cool head. Those guys who'd followed us down the street would be here any moment, and I needed to keep control of the situation.

I wished I hadn't brought Mae. I should have insisted she stay home. I could barely concentrate with the urge to keep her safe screaming at me. "I need to see Hayden."

The man finally turned his shrewd gaze to me. "Who?"

"Hayden Whitling. I know he hangs out here."

The man cocked his head to one side, stringy, dirty lengths of long hair falling over one shoulder. "Don't know anyone by that name."

I ground my molars together, the noise audible. "Just get him."

The man narrowed his eyes. "Told you. I don't know anyone named Hayden."

A chill skated down my spine. From behind me came the sound of footsteps. I didn't need to glance over my shoulder to know it was the guys who'd been following us down the street.

Every muscle in my body tensed, ready for a fight. It had been a lifetime since I'd been here, surrounded by men like this, but it wasn't something you forgot quickly. Where you came from. How you'd been brought up.

"Maybe we should just go," Mae suggested quietly. "If Hayden isn't here..."

"Nah, stay awhile," one of the guys said from behind me. "I can be your Hayden, baby."

Mae curled her fingers into the back of my shirt. The precarious situation teetered on spiraling out of control.

Loss of control wasn't something I was comfortable with. But I was also a good liar. And I could fake it if I had to.

"They mean me, you idiots," a deep voice came from inside the house. "Get out of the way, Winger."

The guys behind me shut up instantly, and Winger, the runty tattooed guy, stepped aside.

Mae gasped.

I already knew why.

The man who appeared in the doorway was easily six foot four. His broad shoulders filled the narrow space, a white wifebeater hugged his chest.

His gray eyes stared out from beneath a black baseball cap.

Eyes that were identical to mine.

Whereas Winger had focused on Mae with barely concealed desire, Hayden's gaze didn't stray in her direction for even an instant. He saw nothing but me. "Hey, big brother. Long time, no see."

"What?" Winger squawked. "You got a brother, Chaos? And since when is your name Hayden?"

Hayden fixed the smaller man with a hard glare. "Are you seriously that fuckin' dumb? Do you really think my mother named me Chaos?"

Winger shrugged and disappeared into the depths of the house. At the jerk of Hayden's head, the five men behind me silently formed a single line and edged around us to follow Winger. One of them even politely excused himself, which had me at a complete loss for words.

Hayden's gaze finally flickered to mine. "Who's this?"

"Mae, meet my brother, Hayden. Or do you prefer Chaos?" I wrinkled my nose. "I don't think I can call you that. Where did that come from anyway?"

Hayden held a hand out to Mae, and she took it. "Nice to meet you," she said.

But his attention was already back on me. I glanced at Mae, and her confusion was clear in her expression. I could practically see her mind whirling with questions, the main one being, how on earth clean-cut, highly educated Liam Banks had a brother who ran a gang.

The answer was long and twisted, and not one to be given right now, when there were more pressing matters at hand.

"I don't know," Hayden said. "Chaos follows me. And so does the name. Winger is a dumbass, but barely any of the guys here now know me as anything else. Been a long time since someone called me Hayden."

I cringed at what felt like a hidden barb. "I know I haven't been around..."

Hayden scoffed. "Understatement of the century. It's been years since I've seen you."

"It's not like you invited me for Sunday night dinner."

"Would you have come if I had?"

"Of course I would have."

"Doubtful."

I sighed. "Look, I didn't come here to get in an argument with you. "

"Nah, you came because you want something. No other reason you'd be here, right?"

I ignored him in the way only brothers could. "Was there a hit out on Jayela Donovan?"

"Who?"

"The cop who was killed in her apartment a few weeks back. Not asking if you did it—"

"Oh, that's rich. Of course you fucking think I did it."

"Can you blame me?"

"You know what, brother? You got a real funny way of asking for help. One that feels a whole lot more like you looking down on me and treating me like the scum on your shoes." He stepped back and went to close the door in our faces.

I stuck my foot out and caught the door with the heel of my hand. "No, stop. Wait. I'm sorry. That was a low blow. I swear, I didn't come here to get into it with you."

"Jayela was my sister," Mae said quietly.

Hayden and I both glanced over at her in surprise. She'd gone completely quiet as the two of us squabbled like we had as kids.

"Please. If you know anything..." Her voice dropped to a desperate whisper.

Hayden studied her, sizing her up, assessing to see if she was worth his time and effort. Or perhaps determining how she could be useful to him in the future if he helped her now. You never knew with him. His gaze flicked to me before it focused back on her, but I didn't miss the flash of pain in his gaze that he tried to bury.

It cut through me like a knife.

"I know what it's like to lose a brother," Hayden said slowly.

The knife twisted. We'd been close once, the two of us. But now there was nothing left of our relationship.

Hayden's gaze raked over Mae. "You got cameras or microphones on you or something?"

"No," I assured him. "Nothing like that."

"Because I will fucking kill you myself if you're lying to me."

I swallowed hard. This man might have been my blood, but he wasn't the kid I remembered. He was colder. Harder.

There was an edge to him that I'd lost or maybe never had at all. "She's a teacher. Not a cop."

Hayden finished his assessment. "Yeah, there was a hit on her. But don't ask me who carried it out because I honestly don't know. Not that I'd tell you anyway, even if I did, but that's the truth."

"Bullshit," I interrupted. "You know. You telling me that someone took out a cop and then didn't run his mouth about it?"

Hayden lifted one shoulder. "Ain't all of us as dumb as Winger. Some of us are smart enough to know when to keep our mouths shut."

"Could it have been DeWitt?" Mae asked. "He said he ordered the hit, but maybe he carried it out, too..."

A slow grin spread across Hayden's face, before a chuckle built steadily from deep inside his chest.

"What's funny about that?" I demanded.

"Everything. DeWitt?" He snorted. "DeWitt is a low-level nothing. He couldn't order a hit if his life depended on it. He ain't got the authority, or the know-how. And he certainly couldn't carry one out. Man is dumber than dogshit."

I frowned. "He's running around Saint View Prison right now, telling everyone he runs your crew. Even the guards have an eye on him. He's got pull. The men are following him."

Hayden rolled his eyes. "He can say what he likes on the inside. And if those other dumbasses in there want to follow his lead, then that's their problem. They've got an IQ of about three between the lot of them. How do you think they all wound up in there, while the rest of us are out here walking around? The dumb go down. The smart stay free. That's how it is around here. I'm telling you now, DeWitt didn't order that hit. Or execute it. He's not the person in there you need to worry about."

"Who is then?" Mae asked.

"Come on. You trying to get a bullet in my back?"

Mae blanched. "Of course not. But someone I care about very much is in there, and if he's in danger..."

Hayden glanced over his shoulder and then stepped out of the doorway fully, closing the heavy door behind him. He spoke to me. "Put a new roof on mom's place, and I'll tell you."

I frowned. "She needs a new roof?"

"The place leaks like a fucking sieve every time it rains."

I ran my hand through my hair, guilt and remorse chewing away at me like a rodent. "I send her checks all the time. She never cashes them."

"Yeah, trust me. That's a bone of contention between her and me, too. I've been telling her for years that she needs to take your money, but she won't. So just pay a fucking company to get out there and do the work."

I could do that. "Done. And anything else she needs as well. Just tell me. I'll get it sorted."

Hayden eyed me. "You actually mean that, don't you?"

"I do. I want to help her. And you, too, if you'll let me."

Hayden shook his head. "That ship has sailed, brother. I'm all grown up now. Don't need your help no more."

We stared at each other, years of history tightening the air around us until the tension was almost unbearable.

Hayden was the one to break it, steering the conversation away from our nonexistent brotherhood. "Anyway. DeWitt ain't your problem. If you got someone on the inside you care about? Tell them to stay away from Scythe. He's ten times worse than DeWitt could ever hope to be."

"Scythe?" I scoffed. "That his weapon of choice or something?"

"If the rumors are true, it is."

I balked. "You serious?"

Hayden shrugged. "He's somewhat of an urban legend around here. That he uses a scythe to slash the throats of his victims. So I don't know if there's any truth to the story or not. But apparently the guy was born with a scythe-shaped birthmark on the back of his hand. He treats it like a calling."

"Jesus," Mae whispered. "My sister's throat was slashed."

"Jesus won't help you with him, lady."

I drew his attention back to me. "And this guy is in your crew? Got a legal name?"

Hayden shook his head. "We don't do legal names around here."

"Okay, well is he here? Can we talk to him?"

Hayden stared at me, then grabbed me roughly by the arm and yanked hard. "What the fuck, Liam? You've been out of Saint View so long you don't get how this place runs anymore. *Can we talk to him?*" He threw my words back at me in a high-pitched taunt. "No, you can't fucking talk to him! Scythe ain't just a regular gangbanger. He isn't hanging around on the streets with the rest of us and doing petty crimes. He's the real deal. The guy is a complete nutjob. A real screw loose sort of guy, you know? You could invite the guy to dinner at your granny's house, and he'd stab her right through the heart for getting a lump in his gravy, then he'd sit back down and finish his meal. He's *that* sort of psycho. The Mafia go to him when they want someone taken out quietly. If there was a hit that nobody is taking the glory for, but the target is dead, it was probably him. The man's reputation is legendary enough. He's swift and vicious. Deadly."

I shook my brother off. “Well how do *you* talk to him then?”

“I don’t. And I hope I never do. He finds you. And if he does...”

A chill skated down my back.

“...you’d better fucking run.”

33

MAE

That night at the men's prison, distraction racked me to my core. For once, I was glad my class was full. I put a blackboard of verb conjugations up, then wandered the aisles of my classroom, studying each man's hands, looking for scythe-shaped birthmarks.

Vincent peered up at me curiously as I hovered over him. "Are you okay, Miss Donovan?"

I scanned his hands quickly. No birthmarks or tattoos, so I forced a smile. "I'm fine. Thank you." And then I moved to the next prisoner to do the same.

Before I'd quite finished checking the whole class, Rowe pulled me into the empty corridor, shutting the class in.

"What are you doing?"

I confessed everything. From going to Saint View with Liam, meeting his brother, and finishing with, "Do you keep records of the men's tattoos and distinguishing marks?"

He nodded. "Tattoos, sure. They're periodically photographed."

"But birthmarks, though? Do any of them have a scythe-shaped birthmark on their hand?"

He frowned. "Scythe-shaped? I've no idea. When we photograph tattoos, we're looking for gang symbols mostly, so we know who runs with who on the outside. It helps us separate rival gangs and keep fights to a minimum. Birthmarks are only photographed if they're prominent and used as identification. There might be a photo of a birthmark on a hand if it's dark enough, but we don't exactly have a 'weapon-shaped' tag on the system, like we do for gang affiliation. It would just be in the guy's regular file."

"So I'd have to go through every man's file in order to find something like that?"

Rowe nodded. "If there was a photo taken at all. If the birthmark is faint, or the intake officer on the day was in a rush, they wouldn't have bothered."

I groaned. "There's hundreds of men in this prison. This is like looking for a needle in a haystack."

"Heath's a big boy. He can look after himself."

"Can't you do something?"

Rowe shrugged. "Like what? There was no direct threat made. This whole prison is filled with violent men, Mae. You can't forget that. Even if we could identify him, this scythe guy is no more a threat than any of the others. They're all capable of messed-up things."

I understood his point, but that wasn't going to stop me worrying about Heath. I couldn't get the things Liam's brother had said out of my mind.

After shift, I retrieved my phone from my locker and checked it, hoping for a message from Liam. There were missed calls and a voicemail, but they were from Tori. With Liam still on my mind, I hit the voicemail button and held the phone to my ear.

"Mae! I just got off the phone with my priest! We did it! The warden at the prison approved two visitors to the infirmary on a

weekly basis to bless the sick, deliver last rites, and take confession from anyone who wants to participate. We start tomorrow afternoon..."

Whoa. We?

The rest of her voicemail was her prattling on about how she'd be assisting the priest during each of his sessions, since they didn't have any nuns who could attend. He wanted a woman to be in attendance when he was working with the female prisoners.

My immediate gut reaction was to ring her back and tell her no.

The exact same reaction she'd had to me taking a job here.

But Tori hadn't been able to stop me, and I knew I wouldn't be able to stop her either. There was such excitement in her message, one I hadn't heard in her voice for a while. She loved her stay-at-home mom role, but she'd lost a little piece of herself when she'd finished up at her social work job. She was missing that part of her life. Tori was a good person to the very bone. Her calling in life was to help other people, and maybe this wasn't the way either of us had expected her to do that, but I knew it would be important to her.

So I didn't call her back and try to talk her out of it. Instead, I sent her a Muppet flailing GIF, Kermit flapping his arms around wildly, to express my excitement. This was good news, I reminded myself. They'd assign Tori and her priest a guard, and she'd be just as safe as I was.

I got in my car, with the intention of heading home. I twisted around the streets, driving without thinking. But it wasn't my house I found myself in front of. Without even thinking about it, I'd blown straight past my own street and deeper into Providence, parking in front of Liam's place. It was late, but I didn't call. I just took the fancy elevator up to his apartment on the top floor and waited for him to open the door.

I didn't even bother with a hello as it swung open. I'd spent all afternoon and evening stewing on what had happened that morning, and I didn't have the energy left for polite greetings. "What's going on with you?"

It was lucky I'd got the words out before my eyes actually registered more than just Liam's face. Because the man wore nothing but soft gray sweatpants, the drawstring loose and hanging low on his hips. His bare chest, that seemed perfectly sculpted by gods, was enough to make any woman forget what words were altogether.

"Hi, Mae, nice to see you, too. What's going on with you?"

"Don't dodge the question."

His eyebrows pulled together. "I'm not. But it's kind of a general question. What's going on with me right now is that I just opened the door and found the woman of my dreams standing there looking smoking hot. Yay for me."

"Flattery will get you nowhere. You know what I'm talking about. What the hell was all of that today? You take me to Saint View and then all of a sudden we're in gang territory and you have a brother?"

He sighed. "You want to come in? Or are we just going to do this in the hallway?"

I eyed his bare chest again, gaze dipping low to the cut ridges of abs and those delicious V lines running down either side of his hips.

When I dragged my gaze back to his face, he was smirking.

God, he was cute when he smirked like that.

"I think we should do this in the hallway." I seriously

didn't trust myself to walk inside with him. I had a feeling that if I did, we wouldn't be talking for long. I could already feel my resistance slipping, even though this conversation was long overdue.

Liam took a step into the hallway. "Okay. If you insist." He took another step, and then another.

I held my hands up. "Hey. Stop there. I know what you're doing."

Liam raised one perfect eyebrow. "I've no idea what you're talking about."

I couldn't help but laugh. "Oh, you know exactly what you're doing."

I moved a few inches backward, trying to keep the distance between us, but Liam was having none of it. He stalked me across the hall, like a panther. A six-foot, tanned, completely fuckable wild animal. My back hit the wall, and Liam followed in close, caging me in, his chest pressed to mine. I got a hand up in between us, pressing my palm over one of his pecs, trying to keep a tiny bit of distance. But Liam had other ideas. His nose ran up the side of my neck and inhaled, sending goosebumps across my skin. His lips landed on my neck, soft and teasing, licking and kissing.

"Yeah. You're right. I do know what I'm doing." His tongue flickered over the shell of my ear, and all coherent thought flew out of my head.

I fought desperately to drag it back in. "Nope." I dodged his tongue, though I couldn't get far with his hands on the wall either side of me. "We're not playing it like this." I ducked beneath his arm and then dodged my way around him, forcing him in a circle so it was his back against the wall. Our positions effectively reversed.

"How are we playing it then?" Liam's look of pure amusement was both infuriating and hot as hell.

I picked up where he'd left off. I closed in on him, pushing my chest against his and my lips to his neck. I swirled the pattern up toward his ear and then let my lips brush over it as I whispered, "We play my way now."

He groaned. "Why does that sound so dirty?"

"Because it can be, if you let it."

"Go on then," he challenged. "State your rules."

"You answer a question, you get a reward."

He chuckled. "Does that reward involve me getting you naked? Because it's really the only reward I'm interested in."

It wasn't exactly what I'd been planning. I'd been planning on getting him a whole lot more naked. But if that's what it took to get him talking, I could probably be convinced. He did look insanely good in those pants.

"Fine. Question first, though."

"I like it when you're bossy."

I liked when he was bossy. But I had a mission. And I wasn't going to be swayed. Well, not swayed too much anyway. I was already anticipating getting naked with him. But questions first. "What's going on with your family?"

Liam slumped back against the wall. "Too broad a question. Be more specific."

"Fair enough. Why did your mom run away from you at the shelter the other day?"

He sighed heavily. "Because they hate my guts? Until recently I hadn't seen either her or Hayden in years." He said it with such sadness that it made me forget the little game we were playing for a moment.

"Why? I can tell from the look on your face, and the way that you talk about them, that it's not what you want. Whatever happened between you guys, just fix it."

He ran a hand through his hair. "You think I haven't tried? It's not that simple. Our history is complicated. I've spent years trying to get them to forgive me. Nothing I do is going to change their minds. It's my fault. I ruined things between us, and there's no going back. As much as I might want to change things, we don't get everything we want."

I wanted to prod more, but I could see that it was hurting him. That wasn't why I'd come here. I hadn't come to pry into his life. I just wanted to know him better. I wanted to understand him.

So I kissed him softly instead. I let my lips part and ran my tongue along the seam of his mouth. He was stiff and unresponsive for a moment, but then he sank in, wrapping his arms around me, and opening his mouth to kiss me back. I pressed against him, his back to the wall, and let our tongues dance.

Just like always, Liam's kisses were everything. The sun, the moon, the air. Everything all rolled into one blinding moment, where it just felt right. When we pulled back, he continued his story without any prodding from me.

"Hayden and I have different dads. Neither of them in the picture, both of them took off after they knocked our mom up. But while Hayden's dad was just some guy from the hood, my dad grew up here."

"In Providence?"

"Yep. James McIntosh Banks. Son of William Easton Banks. The very definition of old-school money. That time you came to my party in high school? That was my grandparents' place. I lived with them through all of high school."

I let my lips drift from his and across his jawline, kissing a trail toward his neck, thinking it might be easier for him to say his truth if he didn't have to look me directly in the face. "Why not your dad? Why live with his parents?"

He scoffed. "Never met the guy. My dad is a piece of shit. Money doesn't make you a good person. Quite the opposite, in fact, if you ask me. He took off the moment my mother told him she was pregnant. Got a job on the other side of the world, denying he was my father."

My heart broke for Liam. I hated my dad, too, but at least he'd never denied that he was my father in the first place. That was a different sort of betrayal altogether.

"So how did you come to live with your grandparents?"

Liam's fingers found the hem of my shirt and slipped beneath it, his warm palm flattening against the small of my back. He stroked tiny patterns there with the tips of his fingers. "My grandfather is a better man than his son. He sent my mom money when I was little. And he visited sometimes. When my mom told him about how well I was doing in school, he started taking an even bigger interest. My grandfather values intelligence above all else. My father was a disappointment to him, and I think he saw me as a second chance to get it right."

"So he paid for your schooling?"

Liam nodded. "Yes. Pulled me from the public school and put me in at Edgely Academy."

There was something I wasn't understanding, though. "Your mom wasn't happy about that, though? Edgely is a great school. Ranked one of the highest in the state. I would have thought she would be happy for you?"

Something clouded Liam's bright-blue gaze. "She was happy for me to get a good education. She cried happy tears the day my grandfather turned up on our porch and declared he was going to send me to Edgely. He'd already bought me a uniform and everything. I just remember her hugging him, and then hugging me, and her tears of happiness soaking through my T-shirt. She'd whispered in my ear about this being my big break, and how this would change my life."

"Sounds like it did..."

"Yeah. It changed it, but I'm still not sure if it was for the better. I moved in with my grandfather, so I would be close to school. That house was insane. My mother's entire house could have fit in the foyer alone. A foyer! Who the hell needs a foyer anyway? What's the purpose, apart from looking grand and letting people know how much money you have? It's a complete and utter waste of space and money."

I had to agree. But I didn't want to interrupt him. "How did that turn into your mother and brother not speaking to you, then?"

His gaze flickered to the ceiling, and his head dropped back on his shoulders. "Because I was a dickhead. I let it all go to my head. I started believing the crap they were filling my head with at school. That Edgely men were made for greatness. And there was more of that at home, as my grandfather tried to mold me in his own footsteps. He'd failed with my father, so he doubled down with me, making sure I excelled. I was his chance for redemption, you know? He'd lost face with my dad being a bit of a wild child. But I was the model student. Top of the class. Star baseball player. Ivy League college-bound."

He paused and finally looked down at me with glassy eyes. "All the potential in the fucking world and at the same time, completely ashamed of where I came from. Of *who* I came from. I stopped telling my mom when school functions were because I was embarrassed. The other kids' moms were trophy wives, perfectly polished and scrubbed in their designer suits. And my mom's shoes had holes in them. With me moving in with my grandfather, he stopped giving her money. I didn't really put it all together at the time, but now..." He sighed heavily. "The wedge just grew deeper and deeper between me and them. Hayden started going down the wrong path, and my mom tried to get me to step in and be a role model for him. But by then I was sixteen, and I had a flashy new car and was busy using it to pick up girls. I didn't want my thirteen-year-old brother cramping my style. And so I started ignoring her calls. I'd groan when her number would show up on my phone and pretend, even to myself, that I was too busy to take the call. Or that I'd call her back later. I never did."

My heart ached for him. The level of disgust and shame he'd bestowed on himself was thick. Anyone could see that. His words dripped with regret and longing. A longing to change the past. Though none of us could do that. I knew that just as well as anyone. "You were sixteen, Liam. Sixteen-year-old boys are dumb. And selfish. And self-absorbed."

"I was embarrassed by them."

I shook my head. "You were trying to fit in."

"Yeah. But in trying to fit in, I pushed them away. I told my mom I needed space, and that I couldn't constantly be worrying about her, and what she and Hayden were doing. I had a head full of exams, college applications, parties, girls, sports, and friends, and I was constantly trying to impress my grandfather. He wanted me to be a lawyer, like him. And I wanted it, too. I'm good at this job, Mae. Really good. But I let wanting this life consume the one I had. I let it swallow me up and spit me back out a completely different person. One who came from money and had every opportunity right there at his fingertips. I was not longer Liam Whitling. I was Liam Banks. And sometimes..."

My heart broke for him. For the decisions he'd made as a boy, and how they affected him now as a man. For his mother and her hurt. For the little brother he'd left behind, not given the same opportunities because of nothing more than circumstance. I trailed my fingers down the sides of his face. "Sometimes what?"

"Sometimes I don't even want to be him. Sometimes I just want to go back to being Liam Whitling. The boy who had nothing but his mother and brother. That kid was happy, you know? Before his greed got the better of him and he forgot where he came from."

I pressed up onto my toes and kissed his lips softly. "You're incredibly hard on yourself, you know? Sixteen-year-old boys make bad decisions all the time. Your mom could have kept trying."

But he shook his head. "It isn't her fault. She was just doing what I asked."

"Maybe so. But what's her excuse for staying away now?"

"She hates me."

"She doesn't. No mother hates her child." Or so I'd been led to believe, anyway. I had no experience with a mother figure myself. Unless Jayela counted. But she'd only been a few years older than me and had never been much of the warm and snuggly kind of person.

"I don't know how to fix it. I've been sending her checks for years, but every single one of them has gone uncashed. I know she gets them. I started driving over there every week and putting them beneath her door just so I could be sure. But still the money sits in my bank account." He threw up his hands. "I don't need all this fucking money. You saw her, Mae! She is eating in a homeless shelter. Why won't she cash the checks? There's more than enough money there to buy food, clothes. She wouldn't have to work as hard as she does."

I squinted at him. "Maybe what she needs from you isn't money."

"Then what?"

I trailed my hand down his chest, rubbing soothing circles over it as I went. "Maybe she just wants your time."

"Then why does she run away every time I do see her?" He grew more and more agitated with every word. He pulled away from me and paced down the short hall. There were no other doors on this level. He owned the entire top floor. "Why doesn't she just stay and let me explain? Let me apologize?"

He caught himself in the middle of the hall. His gaze locked with mine. "Shit. I'm sorry. You don't need me dumping all of this on you after everything you've been through. Fuck. I must sound like that poor little rich boy, right?"

I closed the distance between us, wrapping my arm around him and resting my head against his chest. "No. You sound like a man who made a mistake and wants to make up for it. You sound like a man who misses his family. I know what that feels like." Because I had no one either. I didn't talk to my father, and unlike Liam, I had no desire to. I just wanted my sister back. She was all I'd ever wanted in a family. But now I had no one.

I leaned back and stared up at him.

He dropped his forehead to mine and closed his eyes. Mine drifted shut as well, and we stood there like that, in the middle of the hallway, our breaths mingling, while we both drowned in our feelings. "I don't want to be sad all the time," I whispered.

"Me neither."

His mouth found mine, slow and steady. There was no heat or urgency in his kiss. It was full of heart-breaking sadness that called to the darkness inside me. It called to the heartache I'd buried deep, just so I could function. But his pain urged mine to the surface.

And I clung to him like he was a lifeboat in a thrashing ocean.

He held me the same way. His strong arms circled me, crushing me to his chest, his palms flat on my back and holding me close.

"It's all I think about when I'm alone," I admitted to him. "I think about the way she died. It's my fault."

"It's no more your fault than it is mine. You can't think like that."

"But I do," I said sadly. "I do. I don't know how to stop. It's easier to just throw everything into getting Heath out of jail. Into kissing you. Into arguing with Rowe. Everything is just easier when the three of you are around to keep me occupied. When I'm alone, all I do is think."

Liam kissed me again, and I melted into his touch. He knew what I needed. And I knew what he needed. Our touches grew faster, harder. Within minutes we went from soft and sad, to fast and frantic. I fumbled with the drawstring on his sweatpants, loosening it enough to get my hands down the front. He wasn't wearing underwear, and I took his cock in one hand and his balls on the other.

He let out a hiss. "Mae..."

I stroked him beneath his pants, and he grew beneath my touch. "Please, Liam. I want to touch you."

"We're in the hallway."

"And the other day we were in an alleyway. I can't help when I want you." I dropped to my knees and dragged his sweatpants down his muscular thighs. At least this time there was no chance of being caught. There was no reason for anyone to come up to this floor but us.

He groaned and brushed the hair back off my face. "Mae... What are you doing?"

"Getting you hard?"

It was enough to lighten the mood. And I was grateful for it. Because there was only so much heartache I could handle. And I was pretty sure Liam and I had both reached our max capacity.

He chuckled. "Well, you're doing a good job of it."

I grinned up at him, my mouth hovering mere inches from the blunt head of his dick. "I'll take that compliment."

"Should I give you some more?"

I teased him, letting the tip of him brush over my lips. "Sure. Everybody likes a compliment."

"You've never looked more sexy than you do right now. With my cock at your lips, and your hand wrapped around it. It's taking everything in my power to hold back."

I let my tongue dart out and taste him.

He hissed, and my taste buds yelped in joy at his arousal.

His hand dropped to the back of my head, his fingers stroking through my hair, pushing it back off my face. "You're making it really difficult to just stand here, Mae. I want to... Fuck."

God, he was so hard. Liam with a full erection was the hottest thing I'd ever seen. His dick was big and thick, and his abs flexed beneath my touch. I gazed up at him, watching the flare of heat in his eyes. His fingers clenched into fists at his sides. His entire body tensed. He wasn't joking when he said he was struggling to hold back. But something deep inside me didn't want him to. He was battling that urge to dominate, struggling with a control I'd taken from him. And maybe I was willing to give some of it back.

"You want to what? Tell me."

His breath hitched. "You don't want to know."

"Try me."

He swallowed hard. "Open your mouth."

A surge of heat flared between my thighs. I let my lips part.

He dropped one hand to the back of my head, wrapping the length of my ponytail around his fingers. My breath quickened as he twisted it, a slight tugging sensation prickling at my scalp pleasantly. He tugged it down, so my chin and lifted. "I want to feel your mouth on me, Mae. I want to feel your tongue slide along the ridges, and the head…"

"What else? Tell me," I urged. I discreetly pressed my thighs together, trying to find relief for the aching need growing at my core. I just wanted him to keep talking. Keep telling me what to do. I had no idea why I liked it so much. I'd never been like this with anybody else.

He tugged my hair a little harder. "You really want to know?"

I nodded.

"I want to thrust deep into your mouth, I want to feel it hit the back of your throat. But I don't want you doing anything you don't want to do. So the ball's in your court. I'm going to stand here and not move. No matter what it takes." He let go of my hair and pressed his palms to the wall behind him, his forearm shaking with the effort.

Just like that, I was suddenly determined to make him move. To make him lose control. And so I opened my mouth and gave him what he wanted. I wrapped my lips around the tip of him and let my tongue glide beneath. He was velvet over steel, pleasantly warm, and by far the biggest man I'd ever had there. I started soft and slow, working just the head of him inside my mouth and then pulling away only to repeat the process. True to his word, Liam didn't move his hips. But his head dropped back against the wall, and his eyes closed, his bliss etched into his expression

He'd been wanting this. I could tell without him even

saying a word. He'd gotten me off multiple times and never even let me touch him once. And yet now, as I worked him in and out of my mouth, taking him deeper with every bob of my head, he was finally surrendering. Minute by minute, tiny pieces of his control ebbed away, until I was taking him deep into the back of my throat and loving every second of it. Every minute that passed only made me want him more. I wanted his hands in my hair. I wanted him to pull it like he had earlier. I wanted to make his hips jerk. I wanted him thrusting into my mouth when he came.

"Mae," he groaned.

My core gave a steady thump of excitement. This was it. The moment he completely came undone. I gazed up at him, his dick still deep in my mouth.

His gaze burned. "Put your hand up the front of your skirt," he directed. "Into your panties."

My eyes flared, and arousal built low inside me. I moved away from him so I could speak. Heat blushed my cheeks. "I've never…"

His gaze turned incredulous. "You've never touched yourself?"

I shook my head. "No. I have. Just never…"

"Never with someone watching you?"

Yes. That. Exactly that.

I didn't have to answer. The look on my face must have told him everything. "I want to watch you touch yourself, Mae. My dick in your mouth, and your hand in your panties. Fuck!"

Precum beaded on the head of his cock. I licked it away quickly, delighting in what I was doing to him. What we were doing together. The need building inside me was so intense, I needed the relief. And so I did what he said. I wrapped my lips around his cock, sucking him deep into my throat once more, and pushed my free hand beneath my skirt and between my thighs.

I held Liam's gaze as my fingertip touched my clit. I moaned around the thick length of him, rubbing little circles over myself in just the way I liked.

Liam's breaths grew ragged, and to my delight, his hips jacked off the wall, thrusting shallowly into me.

So when he jerked out of my mouth completely, surprise punched through me. I glanced up at him. "What's wrong?"

He was breathing hard. His gorgeous, solid chest heaving with the strain. He stared down at me. "No. I want more. I want everything."

In one fast move, he had me up off the floor and slung over his shoulder. I squealed in surprise as I hung down his back, then laughed when he had to waddle through his apartment door with his pants around his ankles.

"Shit," he swore, kicking the door closed behind us. "I did not think this through. It was hot in my head."

"I have a perfect view of your ass from back here. It was a good idea, trust me." I wasn't lying. Liam's bare ass was a thing of beauty. I wondered how many squats the guy had to do to get that sort of muscle tone. Probably more per day than I'd done in a lifetime.

He threw me down on his bed, a little cloud of soft mattress, fluffy pillows, and pure-white sheets. I'd barely had time to bounce before he was ripping off my skirt and panties and stepping out of his sweatpants. When I was naked from the waist down, he stood back. "Show me."

I knew what he meant. Quickly, I unbuttoned my shirt and let it fall away to expose my bra. It did up at the back, but I was too impatient to sit up and peel them off. And so I just flipped the cups down and took one breast in my hand, pinching my nipple into a taut peak. The other hand dipped between my legs once more and picked up the rhythm I'd started on my clit in the hallway.

Liam's groan of ecstasy was everything. "Don't stop."

I couldn't now, even if I'd wanted to. He had his hand wrapped around his cock, pumping it slowly while he watched me. In unison we worked ourselves harder and faster, until my moans matched his.

"Liam," I groaned, nearing the edge. But it wasn't enough for me to work my clit alone.

Liam seemed to come to the same conclusion. He reached for his bedside table, opening the top drawer, and pulled out a condom. He made short work of rolling it over himself, and then he was between my legs, hovering over me and pushing them wide.

He notched himself at my entrance, the tip of him sliding through the wetness easily, and my thighs trembling with the need to have him inside me. I worked my clit harder, but it wasn't enough to get me over the edge. "I need you," I whispered.

"I need you, too," he replied. He paused for a moment, and in the silence between us, there were words unsaid. Silent thoughts that made me think that maybe he needed me for more than just a release.

I wasn't ready to go there. Not yet. We'd come a long way in such a tiny space of time, but for now, I couldn't process those feelings. They were too big. Too all consuming. Too difficult to reconcile with other feelings that wrapped themselves around my heart.

But then Liam was pushing inside me, my body welcoming him home, and all other thoughts flew out of my mind. We both groaned together. And then he kissed me, swallowing my moans of ecstasy as his cock stretched me deliciously. He rocked himself in and out of my body, his momentum slowly picking up until his thrusts matched the tempo of my fingers on my clit.

It was me who fell over the cliff first. Ecstasy rushed through my body, starting deep within me and burying its way into every fiber of my being. It tunneled through my core and radiated out through my limbs until every inch of me spasmed and tingled and cried out with joy.

My internal walls clamped down around Liam and sent him flying over into his own abyss. His shout as he barreled into an orgasm was muffled by his mouth on mine, and our tongues tangling, the kisses urgent and needy and messy. He thrust himself in and out of my tight core, riding both of our orgasms out for as long as either of us could stand, until I was oversensitive and begging for mercy.

I wrapped my legs around him and he sank down on top of me. His weight was heavy and warm, a slight sheen of sweat covering both of our naked bodies.

"You know something?" he murmured into the crook of my neck.

I trailed my fingers up and down his bare back. "What's that?"

"I'm really glad I never asked you out in high school now."

I pushed him off me just a little, so I could see his face. He was flushed pink from exertion, but his smile was ear to ear, and that glint in his eyes had me wondering how quickly he'd be up for a second round. "Why is that?"

"Because I've never had first-time sex like that. With anyone. And somehow, I don't think little Mae Donovan, the valedictorian of Providence School for Girls, would have let me fuck her mouth in the middle of the hallway when we were seventeen."

I grinned at him. "And I don't think cocky, arrogant Liam

Banks, valedictorian of Edgeley Academy, could have lasted that long. I heard the rumors about you. One and done, right?"

It wasn't true. I hadn't heard any rumors. But it was fun to tease him.

Liam's mouth dropped open. "Who told you that? I'm going to call them right now and demand a retraction. Just give me a name."

I laughed and pulled his mouth to mine once more. And when he deepened the kiss, I let him show me again that he had the stamina to prove my fake rumor wrong.

34

HEATH

I was sick of other men. So incredibly over their constant talk. There was never a minute alone. Or a minute of silence. Every minute of every freaking day was filled with the complete and utter garbage they spewed. One-upping each other. Talking about the crimes they'd committed and the women they'd screwed on the outside, like each one was some sort of medal to hang around their necks.

I just wanted them all to go away. To leave me in peace.

I didn't want to make friends, or alliances. I didn't want to talk about my past, or a future that might not even exist.

I shifted onto my side on the lumpy prison mattress and propped my book open with one hand. With the other, I shoved a pillow over my head, only leaving enough room to peep out to see the words.

Books were all I had in here. Books and the tiny glimpses of Mae that I got when she was here, teaching her class. But those weren't enough. My memories and my imagination had to fill in the rest.

I tried to focus on the words, but the other prisoners

were particularly loud today. The buzz of a building argument over a card game on the row behind mine grated through my nerves, and someone's obnoxious laugh echoed through the high-ceilinged room. I sighed, knowing it would only be a matter of time before the guards got pissed off and began shouting at everyone to keep it down.

All the more reason to keep to myself and just read my damn book.

It's not like I had anything better to do until Mae's shift started later.

A tugging at my foot caught my attention. I threw off the pillow and sat up, only to feel the cool prison air brush over my now bare toes.

DeWitt's favorite goon, Randall, stood in my tiny cubicle. An unwritten rule breach between prisoners. You didn't enter another man's space uninvited.

And you certainly didn't enter his space, then pull his fucking sock off his foot.

Randall dangled the sock in front of me tauntingly.

"What the fuck are you doing?" I lunged forward to grab it, but the man danced out of my reach and back into the walkway.

He laughed and tucked my sock into his back pocket. "Gonna put it on the door of that hot teacher's classroom so everyone knows not to interrupt while I'm banging her."

Red flashed behind my eyes. My secret was out. Every man here knew that there was something more between Mae and me than I was letting on. And they used it every opportunity they had. I was learning to shove that anger deep inside. Because at the end of the day, they were just words. And ramming my fist into this guy's nose, despite the fact I really wanted to, was not going to get me anywhere but solitary.

I wouldn't give them more fuel by responding.

But I did need my sock back. If I didn't hand in two at the end of the day, there'd be red flags raised. My cubicle would be searched, making sure I wasn't hiding it with the intent of doing God knows what. Strangling someone with it? Knotting a whole bunch of them together and making a rope that I could dangle out a window to escape? I had no idea, but the prison had a lot of little rules like that. They were on top of everything, and always looking for a break in protocol, so they could slam you with a punishment and remind you who was in charge of your life.

So I followed after Randall, dodging around other prisoners, and picking up the pace.

"Maybe I'll use it to tie your girl's hands up, instead, huh, Michaelson? She like it like that?"

The desire to slam my fist into this guy's face grew. Fuck, it would be so satisfying. It would ease the anger building inside me. It skated up from deep within, building in intensity like a wave ready to crash down and completely wipe out everything else.

It was that red haze that blocked out my sight. My hearing.

It blocked out everything else until it was too late.

Randall stopped abruptly. He tossed me the sock.

I caught it, blinking at him in surprise. It made no sense. Why come into my cubicle and start something, only to call it off a moment later? It didn't fit. It wasn't how things worked around here. If you started something, you had to be prepared to see it through, right to the very bitter end sometimes.

The only way things ended around here was if a guard stepped in.

Or in blood.

I froze. Where the hell were all the guards?

Randall chuckled darkly. "Not so tough without your guard boyfriend hanging around, are you?"

My gaze flitted around the large room and saw what I hadn't a minute ago. Men closing in on me, stalking forward slowly, forming a circle, while chaos erupted around us. At the back of the room, three prisoners overpowered one guard, while to the left of the room, all I could see was legs sticking out from the end of the row. I couldn't see the guard's face, so I had no idea if the guy was out cold, or worse. With rising panic eating its way through my center, I searched for the final guard.

Colt, I realized with a flash of panic. He was the young guard, the one who was friends with Pritchard. He swung a powerful punch into the midsection of one prisoner, and then followed with another when the man kept coming at him. He was a good fighter. That much was clear. His strikes were the coordinated lunges of a man who knew what he was doing. And yet no man was any match for a coordinated group attack. Prisoners swarmed him, hyped up by mob mentality and a swirling sense of violence in the air.

War cries echoed around the room, and from somewhere in the back, somebody started up a chant. "Riot. Riot. Riot."

My gaze met Colt's, right as he slammed his fist against the emergency button. Then he was swallowed by the mob.

A blaring siren cut through the din, and a static-laced robotic voice reported a message. *"Code thirty-three. West Wing, General Population. All officers assist."*

I expected fear. I expected the men to back down. But if anything, the frenzy only increased. And the prisoners went into action.

"You picked the wrong team, Michaelson. We tried to

tell you. Me and DeWitt. You could have been in on all of this. You could have been our partner. We want to give you one last shot, because, brother, we don't know where you stand. We saw you and Pritchard and the teach, chatting it up real friendly like in her classroom. And some of us round here are thinking you might be a snitch."

I blinked in disbelief. "What the fuck are you talking about?"

He clucked his tongue, circling me as the other members of his gang crept in closer. "We're thinking you're undercover. A cop or a guard, sent in here to spy. You a spy, bro?"

I wished I was. Because fuck, that would be a whole lot better than being in here on pending murder charges. "You're barking up the wrong tree, *bro*." I spat the term out. Because this man wasn't my brother. No one in here was.

"You disrespect us. We offered you friendship, but you sneer down your nose at us like your shit don't stink." He got up in my face, brave amongst the chaos he'd caused, and a circle of menacing figures drawing closer.

I didn't have to look at them to know they scented blood in the air. They were the sharks. And I was the swimmer.

"I never disrespected you."

"Bullshit." The man's breath washed over my face, rancid from his rotting teeth. "Then get on your knees and show me respect."

The other men chuckled. "On your knees, Michaelson," one of them laughed.

I refused to budge. I had never disrespected the man. I didn't want to join his fucking pack of scumbags. I just wanted to be left the hell alone. They'd taken Pritchard's interest in me as more than what it was.

I could ignore Randall, but I sure as hell wasn't going to kneel for him. "No."

Randall widened his eyes and put a hand to his chest. "No?" he gasped in mock surprise.

The other men chuckled at his antics.

Randall's gaze narrowed once more. "Kneel."

Jesus Christ. The guy was a headcase on a power trip.

They didn't even give me the chance to say no again. Somebody kicked out the back of my legs, forcing my knees down hard into the unforgiving cement floor. Two guys grabbed my arms, and Randall gripped me hard around the chin, his fingers pressing deep against my jawbone.

"You don't want to give me your respect? Then I'll take it."

As the first blows rained down on me, all I could think was that I was glad Mae didn't start for another hour. That she'd still be safe at home. And that if I didn't make it out of this alive, I would go to my death forever regretting not kissing her.

35

ROWE

"I just want it stated for the record that I already had the prisoners clean out this storage room before you even started here. So this is a total waste of time."

Mae glared at me from the darkest corner of the storage closet, dusty boxes and overflowing piles of decades-old junk surrounding her. "I'd seriously hate to see your house if you think this is cleaned out."

She was wrong. There was nothing in my house to even get messed up. It was as minimalist as you could get. I didn't even own a couch. Just a bed, a TV, and a stack of takeout menus. There was very little besides those necessities. Everything else had too many memories attached, and I couldn't stand the daily reminders. "It's fine for a prison classroom."

"I can't teach like this, Rowe! I have no supplies, and you won't let me bring any in."

"You aren't wasting your own money on these men."

"They deserve the chance to turn their lives around. Education can do that for them. Stop talking about them like they aren't even humans." Her cheeks went pink when she got mad. It was half the reason I enjoyed riling her up. Apparently, I was really pushing her buttons tonight because the apples of her cheeks were verging on red.

"If you'd seen their rap sheets, you'd realize that half of them aren't," I commented dryly.

She threw her hands up in the air. "Ugh! You're impossible."

So was she. Impossibly annoying. Impossibly compassionate. Impossibly beautiful.

I tapped my foot. "Let's just get on with it. Your class starts in an hour."

"Thank you, Captain Obvious. I'm well aware. If you'd just back off and give me some room, perhaps I could get this done."

I folded my arms across my chest and watched her pick through the ancient, outdated supplies. I already knew she wasn't going to find what she was looking for. There were no stacks of matching textbooks or clean white writing pads. Definitely no MacBooks or whatever other sort of fancy learning technology she was probably used to having at her private school. But she was also impossibly stubborn and wasn't going to listen to me. I'd already learned she had to do everything her goddamn self.

A siren cut through the air, loud and obnoxious.

Mae froze. "What does that alarm mean?" Worry flickered in her gaze. Her big eyes trained on me, waiting for answers.

Instinctively, I went to her side but held a hand up, signaling for silence, knowing I wouldn't know what it meant either until the call came. "It's probably nothing. Don't worry about—"

"Code thirty-three. West Wing, General Population. All officers assist."

"That's where Heath is!"

My blood ran cold. "No. That can't be right."

"What? What can't be right? What's code thirty-three?" Mae edged in, clutching at my arm.

I didn't even have time to think about how close I was to her. I grabbed my walkie-talkie and hit the 'speak' button. "Colt? What's happening in there?"

"Colt?" Mae whispered, while I waited for a response.

"He's in West Wing Gen Pop tonight," I muttered. "Shit, why isn't he answering? Colt!"

My heart rate picked up.

She swallowed hard. "Tell me what code thirty-three means."

I gazed down at her. "It means there's a riot and the prisoners have taken control."

I glanced around, taking in where we were, and mentally plotting out my next move.

I needed to go and help. But I couldn't leave Mae.

She dropped the ancient pile of papers. "What does that mean? A riot in the whole prison? Or just in Gen Pop? Tori is in the infirmary!"

I shook my head. "What? Who's Tori?"

"My best friend. She's from the church. She's there with a priest and—"

I gaped at her. "Seriously? How the hell did you get that approved? Fuck. It doesn't matter now. I've no idea how widespread this is. And assuming in a situation like this isn't smart. But the call said Gen Pop, so let's not get carried away. She's probably fine in the infirmary. Perry is down there, too. She knows this place better than I do. They'll both be fine for now." My brain worked overtime, assessing the danger and trying to come up with the best plan of attack. In the hallway outside, there was the thump and noise of running bodies. I just hoped they were guards and not prisoners.

"This is bad, right? Like really bad? What should I do? Should I leave? We aren't far from the exit."

She reached for the door, but I grabbed her arm. "No, stop. The main exits all automatically lock when that alarm is hit. No one in, no one out. Not until they get a riot squad in here. They can't risk a prison break."

"A prison break?" she squeaked.

I nodded. "Code thirty-three is a total lockdown."

I finally focused on her properly. On the tremble in her fingers and her rapid breathing. I took her arms, steadying her. "Hey. You'll be fine. It'll probably be over in minutes. These things normally are."

Mae didn't look convinced. There was a huge bang from somewhere deep in the prison, and she jumped a mile. "Heath and Colt are both in there. What if they're hurt? Or worse?"

She didn't have to ask those questions. I was already thinking them.

Another series of bangs and crashes erupted, and the distant echo of yelling. My blood ran cold. Gen Pop was on the other side of the prison. If this thing had been isolated, we shouldn't have been able to hear anything.

They had the doors open and were moving freely about.

The alarm went off again, just as eerily piercing as the first one.

"Code thirty-three. Infirmary. All available officers assist."

Mae's fingers dug into my biceps. "No!" Her eyes were wild when she turned them on me. "Tori's in there!"

"She'll be okay." But it sounded weak even to my own ears. I didn't know Mae's friend, but two women alone in the infirmary with an escalating riot wasn't a good situation.

Training and previous experience had taught me that the infirmary would be one of the first places inmates tried to take over. Any part of the prison that stocked things the prisoners would need to hole up in here for days or weeks on end would be the first places they sought out. The infirmary. The cafeteria. The guards' offices. Drugs, food, and hostages. The three things most popular in a prison riot.

"No, she won't be," Mae yelled. "How many officers will be left to attend that call if they're all in Gen Pop?"

I gazed down at her silently. Not willing to answer the question because I knew she wouldn't like the answer.

"Dammit, Rowe! I've worked here long enough to know how short-staffed you are. There's going to be no one to answer that call."

I whirled on her. "I know, okay? I know! What do you want me to do? I can't be in two places at once."

She shoved me toward the door. "Go! Lock me in. I'll be fine until you get back."

I didn't point out that there was a real chance if I walked out there, I wouldn't come back. I'd been in a riot before. Not here, but it had gone down much the same. Section by section taken over until the entire prison had been overrun.

Prisoners had died. Officers had died. Rory had—

Mae shook me so hard my teeth rattled. An errant tear rolled down her cheek. "You have to go. Please."

I stared at her, the desperation in her eyes, and saw her in a different light. She was suddenly braver and fiercer than I'd given her credit for. She knew she wasn't going to be an asset in this fight, so she wasn't insisting she come with me. But she was brave enough to stay here by herself, more worried about her friend than her own safety.

It was probably foolish, but it was courageous. I respected the hell out of that.

"Please go," she whispered. "I already lost my sister. Tori is all I have left. I can't lose her, too."

There was so much raw emotion in her voice that it wrapped its way around my gut and squeezed. It seeped into my bones and connected with my own old hurts, meshing together and growing stronger as a result.

I knew what it was to lose everything. Everyone.

I wasn't going to let that happen to her.

I knew how hard it was to pick up the pieces afterward. I knew what it was to be so devastated that even breathing hurt. I knew what it was to want to end it all.

I couldn't let that pain consume her the way it consumed me. Because somewhere along the line, she'd become a bright spark in my life. And selfishly, I wasn't ready to let that spark go out just yet.

I made the decision.

"You get yourself in that very back corner. Cover up with boxes in case someone does get in here, okay? I'm going to lock the door from the outside when I leave, but there's an emergency handle on this side, so you can override it at any time. But you don't come out, Mae. You hear me? You do not come out for anything or anyone." I grabbed her by the arms and stared down at her.

Even in that moment, I was overwhelmed by how beautiful she was. And by the creeping feeling that maybe some tiny part of me cared about her.

Fuck. I was lying even to myself. It wasn't a tiny part of me. It was a big part. And it cared enough that it propelled me forward, holding her closer, afraid to let her go for fear this might be my only shot.

An insane urge to kiss her bore down on me. To close my eyes and slam my lips against hers. To hold her tight. Just once.

But that also opened up a cavern of agony inside me, and then the siren came again. Another call for help at the infirmary.

With more reluctance than I'd ever felt in my life, I stepped back toward the door. "I'll come back for you, Mae. I swear it. Do not leave this room."

She nodded, fierce determination in her eyes.

She stepped forward and wrapped her arms around me, squeezing me.

I froze at her touch. And then, fuck me, I let my body respond. I wrapped my arms around her, hauling her close, and cradling the back of her head with my hand. I held her to my chest, inhaling the sweet scent of her hair and marveling at what it felt like to have her in my arms.

"Don't you die out there," she mumbled against my chest. "Or I swear to God, I'll resurrect you just to kill you myself."

I couldn't help the tiny grin that flickered at my lips. "You can't get rid of me that easily."

I didn't quite hear her muffled reply, as she turned her face into my shirt, but it sounded a lot like, "I think I want you to stick around for a while."

I think I wanted that, too. And unable to stop myself, I lowered my lips to the top of her head.

Then I let her go.

I locked the storage closet door and walked out into the chaos of a disaster.

36

ROWE

I locked Mae in the storage closet with a rising sense of dread. Her classroom didn't appear any different than when we'd first entered earlier that evening, but the noises from farther off inside the prison walls gave me chills. Screams. Shouts. Bangs and crashes.

I'd been here before, and it wasn't a place I'd wanted to return to. How the hell had this happened? Though there was no possible way this could have been my fault, an old familiar guilt crushed down on me.

"No," I murmured to myself. I wasn't going back there. I wasn't going to let my head get clouded with flashbacks and PTSD when there were people here who needed me. This wasn't like last time. This didn't have to have the same outcome.

It couldn't.

I locked the classroom door behind me and then cautiously moved into the hallway. I looked left, then right, my hand hovering uselessly at my side. We didn't carry guns. It wasn't safe to. The only weapon I had here was a key ring pepper spray. I already knew that would be mostly useless in this sort of situation. You needed crowd control, not a one-on-one weapon that would only last for one prisoner. But it was better than nothing.

The hallway was empty. So I moved quickly and cautiously down toward the infirmary that joined the men's prison to the women's, snaking my way through empty corridor after empty corridor. My footsteps echoed in the muffled silence around me. But the farther I went, the louder the sounds from Gen Pop grew. With every step I took myself closer and closer to the danger zone.

But Mae's desperation for her friend spurred me on. Perry would be there, too. And I knew as well as every other man in this prison, the two women in the middle of a riot would be like gold at the end of the rainbow. I could only pray they were as hidden as Mae was right now.

But the quicker I got to them and back to Mae, the better. I wasn't going to feel okay about any of this until I got Mae out of here.

I stopped dead when a random prisoner stepped out of a side room. He blinked at me, seemingly as surprised to see me as I was to see him. I pulled out my pepper spray. "Get on the ground, prisoner."

He eyed me, cocking his head to one side. "Nah, bro. How about you just come with me nicely. Boss said we need hostages. And while you aren't the women I was sent to get, you'll do."

"You know that's not going to happen."

"You're not the one in charge anymore. What I say goes now."

He lunged at me, grabbing for the arm that held the pepper spray. But I was quicker. He caught a full face of fiery mist and then hit the deck hard, screaming and clutching his eyes.

I didn't stop to cuff him. They were already in phase two, then. Shit. Phase one of a riot was an inciting incident. Something that happened, a fight or an organized attack that lit things up and got the prisoners all hot under the collar. Most disturbances ended there, with guards regaining control in the space of moments, or minutes at worst. But the fact these prisoners were now on the hunt for hostages meant they'd moved past that early critical stage, and the danger was only increasing with every second that passed. Hostages meant organization. Bringing in as many prisoners as they could, rounding up more guards, and taking control of more sections. They already had control of General Population, the biggest section of the prison by far. And now the infirmary. How many other sections did they control?

A sickening sense of déjà vu washed over me.

This was exactly what had happened at my last prison.

I took off running again. A new determination fueling my muscles. My pace increased with every corner, the sounds of the riots in the distance urging me to move faster. When I skidded around the corner closest to the infirmary, it was at a dead run.

Even from the hallway, the infirmary looked like a disaster zone. Smashed glass and broken bottles spilled out the doorway and into the hall. Sheets and blankets lay in a heap just inside, and as I entered the room, the blood smeared on the floor and wall send shock waves through my body. What the fuck had happened here?

"You stupid sluts! You can't hide in there forever!"

I spun, laying eyes on a single prisoner trying to beat down the bathroom door. My ears suddenly registered the terrified screams of the women inside. Bile rose in my throat. I could only pray that the two of them were locked inside alone, and not with one of this guy's friends.

There was no sign of the priest.

"Get away from them." I grabbed the now empty pepper spray from my belt and held it out like it was a gun, while desperately searching the room for something else I could use as a weapon if it came down to that. I didn't want to hurt anyone seriously. Not even these prisoners. But if it was between them and the women, I knew who I'd choose.

The prisoner shot a glance over his shoulder at me, and then he laughed. "You aren't in charge here anymore, Officer Pritchard. You picked the wrong side."

I had no idea what he was talking about. It was the same thing the other man had said, which only made me surer that this had been an organized attack. "I said get away from the door, prisoner."

The man finally stopped his banging and turned on me. "Or what?"

That was the million-dollar question, wasn't it? My spray was empty, and I had no other way of defending myself. So I was going to have to bluff. "Or I fill your eyes with this spray. You choose. Walk away and keep your eyesight, because you know nobody here is going to administer first aid in the middle of the riot. You'll be waiting hours for treatment. You ever been pepper sprayed?" I didn't wait for him to answer. "I have. And you know what it feels like?"

The man didn't answer, so I just carried on anyway. "It feels like clawing your own eyes out with a rusted spoon. For hours on end, because even with medical attention, that shit burns like you dropped your eyes in acid. You want that? Or do you want to just walk away now and enjoy your tiny taste of freedom before we lock this place down again. Your choice."

The man obviously wasn't as dumb as he appeared because he listened. He edged around me warily, grabbing an armful of medical supplies and shoving them down his shirt before turning and stumbling out of the room.

I waited until I was sure he was gone, checking the hall in both directions, and then locking the main door before rushing back to the bathroom door and banging on it. "Perry! Tori! It's me, Rowe. You can come out. He's gone."

"Rowe?" came Perry's shaky voice. The door opened a crack, and her wide green eyes shone out. When she saw it really was me, she rushed out and threw her arms around my middle. "Oh, thank God. I didn't think he was ever going to leave. It would only be a matter of time before he smashed his way in here."

I squeezed her tight for a moment and then turned to the other woman. "Tori?"

She nodded.

I focused back on Perry. "Where's the guard who was stationed in here with you two? Mae said there was a priest?"

Perry's bottom lip trembled. "It was Simonsen. He shoved us in the bathroom and held them off as long as he could. Father George helped. I don't know what happened to them, though. There was screaming as they dragged them away..."

A sick feeling curdled in the bottom of my stomach. "Fucking savages."

Perry clutched at me. "How are we going to get out? Everything will be locked down in a code thirty-three."

"I've got Mae holed up in a storage closet. I don't think any of the men will think to search for her there, because it hasn't been used in so long, and there is nothing of value inside. Not like here in the infirmary. We need to get out of here. They'll be back for the drugs they've left behind. They're not gonna care about pencils and paper. The classroom storage closet is our best bet for now. Come on."

"You left Mae alone?" Tori accused.

I narrowed my eyes. I didn't appreciate her tone, and my patience was already wearing thin. "Yeah, well. She's stubborn, isn't she? And too selfless for her own good. She insisted that I come and get you first. So can we quit yakking and get back to her already?"

Tori blinked, and then to my surprise, smiled at me. "I like you. You care about her."

"No more than I care about anybody else in this place."

Tori gave me a sidelong glance, and despite the fact I'd only just met the woman, I could tell she didn't believe me. Hell. I didn't believe me. I did care about Mae more than I should, even though I'd promised myself I wouldn't go there again. Caring about people only led to misery.

I was so sick of living with my own misery.

The three of us moved to into the hallway once more, the two women sticking close to my sides. I set the pace, a steady jog, even though my muscles screamed to break into a full run and get back to Mae quicker.

"This is bad. This is so bad," Perry muttered as we jogged along. "Why didn't I call in sick today? I'm an idiot. I had a scratchy throat. I could be lying at home in my own bed right now, instead of running from my smashed-up infirmary to go hide in a closet for God knows how long until the frigging riot police get here. Do you even know how long riots last for, Rowe?"

I grit my teeth. "Hours. Days. Weeks, at worst."

"Weeks!" Tori yelped. "I've got a baby at home."

I took her arm and dragged her along, forcing her to keep pace. "Then keep running so we can get you home to him. Standing out here in the middle of the hall and yelling is only going to end in disaster if we come across a gang of prisoners."

That got her moving. She pulled ahead, and Perry and I both increased our speed to keep up with her.

"How much farther is it?" Tori asked, her breath coming in puffs.

"It's not far. One more hall, and then a right turn." I was encouraged by the new silence. My boots on the solid cement floors echoed in the quiet. Tori's ragged breaths filled my left ear, while Perry's tiny whimpers filled my right. I grabbed her hand. "It's going to be all right. I promise."

We rounded the final corner and stopped dead.

Knee-high flames met us. Orange-and-yellow fire spread right across the hallway, blocking us off, the heat warming my face even from this distance.

"What was that about promises, Pritchard?" The prisoner I'd let go earlier cackled. He stood on the other side of the flames, delighted with his handiwork. And it was only then that I realized who he was.

Milton James. Arsonist. In prison for lighting his grandmother's house on fire.

While she was sleeping inside it.

The woman had made it out alive, which was the only reason James had been left in Gen Pop and wasn't locked up in a solitary cell.

"I did say you were on the wrong side." He turned and sauntered away, like he didn't have a care in the world. "Wrong side of the riot and the flames apparently!" His laughter echoed back.

And there was nothing I could do about it. I stood there, watching the flames grow higher and higher as they licked their way up the walls. Tori and Perry screamed around me, their hands tugging at my clothing and trying to pull me away from the flames that crept ever closer.

But all I could think was that Mae was on the other side of them.

Locked in a closet.

With no idea of the danger she was in.

37

MAE

Rowe had been gone for too long. I wasn't wearing a watch, and my phone was in my locker, but I was sure time had slowed to a crawl. Like I'd promised, I squeezed myself into the very back corner of the closet and dragged boxes in around me, building myself a mini fort so that even if the door was opened by a prisoner, I might get lucky. They might just look in, see the pile of boxes, and not investigate further to find me crouching behind them.

But as the minutes rolled on, an increasing sense of panic crept through my chest, wrapping its way around my lungs and making it hard to breathe. I'd never thought I was claustrophobic, but being locked in the darkness, the air still and stuffy around me, I could suddenly understand why people hated this sort of environment. Occasionally there were noises, or footsteps from the hall outside, but for the most part, there was just silence.

It took every ounce of self-control to not bust my way out of the closet and then the classroom. Worry plagued my every moment, until the beginnings of a panic attack tried to take hold. My throat dried, and my hands turned clammy with nerves.

I took a deep breath and let it out as a long sigh. I was no good to anybody if I hyperventilated and passed out in here. I would be equally useless if I were a blubbering mess who couldn't keep herself under control. So I sucked in one deep breath, and then another.

It was on the third breath that I picked up the scent of smoke in the air.

I went perfectly still.

Shit. Freezing was just as bad as hyperventilating.

I pushed the boxes out of the way and stood, racing for the closet door and pressing my nose to the tiny slits of light that came in from outside.

Definitely smoke.

It wasn't thick, but it was there. I leaned back on the door, my chest heaving with rapid breaths, that panic attack from a few minutes ago just fighting to resurface.

The sprinklers would come on if there was a fire.

But I waited another five minutes, counting down the seconds in my head, both in an attempt to keep track of the time and to calm my racing mind.

The sprinklers didn't turn on.

And the smoke in the air only grew thicker.

I couldn't stay in here. I'd promised Rowe, but all I could think about was being burned alive. Flames engulfing my skin. There was no escape from this closet. There was no window, no additional door. If the fire made it as close as my classroom, I was done for. Nobody but Rowe knew I was in here. Nobody would be looking for me. I wasn't even supposed to be on duty for another hour. With the prison on full lockdown, and the sprinklers obviously not working, how long would it be before firefighters even got in here? I couldn't rely on them. I couldn't rely on Rowe, or Heath.

The only person I could rely on was me.

And I wasn't going down without a fight.

I turned the lock, then opened the door. I blinked in the bright light of the classroom but was relieved to see it wasn't as thick with smoke as I'd initially thought from the darkness of the closet. The air was definitely scented with it, but the fire wasn't right on top of me.

At least not yet. But I wasn't planning on sticking around until it was.

I strode toward the door of my classroom, a plan forming in my mind. I knew where the infirmary was. I'd go straight there, find Rowe and Tori and Perry, and then we'd hole up somewhere and wait this thing out together. Maybe Rowe would know a way of checking on Heath and Colt. One thing I knew for sure was that I couldn't go waltzing into Gen Pop alone. Facing a whole room full of prisoners wasn't an option, but neither was staying in this classroom, alone and with a fire nearby.

I yanked the door open.

"Well, well, well. Howdy, little mouse. Where are you escaping to?"

DeWitt strode forward, pushing me back inside the classroom and letting the door slam shut behind him.

I had no choice but to scuttle backward or be bowled down by him. I didn't want him touching me. I didn't even want him near me.

He glanced around the room. "You all alone? Poor little mouse. So lonely."

"Officer Pritchard will be back any moment," I bluffed, praying it were true.

DeWitt chuckled at that. "Nah. He won't. We took care of

that." He sniffed the air. "Ah. The delicious scent of burning flesh. Or to be more precise, burning officer flesh."

Horror washed over me. "What are you talking about?"

DeWitt shrugged. "He was being annoying. And we didn't need him for the plan. So I let James have some fun. He's really missed setting fires, you know? Crazy fuck. But don't worry. We trapped them in, and the doors are supposedly fireproof. It'll burn itself out, so we'll be fine here. This smoke stinks, though, doesn't it? It didn't smell so bad in Gen Pop, but that might have been because your boy's blood is in the air down there. Randall and the boys were in the middle of a good old-fashioned ass-kicking when I left. I'm not one to get my hands dirty, myself. But Randall's been busting to take Michaelson down ever since he got here. There's really no love lost between the two of them. All good, though! I told them not to kill him. And they listen to me."

He shrugged like it was no big deal.

But I felt like I'd been punched in the stomach. The thought of Rowe trapped by fire was incomprehensible. What if Tori and Perry were with him? And Heath...

Bile rose in my throat.

No!

I wasn't losing any more people, goddammit.

Something inside me snapped. I turned wide eyes on DeWitt and let the fear inside me take hold. It bubbled up as hysterical anger. "Crazy fuck?" I yelled, getting in his face. All traces of mild-mannered school teacher washed away in the smoky air. "What do you think you are? You think you're some big mastermind? You think you're some big dog around here? You're nothing but a common thug."

A muscle in his jaw twitched. "A thug?" His voice dripped with fake disbelief. "Sweetheart. Where did you get that from? I think we all know why I run this joint. I'm a born leader, baby." He waved a hand around. "You see anybody else starting riots successfully? Nah. Just me."

He talked the talk, but I'd pissed him off. It was evident in the way his shoulders stiffened at my accusations. I'd questioned his authority, and he didn't like it. He buried it well beneath his bravado, but it was there. His tells. His little giveaways. They spurred me on, hate for this man swirling and gathering speed until it was all I could think of.

My sister was gone. Stolen from me. The people I cared about in danger now, too.

I saw red. And then I let it loose, nothing to lose.

I ran at DeWitt with no weapons but fingers clenched into fists and a fierce determination that this man would not block my exit for one minute longer. I was leaving this room come hell or high water. I was finding Tori. I was finding Heath. And I was finding Rowe. We were leaving this place together. All of us alive. Because I refused to lose one more person I cared about.

The realization that Rowe meant something to me was startling. It hit me as I slammed into DeWitt and pummeled at his broad chest, scratching and biting, screaming for him to let me go.

But the man was a wall. He didn't budge an inch from where he'd planted himself, blocking the entrance.

His eyes darkened. His fingers wrapped around my slim wrists, his grip punishing. He yanked my arm so hard I was sure my shoulder was on the verge of dislocating.

I yelped in pain, hating I was at the man's mercy. But my own determination refused to let me give up that easily. I slammed my heel down on the top of his foot, satisfied when he gave a grunt of pain.

"Don't be a bitch now," he murmured.

I kicked and thrashed, trying to get out of his grasp, while my shoulder screamed in agony.

"Seriously. Settle down," he snapped, his control on his cool, unflappable exterior unraveling just a fraction.

But then he grinned. An evil grimace full of his rotted, dirty teeth and stinking breath. "I just wanted to take you to your boyfriend."

He spoke with such dripping sweetness that even a blind man would have seen through it. It was the honey that attracted insects, only to get stung by the bee.

I didn't know who he meant. For the tiniest of seconds, fear rushed through me, thinking that Liam was here. But then we'd just been talking about Rowe. Or was he talking about Heath? None of them were my boyfriend. But that didn't stop me from caring about them. From being desperate to know where they were and if they were okay.

I wasn't dumb enough to let DeWitt know that. "I have no boyfriend."

"Oh, little mouse. How you lie. You're all Heath talks about. I thought that would make you happy?"

"You're a liar." I somehow doubted Heath had been talking about me, but that didn't matter now anyway. DeWitt knew there was something between us. The whole prison did. But I wasn't going to fuel the fire.

DeWitt held me tighter, his fingers pressing into my flesh so hard I suspected my skin bled. "I never lie. I am taking you to Michaelson. Right down there in the belly of Gen Pop, where everyone is waiting for me to put on a show. I can't wait to see the look of relief and excitement on his face when he sees you're alive and well." His voice dropped an octave, into a deadly whisper. "And then I'm going to snap your pretty little neck in front of him, so the man learns his place."

Fear punched through me, sharp and deadly. I started up a fresh round of struggles, screaming and thrashing out, trying to fight the hold DeWitt had on me. He shoved me up against the wall, but I twisted, managing to skitter away.

I lunged for the door, freedom mere inches from my fingertips, only to be brought down by a bone-jarring tackle that had me slamming into the unforgiving floor.

I screamed out in pain, DeWitt's heavy weight coming down on my back, smashing my face into the floor. Blood coated my lips, the metallic taste filling my mouth.

But I didn't stop fighting.

I fought as he pulled my hair, yanking my head back. I fought when he flipped me over onto my back and leaned on me so hard I could practically hear my ribs groaning under the pressure.

"I knew you'd like it rough. I was just going to take you down there and kill you. I generally like boys better than girls. But you I have a sweet spot for. And my dick hasn't seen any action for too long. So shut up. And take what you get. You stop screaming in my face, and I'll make it real good for you." His meaty fingers wrapped around my throat, choking my voice into silence. My eyes bulged. Breath burned in my lungs, then caught fire when I could neither expel air nor take it in.

DeWitt chuckled, that evil sound grating down my skin. "That's more like it. A quiet little mouse."

The burning in my chest eased as darkness flickered at the edges of my consciousness. Dimly, I was aware of DeWitt yanking off my pants and fumbling with his own.

With no energy or oxygen left to fight, I prayed I would pass out. Because that would be better than being awake to watch DeWitt take something I wasn't willing to give. Passing out would take me one step closer to death. And right now, with every part of my body screaming, that didn't seem like such a bad thing. Death was one step closer to being back with my sister.

The darkness tried to take me, hugging me close, silencing the world with its seductive whispers.

Something dripped on my face.

And then again, and again.

Slowly, the darkness at the edges of my vision disappeared, and sound rushed back in. The fog in my eyes cleared, and a red rainbow took its place. I blinked again, my oxygen-starved brain fighting to make sense of what was going on.

DeWitt wasn't talking anymore. Every time I'd seen the man, he hadn't shut up. But now, he was eerily silent.

It wasn't a red rainbow.

It was a red slit across the man's neck. A gaping, bleeding gash, where steel had cut his throat.

The dripping on my face was his blood.

A warbled scream came out as more of a croak, and I scrambled backward, sliding myself along the floor and away from the gory sight.

But I couldn't look away. Instead, I stared with horror, as DeWitt bled out on my classroom floor.

Vincent stood over him, one hand still clutched in DeWitt's hair, and a blood-soaked knife in the other.

38

MAE

"Vincent," I whispered, staring up at the quiet, timid man who was by far my best student. He didn't look any different. His hair was as neatly brushed as it always was. His brown eyes alert and intelligent.

He dropped DeWitt's lifeless body to the floor and then stared down at his hands. "Darn it. I've got blood on me. Do you have a tissue, please?"

I blinked. A tissue wasn't going to touch the mess he'd made. Blood was rapidly spreading across the gray concrete floor, darkening it with a sickening, slick stain. But I scrambled to my feet, tugging my clothing back into place as I went, and retrieved a box of tissues from my desk drawer, cautiously handing them over.

Vincent smiled at me politely, like we were at a high tea, rather than standing in the middle of a prison riot with a dead man at our feet and smoke in the air. I didn't know where to look. Down at DeWitt's unseeing eyes. Or at the man who had brutally murdered him in cold blood and now wanted...a tissue.

He pulled a few out carefully and dabbed at his uniform with a sigh of frustration when unsurprisingly, they did nothing to help. Then he glanced up at me. "Oh, sorry. Did you want one, too? You have a little..." He motioned to his forehead.

I put my hand up to touch my own, and my fingers came away with sticky red blood.

DeWitt's blood.

I let out a tiny gasp and grabbed a fistful of tissues from the box Vincent offered, and scrubbed frantically at my forehead.

Vincent watched me curiously. "That isn't helping." He went to my desk and found my water bottle in the bottom drawer. "Look what I've found. Come here. Let me help you."

I shook my head hard.

"You don't want me to touch you?"

It was like he could see inside my head. Or maybe my terror was just written all over my face. But the notion didn't seem to please him.

The last thing I wanted to do was piss off the man with the knife and an obvious penchant for murder.

"You first," I stalled. "Your hands are covered in blood. Much worse than mine. The tissue just smeared it around. Let's get your hands clean first, and then we'll worry about my few drops."

He didn't seem impressed by that idea.

I spoke quickly, keeping my voice as sure and soothing as I could. "Truly. I'm just fine. You first."

He reluctantly nodded and held the squirt bottle out to me. "As you wish."

I took the bottle, careful not to let our skin touch, and tried to muffle a cough. The smoke was getting thicker.

Where the hell was the riot squad? If I could just stall Vincent long enough for them to get to me...

"Squirt some into my hands," he directed.

With trembling fingers, I did so, squeezing the bottle gently, while Vincent cupped his fingers together to make a little pool. When it was close to full, he rubbed his hands together, letting the pink-tinged water fall onto the floor.

I held the bottle up again. "And the backs? You have some, uh...spray on the backs of your hands and across your knuckles."

He nodded and held his hands out. I covered them with water once more and watched as he scrubbed at first the back of his left hand, and then his right with a soggy tissue.

The tissue didn't turn pink from blood like I'd expected. It turned an odd shade of brown. The same sort of brown the water turned when I washed my makeup off at night.

Shock punched through the abject fear keeping my body in a permanent state of anxiety. Vincent scrubbed more at his hand, rubbing off the blood, along with a solid layer of brown goop that might have been some sort of stage makeup.

It left behind not only clean hands but a small, brown birthmark.

Perfectly shaped like a scythe.

Our conversation with Liam's brother, Hayden, came back to me in a rush. *"DeWitt is a low-level nothing. He ain't your problem. If you got someone on the inside you care about? Tell them to stay away from Scythe. The guy is a complete nutjob. A real screw loose sort of guy, you know? You could invite the guy to dinner and your granny's house and he'd stab her right through the heart for getting a lump in his gravy. That sorta guy."*

My blood ran cold. "Scythe—"

Vincent glanced up sharply. "What did you say?"

I pointed to his birthmark, trying to stall. "Your birthmark is shaped like a scythe. Why did you have it covered? It's almost like a tattoo." I forced a smile, though I knew it trembled. "It's very cool."

Vincent gazed down at it, rubbing his thumb over the curved shape of the blade. "They sell makeup at commissary. I always cover it. Bad things happen when I don't."

I didn't know what he meant by that and I didn't dare ask.

But Vincent grew edgy in the silence. The seconds drew out, with the two of us staring, trying to work the other out. I was sure he didn't believe my attempt at casual interest.

Hayden's warning. DeWitt lying dead with his throat slit. My sister the same.

My head spun with the realization that I could be staring into the eyes of my sister's murderer.

It was me who caved first. Me who couldn't keep it together no matter how hard I tried to keep the fear at bay.

Vincent was Scythe. The one Hayden had called ten times worse than DeWitt. At the time, I hadn't understood how that was possible. But now I saw. Now I saw Vincent's silently lethal actions in the cold hard light of day.

And I understood what Hayden had meant.

A sob broke free from my chest. I couldn't hold it in any longer. The terror. The confusion. All I could do was try to keep him talking. Try to remind him that I was his friend. Try to keep him thinking that we were a team.

I swallowed hard and tried not to lose the contents of my stomach when I stared down at DeWitt again. "Vincent, what have you done?"

He blinked, seemingly confused by the question.

I pointed to the body at our feet. The very, very dead body.

"Oh that. He was hurting you. So I killed him. And probably dulled my favorite shiv in the process. Most annoying. Anyway, shall we go?"

My stomach flipped. Vincent's manners and quiet calm had always been out of place, surrounded by loudmouths and extroverts, all vying for the top dog position with their bravado and bullshit. But I'd never found his ways disturbing. Never found them as completely creepy as I did right now. Who killed a man in such a brutal manner, then in the next breath, quietly and politely asked for a Kleenex?

Nobody in their right mind, that was for sure.

"Go where?" I asked, my mind racing. What was it people always said when dealing with kidnappers or people who were about to jump off a bridge? Keep them talking.

He switched his shiv to his left hand and held his right hand out for me. "Well, we can't stay here, can we? I'm not sure if you noticed, but the smoke is getting quite uncomfortable, so I think it's time we departed."

"Departed?" I asked slowly. He was right, the smoke was getting worse every minute we stood here, but his choice of words had my legs trembling. I couldn't stand the not knowing. "Are you going to kill me, too?"

He stared at me, and I could practically see his mind whirring. He tipped his head to one side. "What a curious thing to say. Come now."

He held his hand out to me.

But I couldn't. I'd rather die in a smoke-filled room than be brutally murdered at the hands of a complete and utter psychopath who used words like 'curious' and 'darn.'

I shook my head. "No. No...thank you."

He frowned but ignored my protest. "Come."

I shook my head, drawing whatever tiny amount of strength I had left. "I said no."

That was when I saw it. The change in him. Where he went from Jekyll to Hyde. Bruce Banner to the Hulk. A shield dropped down over his dark eyes, and they narrowed into slits. In one large step, he had his hand around my throat, his blunt nails digging into my neck. "No wasn't an option, *Miss Donovan.*"

He hissed my name like he was some beast from the depths of Hell, and my legs threatened to give out.

Then just as quickly, he let me go, calm expression back in place.

I caught myself on a table, clinging to it for dear life in order to stop myself crashing into the floor again. When he held his hand out this time, I knew better than to disobey him.

With jerky movements, I put my hand in his.

His fingers clamped over mine hard, sharp, and painful.

Possessive.

"That's a good girl," he purred. "I have so many plans for you, Miss Donovan. And the night has only just begun."

The End…for now.

The Saint View Prison trilogy continues in book 2, Solitary Sinners, and book 3, Fatal Felons.

Want to know how Liam and Rowe feel about a threesome? It's in the bonus scene! Check the bonus content tab at https://www.ellethorpe.com/lockedupliarsbonusscene

ARE YOU NEW TO THE SAINT VIEW WORLD?

You already met Colt, Lacey, Banjo, and Rafe in Locked Up Liars. For another wild ride, check out Devious Little Liars and see where their story began.It's full of twists and turns and secrets too!

There's a sneak peek on the following pages.

Elle x

CHAPTER ONE

LACEY

I was about to be arrested.

That was my first thought when a flash of movement outside the window caught my attention.

Extreme overreaction?

Perhaps.

But when you'd illegally let yourself into your school on a Sunday, these were the worries that plagued a girl.

Acting on instinct, I hurled myself off the piano stool and onto the floor, scuttling to the windows overlooking the quad. Maybe they hadn't seen me yet. The late afternoon sun was sinking, and perhaps, if I was lucky, the glare would temporarily blind them. I could make my escape out one of the back doors. There was an exit in the administration hall. Others in the math and history wings. Of course, not one anywhere near the music rooms. Helpful.

Ever so carefully, I lifted to peer out the window, and yelped at the face on the other side. I ducked down again, though there was no chance he hadn't seen me, what with his nose an inch from the glass.

I was totally busted. But at least it wasn't the police.

Lawson's laughter on the other side of the window made me realize how ridiculous I was being. I stood, embarrassment heating my face.

"You want to let me in?" he yelled.

I squeezed my eyes closed but nodded. "I'll meet you at the door."

Scrambling down the hall, I tried to come up with a plausible story that would result in the least amount of trouble. I still had nothing by the time I pulled open the heavy, ancient oak doors of Providence School for Girls.

My uncle stood on the other side, boxes of his work balanced precariously in his arms. He shifted beneath their weight, sending a USB stick and a pile of papers sliding off the top. They fluttered down around our ankles.

I knelt hastily, tucking the USB stick into my pocket and gathering up the runaway pages. I glanced up at his familiar face. "Before you say anything, just remember, I'm your favorite niece."

"You're my only niece," he grumbled, but there was still a hint of laughter in his voice.

I put the papers back on top, then took the box from him, lightening his load. "Which means you won't have me arrested?"

He kicked the doors closed behind him. "Well, that depends on how quickly you start explaining why you're at school on a Sunday night, instead of at Meredith's, which is where you said you were going. How did you even get in here without tripping the alarm? If you broke a window, I won't be impressed." He walked toward his office.

I hurried to keep up. "No, no. All windows are intact. I used the code."

"What? How do you even know it?"

I snorted, then remembered I was probably about to be

grounded until I turned eighteen. Which, admittedly, was only a couple of weeks away. But still. I tried to force my expression into something more suitably chastised. "Sorry. But you've been driving me to school and unlocking that door in front of me for the past three years. The code is my birthday. Just like all your passwords."

That resulted in a withering look, but I knew he wasn't really angry at me. We wove through the administration offices until we reached Lawson's, his gold-plated Principal nameplate on the door. He unlocked it, and we both dumped our boxes on the table.

Then he turned to me, folding his arms across his chest, giving me his best principal's glare. "How long have you been sneaking in here for?"

No point lying about it now. "Months."

His mouth dropped open. "To do what? Please don't say drugs. If you say drugs, I swear, I'm going to take you down to that police station myself."

I sniggered. "No. Something much worse."

"Sex? Booze? What could be worse?" He narrowed his eyes, but they crinkled at the corners. He was trying not to laugh. "Are you running some sort of illegal cock fighting ring out of the gym?"

I raised an eyebrow. "No, but wow. Thanks for the ideas. If college doesn't work out for me, I'll be sure to consider those options. I've just been practicing in the music rooms. All alone. No sex, drugs, or farmyard animals of any kind."

My uncle frowned and grumbled. I'd won him over. He knew how important music was to me. "So. No police?"

His expression morphed into fatherly affection. He put his arm around my shoulders and kissed the top of my head. "What do you think? I'm hardly going to call the police when I'd be the one to pay your bail. I've got work to do. Go on, go do your thing. But set your alarm and meet me back here in two hours. You know how you lose track of time when you play."

I breathed a sigh of relief. He so rarely lost his temper, and almost never at me. I couldn't have stood it if he were angry. I kissed his stubbled cheek. "Love you..."

Not for the first time, the word 'Dad' formed on my lips. But at the last moment, I swallowed it down. Instead, I gave him a grateful wave and hurried back to the music rooms.

When I got there, I shut the door behind me and made a beeline for the piano, running my palm over its gleaming black surface. This was my happy place. And it filled something inside me in a way that nothing else did.

Pulling my phone from my pocket, I set the alarm so I wouldn't be late.

Then I pressed my fingers to the keys and closed my eyes, the first lilting notes lifting to the air. Time ceased to exist until a blaring alarm cut through my bubble.

I lost focus, hit the wrong key, and the entire song unraveled. "Dammit!" I slammed the keys hard.

I glanced at my phone and silenced the obnoxious beeping. In the blink of an eye, two hours had passed, and the real world came rushing back in. The sun had set, leaving me in near darkness, and I hadn't even noticed. Patting the top of the piano like it was a dog who'd just completed a new trick, I murmured, "Until next time."

In the corridor, I stopped dead as I caught a whiff of something unpleasant. "What the hell..." I murmured, wrinkling my nose. I took a few more steps, then froze.

Smoke.

I peered into the darkness, trying to remain calm while my brain scrambled to find logical conclusions. It was nearing the end of summer. People could be having barbecues nearby, and the smoke might have just blown in on the breeze. Or perhaps a wildfire had started. The smoke alarms weren't going off. Nor were the sprinklers. I picked up the pace, heading for the admin offices. The entire time, I scrabbled with my thoughts, fighting against the obvious. Pushing myself to believe those excuses, because what was right in front of my eyes was too scary to comprehend. I rounded a corner and stopped dead.

There was no denying it anymore.

The building was filling with thick, acrid smoke.

Something instinctual pushed me forward, and my feet went with it, instead of listening to the panicked voice in my head screaming to turn and run in the opposite direction. I fumbled for my phone, pulled it out, and dialed nine-one-one. Smoke invaded my chest and eyes. I coughed, trying to clear it while fear clawed its way up my spine.

"Fire!" I gasped when the operator answered. "Providence School for Girls." Racking coughs took over. I hung up, but the farther I got, the thicker the smoke became, until it didn't matter if I spoke or not. I held my arm over my mouth and nose, trying to keep it out, but it was a losing battle. My lungs protested, but I moved on, my pace increasing until I was running. I skidded around the corner, bashing my hipbone on the wall. The darkness was disorienting. The visibility next to nothing. I couldn't see farther than a few steps ahead of me.

"Lawson!" I yelled, immediately regretting it when smoke filled my mouth and nose. It got thicker with every step. I coughed again and ran my hands over the wall where I thought the light switch should be. I came up empty, my nails scratching over nothing but drywall.

I spun around, confused now at exactly where I was. I needed to get to my uncle. I knew, that if there was a fire, he would have come for me. Called me. He knew where I was. And there was only one way to get there. We couldn't have missed each other. I pushed my legs harder, not certain that I was even heading in the right direction, but I had to try.

Suddenly, the room around me opened up, and I nearly wept with relief as I recognized the foyer. But there was no time for that.

I'd found the source of the smoke.

Flames licked the walls.

"Lawson!" I yelled again, tasting ash. Panic surged, adrenaline kicking in and powering my movements. My brain short-circuited, whether from lack of air or fear, I didn't know. The one thing I was certain of was that I couldn't lose another parent. I couldn't add my uncle to the broken part of me that had existed ever since my birth parents' disappearance. He was the only father I really remembered. And he wouldn't have left without me. I knew that without a doubt. He wouldn't have left me there to die.

Which meant he was still inside.

I ran in a crouch toward the flames. They grew with every second that passed. "Laws—" I couldn't even get his name out this time before the lack of air stole my voice. I held my breath and rushed toward his office, throwing open doors as I went and dodging the deadly heat.

I skidded to a stop at the glass window of the principal's office. A scream curled up my throat but came out silently.

Lawson's still form lay facedown on the floorboards.

Flames billowed up around him, higher in here than anywhere else. They crawled across the ceiling, like slithering beasts of orange fury. I bashed on the window so hard it should have broken, desperately yelping my uncle's name between racking bouts of coughing.

Overhead, a beam cracked.

Sparks flew and I flinched away. I tried again, lunging for the door, but the heat drove me back. Tears streamed down my face. "Help," I croaked.

I couldn't save him alone. He was right there, the flames getting ever closer, and I couldn't reach him. I stumbled back the way I'd come, dropping to my knees and crawling when my feet wouldn't take another step. My eyes stung. My gaze flitted around the smoke-filled room, but my head grew cloudy.

With a sudden certainty, I realized we were both going to die.

There was no way out.

I closed my eyes. At least the last thing I'd done was something I loved. I remembered the way it felt to have my fingers flying over the piano keys, the song soaring, not only in my ears but in my heart. When the flames took me, that's where I'd be in my head. In the place I was happiest. The only place I had true peace.

Something grabbed me.

Not something, someone.

I dragged myself back into the present. There was somebody else here. Someone who could help. Hope surged within me.

"My uncle," I choked out.

Startled by hands on my bare skin, and my body being lifted from the floor, I tried to force my stinging eyes open. But my vision was so blurred I couldn't make out a face. I turned into the person's chest, and my gaze focused instead on the thing closest to me. Letters floated across my vision, a mere inch from my nose.

The man—it had to be a man, his body had none of the softer curves of a woman—didn't say anything, but gripped me tighter while he moved through the crumbling building.

Heat seared at my legs, my arms, my face. I couldn't do a thing but fist my fingers into the material of his shirt and hold on. The embroidered feel of the letters scratched, in contrast with the softness of the fabric.

He muttered something that sounded like, "Hold on, Lacey."

A thought floated through my head, but it was too hard to grasp. I wanted to chase it, grab it, and force it to make sense. But I was too tired. I watched it go, disappearing into a smoke tendril.

My body jolted against his with each step. I wanted him to run. I wanted him to get me out of this place, but it all just seemed impossible now. Everything hurt. My lungs screamed in pain. It was too hard to hold on. My grip on his shirt loosened.

"Lacey!" he yelled, but his voice was far away.

I closed my eyes and let the darkness take me.

To keep reading, check out Devious Little Liars here: https://mybook.to/DeviousLittleLiars

ALSO BY ELLE THORPE

Saint View High series (Reverse harem, romantic suspense. Complete series)

*Devious Little Liars (Saint View High, #1)

*Dangerous Little Secrets (Saint View High, #2)

*Twisted Little Truths (Saint View High, #3)

Saint View Strip series (Male/Female romantic suspense)

Book 1, (Boston and Eve) coming September 14, 2021 in the Hate To Want You Limited time anthology. Preorder for 99c.

Dirty Cowboy series (Male/Female small town cowboys. Complete series)

*Talk Dirty, Cowboy (Dirty Cowboy, #1)

*Ride Dirty, Cowboy (Dirty Cowboy, #2)

*Sexy Dirty Cowboy (Dirty Cowboy, #3)

*25 Reasons to Hate Christmas and Cowboys (a Dirty Cowboy bonus novella, set before Talk Dirty, Cowboy but can be read as a standalone, holiday romance)

Buck Cowboys series (Spin off from the Dirty Cowboy series)

*Buck Cowboys (Buck Cowboys, #1)

*Buck You! (Buck Cowboys, #2)

The Only You series (Contemporary Romance, series complete)

*Only the Positive (Only You, #1) - Reese and Low.

*Only the Perfect (Only You, #2) - Jamison.

*Only the Truth - (Only You, bonus novella) - Bree.

*Only the Negatives (Only You, #3) - Gemma.

*Only the Beginning (Only You, #4) - Bianca and Riley.

*Only You boxset

*Only the Lies. Free when you join Elle's reader newsletter below.

Add your email address here to be the first to know when new books are available!

www.ellethorpe.com/newsletter

Join Elle Thorpe's readers group on Facebook!

www.facebook.com/groups/ellethorpesdramallamas

ACKNOWLEDGMENTS

Firstly, a big thank you to Jira, my husband. He's not a writer by any stretch of the imagination, but he spent several days brainstorming this series with me, feeding me ideas that I then ignored completely and went off on my own tangent, much to his annoyance. But that's how writers brains work. You give me the spark, I'll give you the fire. I couldn't have written this book, or any book without him and his support. He truly is my number 1 fan, and I'm his.

To my awesome readers - If this was your first trip to Saint View, welcome! If you're a regular around here, thank you for loving this world and these characters like I do. Did the Colt, Banjo, Lacey, and Rafe scene kinda give you the warm and fuzzies like it did for me? I miss our forgy crew and was so happy to bring them back in Locked Up Liars.

Thank you to my writer besties - Jolie Vines, Zoe Ashwood, and Sara Massery for your critiques, sprints, advice, and friendship.

Thank you to my awesome editor, Emmy Ellis at Studio ENP, and to my proofreader Karen Hrdlicka. Big shout out to Louise O'Reilly for reading this book multiple times, and back when it was a complete mess of a first draft. Thanks for keeping me from deleting the entire thing! lol. And a big thanks to my other beta readers, Shellie and Dana. Your advice is always valued and appreciated.

And to my kiddos, Thomas, Flick, and Heidi. Thank you for being my daily inspiration to work hard and reach my goals. Love you guys.

Elle x

ABOUT THE AUTHOR

Elle Thorpe lives on the sunny east coast of Australia. When she's not writing stories full of kissing, she's a wife and mummy to three tiny humans. She's also official ball thrower to one slobbery dog named Rollo. Yes, she named a female dog after a dirty hot character on Vikings. Don't judge her. Elle is a complete and utter fangirl at heart, obsessing over The Walking Dead and Outlander to an unhealthy degree. But she wouldn't change a thing.

You can find her on Facebook or Instagram(@ellethorpe-books or hit the links below!) or at her website www.ellethorpe.com. If you love Elle's work, please consider joining her Facebook fan group, Elle Thorpe's Drama Llamas or joining her newsletter here. www.ellethorpe.com/newsletter

facebook.com/ellethorpebooks
instagram.com/ellethorpebooks
goodreads.com/ellethorpe
pinterest.com/ellethorpebooks

Printed in Great Britain
by Amazon

83325129R00202